VULTURES

ALSO BY LUKE TARZIAN

ADJACENT MONSTERS

The World Maker Parable

ANTHOLOGIES

Dark Ends

VULTURES

A SHADOW TWINS NOVEL

LUKE TARZIAN

PRAISE FOR VULTURES

"Highly imaginative and powerfully original."
—*Clayton Snyder, author of THE OBSIDIAN PSALM*

"One of the most stunning debuts I've ever read."
—*Justine Bergman, WHISPERS & WONDER*

"Vivid characters and evocative magic woven together in a deep, intricate setting. A fantastic debut!"
—*Christopher Husberg, author of DAWNRISE*

"Complex, dark, emotional, and raw."
—*Justin Gross, FANFIADDICT*

"A stark fantasy…at times, it felt like I was reading someone's nightmare."
—*Jodie Crump, GRIMDARK MAGAZINE*

To mom.
Who believed in me before I believed in myself

I miss you

ARIATH

HELVEDEN

AVAR

THE HEART
OF MIRKÚR

VARE

ULM

THE PHA

TE VÉTUI
THAE

OLD JÉMOON

BANEROWOS

THE ENOX OCEAN

TAL

NALDUNAR

XIAN MOUNTAINS

S
LE

DURENAR

ACT ONE

MISERABLE MARIONETTES

"From chaos, death. From death, deliverance."
—*Unknown*

1

CORPSES

Theailys An retched and the odor was almost as foul as that of the mangled corpse a few feet from where he knelt. A fantastic way to ring in his thirtieth year, to be sure. His younger self would have been surprised, horrified by the headless torso and the limbs strewn across the grass, by the gossamer threads of shadow leaking from the wounds—but that was then. Blackouts and mutilated bodies had become commonplace these last few years and it was hard to find shock in something so perversely routine.

Ignoring the carnage, Theailys stood and started through the moonlit trees. *This has got to stop,* he thought, though he knew the words held little weight. The breathing exercises his mother had taught him as a child did little to quell the murderous voice in his head, and his medication was as useful as a torch in rain. Had Theailys' victims been human he was sure the Faithbringers would have locked him up ages ago. Keepers, sometimes he wished the corpses had been, if only to validate his guilt.

He arrived at Helveden's southern periphery gate. A cold sweat rose from his pores. Nearly two dozen corpses lay strewn across the road; blood stained the cobbles black in the dark of night. Theailys had never before seen this many after a blackout. He had never seen *human bodies* after a blackout.

What did you do? he hissed inwardly.

The voice in his head giggled, manifesting as a spindly white-eyed silhouette. It'd taken to calling itself Faro, a once common name made infamous four centuries prior by the wartime slaughter and treason of Faro Fatego. History told he too had seen shadows, had whispered to the voices in his head. Taking that into consideration it was an aptly appropriated name.

Answer me, Theailys growled as they walked in step.

"You—demon!"

Armored footsteps clanked his way. Theailys blinked, then found himself swarmed by half a dozen Faithbringers, collared by the tips of their crystalline longswords as Faro paced circles around them; the Faithbringers could not see him. Their blades were slick with blood and their white half-plate bore signs of conflict. Theailys sucked in a ragged breath, then exhaled.

"Did you call the lokyns here?" growled the lead Faith-bringer.

"No." Theailys stole a glance at Faro, who had taken to

licking the Faithbringer's cheeks. He took another breath to compose himself. "What reason would I have for doing so?"

"You tell me," the Faithbringer said. His face twitched and Faro snickered. "The enemy are *your* ancient brethren."

"Aren't you an astute one?" Theailys crossed his arms. "Yes, my people are a lokyn sect, but we are no more the enemy than you are." Then, stepping forward so the sword tip touched his throat and drew a dot of blood: "Recall it was the mirkúr-wielding *human* Faro Fatego whom the enemy tasked to lead its brood, to whom our city nearly fell."

The Faithbringer snarled. Theailys had touched a nerve, though not one tender enough to provoke assault, not that the Faithbringers actually had grounds, nor were they dense enough to severely maim the only man who could finally bring an end to the new lokyn war. The Faithbringer sheathed his dragon's tooth of a blade, the others following his lead, then grabbed Theailys by the collar of his robes and shoved him toward the gate.

Theailys crossed the threshold, the southern farmlands stretching out before him, vast and gold, the late-night air imbued with an amalgamation of wet grass, rot, and death. As his blackouts had become commonplace so too had this perfume. It would remain as such so long as the lokyns ran amok.

"You could reap the demon scum.. Keep their essence for your own," Faro said. *"The power of those blackened souls and the mirkúr they possess—"*

No, Theailys thought. *Keepers only know what I do when you take control, but I refuse to reap while I'm awake, not until I have to at least. Not until I'm standing at the Heart of Mirkúr with The Keepers' Wrath in hand.*

Faro snickered. *"Oh, my Flesh..."*—Theailys *hated* the byname—*"You amuse me so! You truly expect your little power focus to imbue you with the strength to reap the barrier that yet surrounds the Heart!"*

Considering the recreation of The Keepers' Wrath has been my life these past five years, yes, I do, Theailys thought as they continued on. *Pray tell, what do you find amusing about that?*

"History," the white-eyed shadow said. *"I sometimes read while you're asleep."*

Better than maiming, Theailys thought.

"Debatable." Faro grinned at Theailys. *"My amusement though, dear Flesh, is in the irony of you taking up the very weapon Faro Fatego used to nearly bring your country to its knees."*

The irony of this had not been lost on Theailys. In fact, it had nearly caused him to abandon the endeavor completely on several occasions. As far as Theailys was concerned the end of this war couldn't come soon enough. With any luck, soon enough was perhaps three weeks away, four at the most.

He held his hand out to Faro. The grinning shadow took it gleefully and the two were made one as they entered Helveden proper, abuzz with the apprehensive merriment evoked by wartime fear and drink. Here the farmland stench dissolved, replaced by horse shit, piss, and bile. Theailys yawned, continuing up the oak-lined promenade, heading northeast toward the Hall of Illumurgists and sleep. He had gone perhaps half a mile when he heard his name.

A pale man in black Hall robes approached from the west. He carried a slip of parchment. "Mistress Khal and Queen

Ahnil require your immediate presence at the Bastion," he said, fingering the hour-old timestamp. "The, um…requisitions team has, um…returned."

Theailys raised an eyebrow. He'd not been expecting them for another week. He yanked the summons from the man and scanned it hastily, groaning. The requisitions team had returned, indeed—as body parts in silken sacks.

THE QUEEN'S council sat sequestered in the Bastion's war room. They'd convened an hour prior to Theailys' arrival, but his tardiness was the least of their concerns.

"This is bad, to put it mildly," Mistress Khal said. The Master Illumurgist sat parallel to Theailys, brow furrowed. "If word gets out about this people will call for blood and the generals may very well oblige them."

"At which point we'll have grossly smeared our covenant with the phantaxians," Theailys said. "The…remains they sent us were a sign, a simple warning to respect the laws laid out on either side, not a declaration of war."

"Yes, but do you really think a people festering in fear will see it like that?" Khal asked.

"Of course not," Theailys scoffed. "Our country is historically, barbarically rash. Any non-human is a perceivable threat. The phantaxians were forcefully exiled from the enclaves because of a plague unique unto their race and the dissident are routinely beaten and hung. Just yesterday a *child* was found strung up in the western farmlands. A *child*!"

Theailys stood to pace the room, hands clasped behind his

back. "Regardless—" He heaved a sigh. "Regardless, this business sets completion of The Keepers' Wrath even further behind schedule than it already was."

"You have a thought, then, brother?" asked Searyn, Theailys' twin sister and Faithbringer general.

Theailys offered the room a reluctant nod. "The conception of this weapon was my doing; I'm the only one who can wield it. I'll fulfill the requisitions myself. Time is of the essence and we can ill afford offending the phantaxians again. I hold favor with their king; that should help to some degree." He paused. "If my queen and council approve, of course."

They did, unanimously.

"I'll need three weeks, four at the most depending on how smoothly things go," Theailys said to Searyn. Round trip, it was about a three-week undertaking, but it was necessary to have a bit of a cushion considering the state of things. "Will your forces be able to hold ground near the Heart?"

"It's doable, though the quicker you are, the better. Our numbers are stretched thin as of late," she admitted, grimacing. "Te Mirkvahíl is dead by my own blade, which makes things a bit easier, but recent reports suggest the rate at which the Heart of Mirkúr is spawning lokyns has increased tenfold."

"These are substantiated by the frequency with which they slaughter villages in the west," Queen Ahnil said. "Not to mention the prevalence of their attempts to breach our walls."

"Understood. I'll make preparations to depart in two

days' time." Theailys rubbed his eyes and stifled a yawn. "If there is nothing else…"

The queen obliged him with a nod. "You are free to retire."

Theailys touched his right hand to his left shoulder in the formal salute and withdrew.

Footsteps trailed behind him, soft against the stone floor. "Feeling all right, brother?"

Theailys slowed to walk in step with Searyn. "Relatively speaking. It was only one corpse this time."

"A good day then." Searyn pushed a loose strand of auburn hair behind her ear. "You aren't tired."

"No." There was no point in lying, Searyn could read him like a book. "Just distracted. Three years to the day. Three years since…" Theailys tensed his jaw. Even after all this time he still had difficulty saying his wife's name. Part of it was grief, but most of it was guilt. He swallowed the lump in his throat and allowed a ragged sigh to escape his lips.

Searyn offered a sad smile and squeezed his arm. "Do you want to talk about it?"

"Not really," Theailys said. "If I do it'll be impossible for me to focus. But…"

Searyn raised an eyebrow. "But…?"

"Sometimes I think myself a fool to have embarked on such an undertaking," Theailys said. "History has not been kind where The Keepers' Wrath is concerned. Have you heard of Anasharon Anor?" Searyn shook her head. "She was Faro Fatego's wife, and in his quest to forge this weapon he accidentally reaped her soul, same as I did to Anayela."

"Perdition," Searyn murmured. "That's awful."

"War is awful," Theailys said, shoving his hands into his pockets. "But you know that more than most..." The question sat on the tip of his tongue. In all the months since Searyn had returned there was one thing they'd yet to speak at length about. "What was it like running your blade through that monster?"

"Awful," Searyn said. She offered nothing more and Theailys knew better than to press, especially at such a thing as this. "Are you heading off to sleep?"

"Not yet," Theailys said. "The burial grounds."

"I'll take my leave." Searyn kissed him on the cheek. "Try not to linger longer than you need."

"Hmm."

Presently Theailys withdrew into the cold night, starting south for the burial mounds. They were swathed in thick mist by the time he arrived, analogous of the pressure in his chest. Privy to this parallel, Faro roused from slumber with a shriek. Theailys offered nothing in response. The past three years had numbed him to the sound.

"*Mmm. Fun,*" Faro hissed as he took shape to Theailys' right. "*Smells like fun here with the dead, my Flesh. Have you come to kiss your Anayela's corpse?*"

Theailys rubbed his thumb against his index finger. A wisp of illum bloomed to light his way along the path. Faro snarled as they continued on. His abhorrence for Theailys' use of illum, minimal as it was these days, was perhaps as strong as Helveden's fear of Theailys' ability to wield mirkúr. The power of betrayers and demons, the people said. The weapon of Te Mirkvahíl.

A face from nightmare memory flashed across Theailys'

mind. He clenched his teeth. *Maybe they were right.* He wiped his nose on his sleeve.

"*You see, Flesh? Light makes you weak. You could be stronger if you snuffed it out, silenced it like night does the sun.*" Faro grabbed Theailys' hand. "*Let me show you. Let me help you feel while you're awake.*"

Theailys yanked his hand out of the shadow's grasp. *Not. Here. Keepers, anywhere but here!* He refused to let this darkness take control where corpses slept. Where Anayela's body lay at rest. He'd already let the mirkúr take her soul—the best he could do now was to keep it from tasting her dead flesh.

"*Are you sure? Not just this once?*" Faro pled, stroking Theailys' face and arms. "*I could ease your suffering with just a thread, a string of smoke to make her rise—*"

Stop. Theailys' fingertips were cold; the mirkúr was aroused.

"*—and you could hold her in your arms, my Flesh.*"

Theailys gnashed his teeth together as the world spun into obscurity. *Please!*

"*Dance beneath the starlight like you used to do.*

Before you reaped her soul."

A RAVEN LANDED *on the branch of an oak tree. It bore no leaves and its bark was the color of old ash. Theailys held his arm out and the raven came to him. It cocked its head, its beady eyes unmoving.*

"*Varésh,*" *Theailys said, acknowledging the creature by its name. He stroked its head, the feathers soft, if not a bit oily. "The world sits in your eyes.*"

The raven's eyes fluctuated cyclically from black to white.

"The darkness and the light," Theailys said. "You have seen it all."

Varésh squawked.

Theailys chuckled. "Why fly so far? What do you hope to find?"

Varésh clucked, flapping his wings.

Theailys sighed. "If you must. What do you make of dreams, old friend?"

Varésh hopped along Theailys' arm until he rested on his shoulder. He snapped his beak at a measured pace.

Theailys nodded. "I see. Is this always so? Is there always an ounce of truth to things we dream or is this simply your opinion, bird?"

Varésh clucked, taking flight. He landed on a tree branch, then bird and branch erupted into flames. Theailys simply stared. He took a seat in the grass and watched the oak tree turn to ash. From the ruin arose a slender silhouette. Theailys eyed the faceless shape, unmoving as he too caught fire and burned to ash, his remnants scattering in the wind.

STARLIGHT TWINKLED INTO BEING. Theailys jolted upward from the dirt, a scream caught in his throat, subdued only by his need to gulp the wet air. He trembled as the silhouette persisted in his thoughts, leering with her eyeless stare, taunting wordlessly just as she had done every week for the past three years. A monument to Theailys' failure.

He retched—a near certainty after a blackout—then scanned the area for remains. Keepers only knew what Faro had made him do. He saw nothing, but his heart thumped wildly when he realized Anayela's burial mound stood several feet from where he knelt. He pushed himself to his feet, knees knocking together, and approached. His stomach dropped, and urine dripped down his legs.

Mirkúr tendrils clung to shards of broken earth. Where once his wife had lain was now a vacant tomb.

Anayela's corpse was gone.

2

IRE

Serece yanked her crystalline blade from the lokyn's forehead with a grinding squelch. The demon's essence turned to ash and scattered in the wind, leaving behind the rotted remains of whomever it'd possessed. Disgusting things, these parasitic shadows. Absolute abominations of nature.

She pressed east, distant shrieks muffled by her hood. She hoped they belonged to lokyns falling prey to phantaxian blades, but the demons were so horrifically adept at mimicking voices it was sometimes hard to tell. A sound in the darkness of the pine trees ahead slowed her pace. She advanced in a crouch, fingers dancing on the hilt of her dagger.

"Serece."

Serece kept on, eyes narrowed, heart thumping. The voice sounded like Sharya.

"Temper Yssa," Serece recited, grip tightening.

"Don't let it harness you," Sharya replied.

Serece took a deep breath.

Then launched a crystalline throwing knife in the direction of the voice. The unseen impact drew a guttural wheeze. When after several seconds no retaliation came, Serece entered the trees to collect her knife.

She looked at the naked corpse, at the blade hilt-deep in the black, rotted skull. It was a lesser demon; the others didn't fall so easily. She yanked the weapon free and spat.

"Sharya doesn't speak using contractions, víthurstyg."

Serece continued on her way, the night now still and quiet. Her ears twitched occasionally as they always did when she was anxious. She arrived at the village square whereupon she found Sharya and her adoptive sisters, Sorin and Taür, gathering the newly dead.

"The others?" Serece asked.

"Lighting pyres in the east," Sharya said. "What of the west?"

"Abandoned," Serece said. "Save a couple of lokyns." She looked at the corpses. "Were there any survivors?" Sharya heaved a sigh, and Serece understood. Her chest tightened and her free hand balled into a fist. "This is the third village this week. I—"

"Should suppress what anger you have stewing and refrain from asking *why*," Taür suggested. "The lokyns kill for sport. It's as simple as that."

Serece frowned. "I know, and I've never questioned that. What strikes me as odd, *sister*, is their very existence. The Ariathans claim to have finally slain Te Mirkvahíl, yet its progeny infest our lands like the plague does our flesh."

"You assume the demons' lives are bound to Te Mirk-vahíl's own," said Sorin, "but there is no evidence to give credence to that belief. Te Mirkvahíl was the puppet master, the head of the serpent if you will, and when you rend a serpent's head from its body it will cease to function properly. For just a moment it will writhe, its actions uncontrolled."

Serece looked to Sharya for support, but the captain offered nothing more than a shrug and small shake of her head.

Serece turned her back to the women, grumbling. "Father believes me."

"*Of course* he does," Sorin said. "Now that Rejya's dead who better to indulge his theories than the royal bastard, hmm?"

Serece wheeled around and smacked Sorin across the face. The shorter woman yelped and staggered to the side, strands of silver hair peeking out from beneath her hood. She glared at Serece, cold blue eyes shifting back and forth between shock and anger.

Sharya stepped between the two, glancing disgustedly at each in turn. "You are childish with your words," she said to Sorin. To Serece, "And you are quick to give yourself to anger. In doing so you both disrespect the phantaxian tenets and put us in danger of provoking Yssa's wrath."

"Idiots," Taür muttered, rolling her eyes.

Serece drew her hood further past her eyes. Rejya's narrow-eyed image took shape in her mind, chiding her with pursed lips and a tilted head.

I know, I know, Serece thought. *Temper Yssa.*
Temper fury.

Rejya's image arched an eyebrow. *"If you know,"* she seemed to say, *"then why do I still sense Yssa feeding off of you?"*

To that, Serece had no answer, and she let the memory of her fallen sister dissipate with shame, a centuries-old emptiness welling in the center of her chest. A void created first by her infant daughter's death, followed by Rejya's death, then widened by the gradual loss of friends and family as the years had passed. She chewed her lower lip, sniffing back tears, then finally let a ragged breath escape and linger in the air.

"I'm sorry."

Sorin shrugged at the apology—she was prone to holding grudges. She brushed past Serece and set to helping a trio of newcomers erect the funeral pyre. Taür followed suit, the pair whispering back and forth.

Half an hour later the pyre blazed, and thick, acrid plumes of smoke carried fallen spirits upward to the Second Life. Or so Serece had always been told they did, and in this instance, liked to believe.

"Burn the buildings," Sharya ordered, handing Serece a torch.

Serece made for the structures north of the square, their pane-less windows not unlike the lifeless eyes of the bodies charring on the pyre behind her. The timber had begun to rot, its soul and structural integrity compromised by the degenerative nature of the mirkúr. To leave the village standing was to sow a plague.

She set fire to the building nearest her, listening to the rot and darkness crackle as the flames began to feast. Black smoke rose to meet the night. Serece walked the village at a measured pace, leaving conflagration in her wake and ash to fertilize the earth. She hoped, in time, something beautiful might grow, though in a frozen hellscape like the Phantaxis Mountains that was little more than wishful thinking.

An hour later they withdrew, the ash-dusted snow the only hint of what'd transpired.

The descent into the Érahnjë Valley was a silent, single-file down a switchback stairway in the rocks. Serece trailed several yards behind the rest, ears twitching madly, fingers dancing on her daggers' hilts. The air smelled mostly of virgin snow and pyre smoke, but beyond that, past the hint of pine, hiding in the darkest crevice of the night, Serece discerned the source of her unease—a scent like kindling aflame. It stoked her still-simmering agitation toward Taür. The atmosphere crackled and Serece cursed.

Yssa was about to go berserk.

Serece hissed, chiding herself mentally as she shoved past her pale-skinned kinsfolk to inform Sharya. She was almost there when a guttural shriek destroyed the midnight calm, like a thousand children screaming their demise. A half dozen plumes of smoke javelined from the sky, making impact in the valley at the stairway base. Snow and rock flew all directions; the phantaxians drew their blades. From the flurry manifested six slender silhouettes with eyes like full moons— the Shades of Yssa, phantaxian rage and frenzy made manifest. Each held a broadsword. Each reeked of flames and death. Each had been present thirteen years ago the night that Rejya died.

The Shades erupted toward the phantaxians. Normally a narrow corridor or stairway such as this would have offered a distinct advantage, but the Shades' fluidity and incorporeal nature negated this.

Serece danced beneath a cleave. Using the momentum, she thrust upwards and sheathed her dagger in the lower jaw of the Shade, its ethereal composition beginning to harden at the touch of her crystalline blade.

It shrieked and kicked Serece square in the chest, knocking her back. She slipped on the icy stone, lost her footing, and tumbled over the edge of the stairway. She hit the ground with a *thud*, the force of impact from the near ten-foot fall knocking the wind from her lungs. For a moment the world swam in and out of focus, the skirmish above a swirl of black and white, light and dark as crystal screamed through smoke.

A deep baying snapped Serece from her trance, just in time to see Sorin's body soar past her into the valley. Serece screamed and scrambled to her feet. Equilibrium not yet intact, she tripped and rolled down the hill, coming to rest a yard from where Sorin's body lay sprawled. Serece bellied herself to her sister's side, a ragged gasp escaping her mouth.

Blood stained Sorin's pale skin and silver hair. Her eyes, once the coldest blue, were a swirl of fog. Serece could see no wound, the little good that did. She brushed her hand over Sorin's eyes, closing the lids. Then, choking back tears and swallowing the lump in her throat, she rose and started up the hill.

She crested, teeth bared, lips curled back in a rictus of rage, and—

TAÜR LAY BLEEDING in the snow, her entrails hanging from her gut. She was not long for the world. With every blink the darkness became more profound. Every breath came weaker than the last. She rolled her head to the right, toward the stairway in the rock, and watched the Shades pin Sharya with their blades. Taür reached weakly, desperately for her friend, though there was little use in doing so. 'I see, and I feel,' was all it meant.

She started, wheezing at a breath on her neck, but she kept her eyes on Sharya, now limp and bleeding in the snow. Taür knew what had found her and she felt no inclination, no desire to gaze upon the thing that'd come to take her life.

Yet still she turned, if only to look her spellbound bastard sister in the eyes and curse her name, to rue the day their mother's faithlessness and general loathing of Serece had brought this pawn of ire to life. Behind Serece loomed the puppeteer, a black wolf wrought from smoke. An Avatar of Yssa, Serece's unbounded rage made manifest.

Taür grasped for the buckle of Serece's cloak and pulled her close so that their noses touched, so she could see coherence flood her sister's eyes as clarity left her own. "I…h-h-hate you." Taür coughed blood, taking care to spit a generous amount in Serece's face. "Always…did."

The first blade entered just above her hip, the second through her gut and into her spine. At the very least her physical pain had dispersed. *I hope this night haunts you for the rest of your days.* She closed her eyes, a muffled shriek the final sound she heard before the darkness took her home.

SERECE BLINKED. The night was still and she lay sprawled on her back, daggers clutched in her hands. The pain came first to her chest, then to her head, like a blade sheathed slowly in her flesh, then twisted. The image of a black wolf in blood-spattered snow flashed across her mind, followed by her sister's battered corpse. The scent of iron clung to the air, to her skin and garb, and Rejya's words rung loudly in her head: *"Temper Yssa. Do not let it harness you."*

Trembling, Serece lolled her head to the left, met by the moonlit dead and a massive wolf formed from smoke. It approached, each footfall leaving threads of shadow in its wake. It sniffed Serece, then raised its nose and bayed. The sound exhumed bits and pieces of a fractured memory. She had heard this howl the night that Rejya died; she had bathed in the blood drawn by her blades.

Not again, she thought. She tried to scream but was too weak. *Fuck. Not again!*

Tears dripped slowly from her eyes. Tears of sorrow and despair. Tears wrought by fear of an old truth she'd done her best to bury and the guilt that'd festered all these years. She had to tell her mother and father now, for her sake and for theirs. But how would they react? How would they look at her when she told them she had slaughtered Rejya and Taür?

3

WRETCH

Wine and whiskey were an awful mix.

Theailys tossed the wretched cocktail back, then wiped the dribble off his chin. It was a day for drink. A week, propriety be damned. He'd searched for Anayela's corpse until the sun shone bright and all he'd found was misery and worry in a mystery that never should have been.

What, he snarled inwardly at Faro for the umpteenth time, *did you make me do? What happened at the burial mounds last night you sadistic prick?*

And, for the umpteenth time, Faro held his tongue and refused to manifest, undoubtedly amused by the desperation his cruelty had wrought. Had the implications of his silence not been so severe, it would have been a welcome change.

Theailys growled and started from his chamber at the Hall. There still much to do before his departure tomorrow and Keepers knew stewing in the darkness with a drink or five would accomplish little, if any, of the tasks at hand.

"You reek something fierce," Mistress Khal said when he approached her in the courtyard several minutes later.

"Good old liquid vigor." Theailys wiped his nose with his forearm and cleared his throat.

"A shit brand I'd guess," Khal scoffed. "You look like you've not slept in days."

Theailys relayed to her the previous night's events as best he could.

She nodded. "So that's what's got the Faithbringers in fits today."

"By 'fits' do you mean they're going door to door and snarling at the dissident again?" Theailys said. Khal's grimace confirmed his assumption. "Great. Don't suppose they'll overlook me just this once?"

Khal shook her head. "Not a chance."

They started on their way.

"You've spent time trying to interpret dreams," Theailys said.

Khal shrugged, the late-morning sun a glint in her amber eyes. "I have. Certainly not enough to have mastered illumancy, but enough to more or less make sense of what I see. Something on your mind?"

Theailys told her about the raven, silhouette, and flames.

Khal thumbed her chin pensively. "There are some who believe dreams are more than dreams. That they are cries from the subconscious, distortions of truths, either yet to come or those that have already come to pass."

"Funny," Theailys said. "The bird said roughly the same thing."

"Interesting," Khal mused. "Considering."

Theailys arched an eyebrow. "Considering…?"

They passed into the shade of the oak-lined campus entry lane. Khal took a deep breath, savoring the fresh air. "Considering," she said, "ravens are often times depicted as tricksters. In illumancy they are seen as omens of ill tidings."

Anayela's missing corpse certainly qualified as such, but it didn't necessarily fit the narrative of his dream. Theailys frowned. "Maybe it's just old wounds unstitched. Old wartime fears." This wasn't the first time he'd had the dream. It'd been a regular affair with the occasional variation when Searyn went away to fight, and after Anayela's death. Now? Maybe it was the dread of failure—what would happen if The Keepers' Wrath didn't work? Thoughts of civil war, of Helveden choked by flames and ripped to shreds by demons turned Theailys' skin to gooseflesh underneath his robes.

"Maybe," Khal said, giving Theailys' shoulder a gentle squeeze. "Probably. Keepers know these last years have been rough. For all of us." Like Theailys, Khal too had lost her wife, and occasionally they would share a drink or eight and reminisce about the days before the shadows had begun to laugh.

They passed beneath the archway, nodded at one another, then departed opposite directions, Theailys southward for the farmlands and the sanatorium manor in which Searyn resided. A spur of the moment detour before wartime responsibility: it was the five-year anniversary of their older brother's death.

"I WAS HALF sure you'd forgotten," Searyn said. Her auburn hair was pulled back in a braid, making apparent the myriad scars on her pale face.

"Almost did," Theailys said, as they started for the apple grove behind the house.

Searyn smiled softly. "I suppose I don't blame you, considering." A Faithbringer general, she was undoubtedly privy to what'd transpired in the burial mounds. "How're you feeling?"

"Somewhere in between exhausted and drunk," Theailys said. "Garnished with disgust and fear. The usual, pretty much." He yawned, and his breath tasted like a foul amalgamation of liquor and bile. "How about you?"

"Well enough that Warden Mira granted me this walk," Searyn said. "Sniffed my smoke this morning, so the voices are asleep. Sky's not falling toward me anymore." She heaved a sigh. "War's a bitch. Phrenzka's worse."

Theailys took Searyn's hand, giving it a sympathetic squeeze.

They entered the grove a short time later, halting in the center before a polished black stone embedded in the earth: their memorial to their brother, Mar. Searyn knelt and caressed the stone, chewing her lower lip. Eventually it began to quiver, and she choked back whatever she'd been about to say.

Theailys sat beside her, legs crossed, gazing at his reflection in the smooth surface. "I think we were about seven or eight years when we found this stone on the beach. D'you remember?" Searyn tensed her jaw, nodding. Theailys sniffled, then chuckled. "You thought it would be a stupid birthday present. Said it was too pretty, and…" Again, he sniffled, sighing raggedly. "Shit."

The tears came steadily, silently. This time, Searyn took *his* hand and squeezed, hard enough to make it go numb. It'd been a dark day, Mar's death; Searyn had watched him fall. Theailys still had her tear-stained letter, splotchy ink and all. 'Went a hero,' she had written. 'Saved us all.'

"I'm sure he's watching over us from Rapture," Searyn said finally. "With mother and father, no doubt."

Theailys nodded, despite the pain radiating from his skull down into his back and arms. Despite the ethereal giggle signaling Faro's presence. He clenched a fist at the tickle of frigidity in his fingers, breathing deeply just as his mother had taught him as a child. To his relief, Faro faded back to the corner of his mind from whence he'd come.

"Promise me you'll be careful," Searyn said. "When you leave the city."

"My neuroses forbid me from being otherwise," Theailys said.

Searyn turned and looked him in the eyes. "*Promise me,* Theailys. Things are dark these days, even with Te Mirkvahíl dead, and the last thing I need is for my light to burn out." Her nails dug into the top of his hand. Her left eye twitched. "*Please.*"

"All right…all right." He pulled Searyn into a tight embrace. "I promise. You too, yeah?"

"I swear," she whispered into his shoulder. "I swear."

Clouds had gathered by the time they returned to the sana-torium—so had the Faithbringers. Adorned in bone-white plate they approached, hands resting on the hilts of crystal swords, the air about them tense with zealous ire.

"General Khoren has called for your arrest," the first proclaimed, voice distorted by a faceless helm. "For your desecration of the burial mounds." Then, snidely: "Imagine my shock—the dissident at the root of such abominable affairs. I never would have guessed."

Searyn gaped at Theailys.

"I wore that very expression just hours ago," the Faith-bringer said. "A strange and horrible thing to learn your commanding officer is the very wretch her people swear they are not."

Her people.

It was Theailys' turn to gape. Had he heard the Faith-bringer right? He looked at Searyn, whose expression was a cross between disgust and incredulity, peppered with unease. "...What proof do you have?" he asked. It was an inquiry, the strength of which accompanied his sister's mien, which was to say that neither was particularly confident. The Faith-bringers had *something*, lest they wrongly swarm a wartime sanatorium. But what?

The lead offered a writ. "General Khoren's command, complete with testimony from Wardens Mira, Lee, and Drahl." Searyn's handlers, as it were. "They spied you drag-ging bodies from the burial mounds. They found you *hanging corpses in a barn*." The Faithbringer paused. One produced a pair of shackles and the others drew their blades, as if anticipating noncompliance. "They saw you *wreathed in* and *wielding* mirkúr."

Searyn put a hand to her head and frowned. "I...don't remember *any* of that."

"A shame," came the distorted, disgusted reply, "that your mind prevents you from reliving sin. If I could make it so, you would dream it every night as retribution. I suppose tattooing the faces of the defiled to your flesh will have to do."

Theailys tensed his jaw and grimaced. An archaic practice, that. The oldest and still highly popular form of branding murderers and the like. He turned his gaze away—how could he look at her? Memory or not, the deposition in the writ was clear—his sister had profaned the dead.

So they *say, you idiot,* his conscience snarled. *This is Searyn —your* twin sister. *Are you going to fall in with these xenophobic, virtue-preaching fucks, or are you going to do what you do best?*

Theailys furrowed his brow and set himself between Searyn and the lead Faithbringer. "Show us proof." He smacked the writ. "This is just ink. General Khoren's opinion of the dissident is the worst kept secret in the country. Show. Us. *Proof.*"

The Faithbringer backhanded Theailys across the face and he dropped to the grass, blood trickling from the corner of his mouth. The Faithbringer pressed the toe of its boot to Theailys' neck, the tapered point of the sabaton resting on his spine. In his periphery Theailys watched them place the shackles on Searyn's wrists. Crystalline like their blades, thus impervious to demonry.

"Foster incredulity all you want," the lead Faithbringer said as they withdrew. "It will not absolve your sister of her wicked truth. There is no exoneration for your kind, nor will there ever be."

"Theailys…" Searyn's eyes were wet as she was led away.

He pressed himself to stand, to give chase, but they were far too quick in mounting up and starting from the grounds. Theailys stood there, shaking, tiny threads of mirkúr streaming sadly, ineffectually from his hands as Faro cackled in his head, as Searyn vanished overtop the farmland hills.

You could have stopped them, Theailys snarled.

"Indeed, my Flesh," Faro said. *"But you forbade my interference where the Faithbringers were concerned long ago, so I did not."*

Theailys clenched his fists. *…I hate you.*

Faro cackled. *"Self-loathing manifests in such peculiar ways. Like a voice inside your head or a shadow at your side. Embrace me. Embrace us, my Flesh. Free yourself of reservation—be your best self."*

Not if that means reaping, wielding demon smoke, Theailys thought. *I refuse—*

"Because you are weak," Faro sneered. He took shape in an instant, bringing Theailys to the grass with but the twitch of a wispy finger. *"This is what weakness looks like: on your knees as* they *take everything away. As* they *destroy and desecrate your kind. Do not fear your strength—find strength in your fear, as Khar Am once said."*

At that, Faro fell away, leaving Theailys warm with moderate rage at the scrutiny and xenophobia his people faced and rightfully puzzled by the voice's sudden clarity of speech. Where had *that* come from? And quoting the Faith-bringer Khar Am of all people? What. In. Perdition.

Theailys stood, spat, then began the slog to Helveden proper, thoughts an anxious whirl and taste buds screaming for a drink.

CAILEAN CATIL WAS SMASHED. To the point his flayed left arm didn't make him feel inadequate. To the point his left hand didn't seem a lump of scarred and fissured flesh with what some *might* consider fingers. He sauntered into the Nasty Rabbit Tavern and grinned at the irony of having ever thought himself a handsome man. The myriad sun-red scars, the thrice broken nose, and crystal eye—now so common-place Cailean could not recall his Keeper-given face, not even in his dreams.

He scratched his stubbled jaw, then produced a flask and sucked down what little drink remained: hot whiskey, with the taste of warfront piss. He wiped the dribble from his mouth and chin as he started toward the tavern door.

The low-lit room was welcoming to Cailean's good eye, the amalgamated stench of alcohol, mirth, and misery to his nose. He took up his usual seat beside the window and leaned against the booth.

"You look like shit," a blurred face said not long there-after, its owner dropping down opposite Cailean.

Cailean rubbed his eye, chuckling wryly as the face forsook its haze. "Theailys An. Could say the same of you." The dark-haired, gray-eyed fucker heaved a sigh and signaled for drinks. Cailean raised an eyebrow. "Really—you're uglier than usual you depressed sod. What's wrong?"

Theailys opened his mouth and out spilled a day's worth of misery with a dash of guilt and an extra pinch of fuck you for General Khoren.

"Oh," Cailean murmured. "Oh." He downed the rest of his ale, grimacing. "Shit." Then, lowering his voice: "Zealous hilt stroker probably framed her. Khoren's been looking for a reason to invalidate Searyn ever since the marshal made her Second General."

Theailys drank.

Cailean leaned back against the booth. "I was looking for you earlier at the Hall. I'm coming with you." He grinned wide at Theailys' tensing. "Heh. Searyn's orders. Queen's too." Cailean pulled his knife out and began to play. "Don't worry. Won't say anything mean about those paleskin bastards 'less the situation warrants it."

Theailys glared. "I've no qualms with letting the phantaxians send you back to Helveden in a silken bag if you call them that. Country over person, Cailean. I'll let them gut you if it means procuring the argentium I need."

Cailean chuckled, fingering the knife. He knew Theailys wasn't joking.

"Try smoke sometime," he said, standing. "Takes the edge off reality."

Cailean dropped seven silver square on the table, then tottered happily toward the pelvis-thrusting, rabbit ear-wearing men at the far end of the room.

THEAILYS SAT in the Hall courtyard with Mistress Khal. The moon was full, the air perfumed with honey-scented smoke. What an absolutely shit day it had been. First Anayela's missing corpse, then Searyn, now Cailean. Keepers scorch the earth, but why in Perdition did that drunkard piss stain have to tag along? They weren't friends, and the last time they had gone somewhere together they had nearly come to blows.

Theailys took a whiff of smoke, held it for a seven-count, then blew it out.

Khal snorted, took the pipe, and took a hit. The smoke escaped her lips in wispy tendrils as she fixed her eyes upon the moon. "Do you think they're up there? Ridge and Anayela? Hell, *everyone* who's ever been ascended? Are they up there in the halls of Rapture, looking down on us, or is it all just one big lie?" She looked at Theailys, strands of raven hair falling past her bloodshot eyes.

"Yes," Theailys said, "and no. I think...I think they're up there so long as we put stock in the concept of Rapture. The moment we lose faith and decide it's something fabricated by the Church, Ridge and Anayela cease to exist. Spiritually, I mean."

"Makes sense," Khal said. "Are you ready for tomorrow?"

Theailys offered a sardonic guffaw. "Funny. Did Searyn teach you that one?"

Khal took his hand and squeezed it sympathetically. "I'll keep an eye on things—on Searyn. You just make sure you keep a level enough head to see this through."

We're fucked if you fail, Theailys knew she meant.

He nodded. Then, taking a page from Cailean's book, he produced a flask and knocked the medicine back.

4

EXILE

The temple was empty save a figure cloaked in mourning red and white. Dawn light entered through the crescent moon- and star-shaped windows, casting pictures on the polished azure floor. Serece walked at a measured pace. Her head and muscles ached, half from battle, half from an hour-long council inquisition during which she had taken fault for the slaughter of her party through infected Yssa. Thankfully her wounds were clean and she was freshly bathed—she dared not confront her mother garnished in her sisters' blood.

Artemae turned to acknowledge her, midnight eyes bloodshot, wreathed black with grief and restlessness. She wore two snow roses in her braided mane of silver hair to commemorate Taür and Sorin; she had done the same for Rejya. "Here you are," she whispered, boring into Serece. "Here, while they are gone."

Serece swallowed. "Mother, I…" She approached,

reaching for Artemae's hands, but her mother turned away. "Please don't put your back to me." Tears welled, and Serece bit her lower lip to hold them back. "Do you wish them here instead of me? Rejya, Sorin, and Taür?"

"Always."

The floodgates cracked. Serece tensed her jaw. "I am sorry to disappoint you—again."

Artemae said nothing as she started toward then knelt before the argentium effigy of Vol'anan. "Mother of Souls," she whispered, hands to her heart, "ferry our fallen to the fair skies above. Love my daughters in the Second Life as fiercely as I did here in the First."

Serece knelt beside her mother, a prayer resting on her tongue, but Artemae gripped her arm. "Stand. Beg nothing of our Mother lest you wound her ears. You already test her patience with your presence in this place."

Serece obeyed, tears trickling down her cheeks. She retreated several steps. "You and I were never close," she said. "You always favored Rejya. You saw the best of yourself in her as we grew. You saw your courage and your will to lead, your tactical prowess. Your unwavering loyalty and compassion for our people even as this flesh-plague started civil wars. In Taür and Sorin, erudition. Wonder.

"But in me?" Serece said, sniffling. "In me you saw your failure—nothing more than a mistake. You told father as much and yet he loves me like his own." Her body quaked. "I was the silent fury your infidelity produced, a stain you would have washed away had you been able. But you couldn't, and it festered, and now everything is *so much worse!*" She strode to Artemae and yanked her up by the hood. "LOOK AT ME!"

Artemae wheeled around and wrapped her hand around Serece's throat, face contorted in a familiar rictus of rage. "…*You…*" Her arm shook, and she relented her grip. She released Serece and brought her hands to her mouth, eyes wet, wide. "*You took my girls.*"

Tears flowed like a river in spring. "I-I didn't m-mean to," Serece whispered as she again reached for her mother's hands. "Mama, please… I don't want to be like this, so angry all the time. *Please…*"

Artemae brushed the gesture off, gazing pensively, furiously past Serece. "The council…your father…"

"Are already aware," Serece murmured. She thought to reach for her mother again but decided doing so to be fruitless. Instead she clasped her hands behind her back, eyes fixed on the floor.

Serece held this position a long while after Artemae had withdrawn from the temple. Eventually she dropped to her knees, prayed to the Mother of Souls, and wept for the dead sisters her rage and envy had poisoned her against.

———

Day yawned into dusk, dusk into night. Serece stood atop the highest spire of the Citadel, the courtyard pyres little more than orange dots from this high up. She had been refused admittance to the funerary rites for Sorin and Taür on pain of death, and a part of her—a far larger part than Serece was normally comfortable conceding to—accepted this decree despite its implications.

Pariah. Witch. She chewed the inside of her cheek, snorting at the hypocrisy of such a thought. *As if I'm the only whose rage has ever summoned Shades or loosed an Avatar upon the land.* After the onset of the plague and their violent expulsion from Ariath, the phantaxians had been forced to weather what was known historically as the Year of Shades, during which they'd lost a quarter of their population to Yssa's frenzied manifestations. Tempering that bestial energy was nigh impossible when it was siphoning rage from nearly one hundred thousand people. *Though I suppose none of* them *ever killed the queen's daughters.*

Daughters. Daughter. Serece lingered on the word, remembering her own, her little Vhora, dead before her second month. She gnashed her teeth at the memory of that night, of the plague devouring her girl, and choked it back to the darkness of her mind. She supposed she could handle being a failure in her mother's eyes—that wasn't likely to change. But to have failed *as a mother...* Keepers, but the knowledge was enough to make her want to rip her heart from her chest. A parent wasn't supposed to bury their child.

Serece sniffed back tears and watched the smoke rise, its wispy tendrils twisting in the breeze as they reached toward a tapestry of stars. There was peace to this ethereal dance. Momentary, peculiar, but profound enough to make her wish it would remain. To wonder how she could bend to persistent anger and the weight of her mother's contempt when she had tasted something so pure.

Her ears twitched. She looked to the doorway, then felt her body relax. "Father."

Undrensil peeled back his hood and approached, a weary smile drawn tight to his lips. His cheeks were dry, but she could sense the sorrow swirling in his sulfur eyes. To all, perhaps save Serece, he was a master at suppressing his pain. He pulled her into his arms, resting his chin atop her head, and Serece allowed herself to melt into his chest.

"What do you plan to do?" His voice was deep, his words soft.

Serece offered a watery chuckle. She only ever came here when considering something bold. "You know me well, papa." She took a deep breath and heaved a long sigh.

Undrensil pulled back and tipped her chin up with his thumb. "You mean to leave."

"To stay here is to exist alone in a crowded room," Serece said, taking his hand. "To be marked a pariah. I accept responsibility for my sisters' deaths, and I surely deserve the odium thrown my way, but..." She squeezed tighter. "Te Vétur Thae harbors far too many means to provoke my temper, especially now. I fear I'll only strengthen Yssa and expedite its next manifestation."

Undrensil nodded, swallowing the lump in his throat. "Where will you go?" Worry flashed in his eyes. "Not Banerowos, I hope?"

Serece shivered at his mention of the dead city, silently cursing him for having said its name. Losing Vhora had been bad enough, but what Serece had tried to do in Banerowos had etched a permanent sickness in her mind. Things dead were better left so.

"No," Serece said. "Somewhere I can hide. Where I can think." She leaned in to hug her father once more, whispering, "I don't want to harm anyone else. And I don't want to *hurt*."

He held her, and they stood there in the gentle night until long after the funerary smoke had died. His kindness, his gentle nature and enduring acceptance of an angry young woman without his blood—Serece would miss that, miss *him* dearly.

"I'll come back," she said finally. "I don't know when, but I promise you I will."

"Do what you need," Undrensil said, stroking her hair. "I just want you to smile. I can't remember the last time I saw happiness in your eyes." He kissed her forehead, then left Serece to the night and her thoughts.

She remained a while longer, arms resting on the balustrade, eyes fixed to the distant peaks in the east—the Frostlands, where she and Rejya had first come to blows. Where they'd nearly killed each other twice, then wept apologies as they shirked the Avatar and Shades their dual exasperation had invoked. Mortality and kinship had a strange relationship, and Serece could not help grinning at the memory of that night.

Adrenaline coursing, she withdrew to pack her things.

THE TOWN WAS a necropolis of hoarfrost and ice. It had been this way for centuries, since the night Phantaxis died and the onset of the plague. The snow here in the Frostlands was exponentially colder than it was in Te Vétur Thae and the lower plateaus of the Phantaxis Mountains. Serece peeled back her hood and rolled up her sleeves. The increased frigidity soothed her flaking, plagued skin whilst renewing her verve. For that, she loved the snow. Craved it like a drunkard does the drink.

She abhorred it too. All phantaxians did, whether they cared to admit so or not. As the snow prevented the plague from further consuming their flesh, it kept them leashed to the Phantaxian peaks. Confined to a bar-less cell. In that respect the phantaxians were a race of wretched immortals. *One day,* she thought. *One day I'll brave the expedited rot and see what lies beyond the snow and rock.* But for now, it was time to see what lay beyond persistent loneliness and rage.

Serece wandered through the moonlit ruin. Eventually she came across the jagged half-collapsed skeleton of a temple. She ducked under the door and into the rime-infested ante-room, familiarity peaking as she eyed the tarnished statues of the Keepers. Even now, despite their ruin, they stood tall and proud.

Beyond them was a cracked and crumbling pedestal, the sight of which stirred odium in Serece. Before the time of plague and endless snow the pedestal had borne the effigy of the god who'd doomed them to this hell. *Curse you,* she thought. *I hope your soul still burns for what you did, Phantaxis. I hope our eternal suffering was worth whatever you achieved by meeting with Te Mirkvahíl.* She closed her eyes and took a breath. Push away the anger—that was what she had to do, what she had come to do. Temper the inner flame to keep the beast at bay.

"I knew that one day you would come," said a voice within the darkness of the passageway ahead. There was a softness to the tone, a gentle urgency. "It was written in the light, whispered of in shadows." A woman emerged, skin bruised and mottled by the plague, azure eyes aglow. She was gaunt, but not unhealthily so, and in her hand, she held a tiny bag. "You look older in the eyes than I recall, my girl."

Serece's heart thumped against her chest. The only one who'd ever called her that was… *"Aunt Fiel?"* She closed the gap and wrapped her arms around the taller woman's neck. Fiel chuckled, a strong arm around Serece's waist. "I thought you were *dead,*" Serece whispered. "Mother said—"

"Bah," Fiel spat. "Artemae says a lot of things. That does not make them true." She pulled away and took Serece's hand. "Bad energy is all my sister is, and you, my dear, deserve much more than that, thank the Keepers Undrensil is good of heart." Again, she spat. "Come now. Time to rest, Celestials know that sleep will soon be scarce."

5

PRESAGE

"Are we there yet?" Cailean said. He gave his black shaghound a pat on the neck and the giant dog barked its approval. Keepers, but these beasts were beautiful. Nothing like riding a hound the size of a bear into battle to make a man piss himself with excitement.

"You asked me the same thing an hour ago," Theailys said. "What do you *think*?"

Cailean scanned the vast plains, tall grass bent beneath the will of the rain. "I think," he said, "I can hardly feel my ass. My pants are soaked through and last night was the hardest fuck I've had in a while. Imagine trying to fit a tree trunk—"

"I *really* don't want to," Theailys interjected.

Cailean chuckled. "I also think my flask is dryer than the desert lands of Nevithal."

Theailys rolled his eyes, reached into his coat, and produced a wineskin that had quite clearly been shown love over the years. Cailean grinned and yanked it from his hand. He uncorked it and took a meaningful sip, letting the liquid set fire to his bones in the best way it could.

"So. Where's your shield?" Theailys asked.

Cailean's left eye twitched. "Elsewhere." He took another swig from the skin, hoping it would dispel the perpetual itch the crystalline barrier's absence invoked. "Why?"

Theailys shrugged. "Just curious. You *are* a Warden, after all."

"Hmm. How 'bout that," Cailean mused wryly. "I s'pose I am."

Theailys frowned. "Fine. Sorry I asked."

Cailean drank the rest of the wine but it was of little use. The memories scratched for release like a bitch at the door. So much light. So much blood. And the screams...well. Those were something else entirely, like a newborn child flayed alive then cooked in a pot (and fuck all if *that* wasn't the most horrific thing he had seen in his life). He eyed Theailys, cursed with demon smoke, and felt envy. Confined to the Hall and subject to blackouts—this prick had it *easy* compared to those who had fought on the front. Cailean gnashed his teeth. *What I wouldn't give for some fucking amnesia and a second dead eye.*

Or a quick end to this miserable life after war. A blade through the heart. An axe to the neck. A mace to the skull. Whatever it took to move on.

Whatever it took to forget.

Avar smelled of fresh rain and apple pie, of wet stone and dirt. Cailean let the myriad perfumes consume him as he brushed off memories of war and dreams of blood. The click-clack of horseshoes and the buzzing din of people bustling to and fro quelled screams and snapping bones, shaghound barks the cackling of demons. Keepers, how he'd missed this place.

He drank alone at the tavern bar, Theailys elsewhere, arguing with demons of his own. *Least that boy has company,* Cailean thought as liquid fire warmed his flesh. He paused to reconsider his impression of Theailys, then shrugged. At this point a silhouette that whispered murder seemed a better corollary of war than did the nightmare memories it evoked. *And I'll bet the conversation's interesting too.*

He drank deep, inebriation stimulating further specula-tion. Was the voice, the shadow Theailys whined about, his demon smoke made manifest or was it wrought by phren-zka? The two men were less friends than they were acquain-tances, so conversation on the topics of mirkúr and mental illness rarely came up, if ever. Searyn had mentioned her brother being subject to this thing since childhood but that shed little light on Cailean's curiosity.

Maybe one's a product of the other. He snorted into his mug. *Shit, but I sound smarter when I'm drunk.* His thoughts drifted to Harbanan, a city on the other side of the world, and an old life where one's strength was relative to the potency of the whiskey they drank. An odd, nightmarish epoch, that. "Bar..." he half whispered, half slurred. "Once marked, always marked..." Another drink, and a memory surfaced with the force of a breaching whale.

A DUSTY PURPLE and orange dusk provided light as they departed Avar and rode for Ulm. Cailean's head ached something wretched as they rode, but then again it usually did. He ignored the feeling as best he could and snuck a glance Theailys' way. "How you feeling?"

"Well enough," Theailys said. "Rough morning. Thoughts were, *are* occupied by…you know." He heaved a ragged sigh. "Do you think there's a modicum of truth to any of it? To Searyn…" Cailean heard him swallow his nausea. "To Searyn…"

"Desecrating the deceased? Profaning Anayela's corpse with demon smoke?" Cailean scratched his cheek. "Dunno." Bar flashed across his mind. "Maybe." He squeezed his eyes shut tight until the monster vanished from his thoughts. Then, he opened them and let the pastel dusk tattoo itself to memory. "One thing I've learned in all my years? Nothing is ever as it seems." He swallowed the lump in his throat. "You guard your heart and guard it well, my friend. Once you let the devil in there ain't no letting go. Once marked, always marked."

CAILEAN SAT in the tavern at Ulm, predictably of course. Unpredictably, he hadn't had a single drink, though the night was young enough that things could change. *Keepers, why am I even here?* He snuck a glance at the bar, at the woman tending to the myriad inebriated fucks. She'd grown older in the eyes; she appeared stretched thin as some might say, though her hair was as beautiful as ever, like deep red fire. She looked angrier as well, though that could have been because the woman two stools to the left had just retched rum and wine.

Fuck it. Cailean stood and strode across the room. He took up the lone remaining stool and rested his elbows on the bar. "Doing all right, Leyandra?"

She paused in her attempt to clean the vomit. "Five years," she hissed. "Five years without a word, and you have the audacity to ask if I'm *all right*?" She wiped away the rest of the muck and tossed the rag at Cailean's face. "Fuck off."

Cailean ducked and it smacked the floor behind him. He sighed, resting his cheek against his fist. "I deserved that." Leyandra crossed her arms and glared. "Deserve that look as well."

"Truthfully, you one-eyed shit: why're you here?"

"Here specifically, or…?" Leyandra's glare persisted. Cailean grinned. "Heading south to freeze my sack off on phantaxian turf and fuck their king. Got a war to end and what not."

Leyandra raised an eyebrow. "And the key to doing so is, what…a rectal climax?"

They stared at one another for a moment. Then Cailean winked and Leyandra sighed, unable to subdue her smirk. "You have a one-track mind, you stubbled bastard." She leaned over the bar and kissed his cheek. "I've missed you. Not a soul here besides me who's danced with Galska Nuul. Drank myself to sleep too many times to count while trying to make the memories disappear."

Cailean nodded, wincing at the mention of that bastard fallen angel. "Yeah, me too. They're a bitch."

"You find what you were looking for?" Leyandra asked. "In the shit, against Te Mirkvahíl?"

"Just more of the same. Entropy, death…" He glanced at his mangled arm. "Failure."

Leyandra produced a bottle of wine from under the bar. Already uncorked, she took a generous sip then passed it off to Cailean, who sucked down half before he set the bottle to the side. She gave his good hand a gentle squeeze. "Sorry to hear."

"*You* look *miserable*." Theailys took perch on the empty stool to Cailean's left, his eyes bloodshot, a stupid grin stretched across his face.

"Who are you?" Leyandra asked. "And what the hell have you been smoking?"

"Horse shit by the smell," said Cailean, wrinkling his nose. "Ley, this idiot here's Theailys An. He's coming with me to fuck the phantaxian king."

"For argentium!" Theailys added with an interjecting index finger. "To make a *weapon*."

"Perdition…" Cailean sighed, "how much did you smoke?"

"Probably a bit too much," Theailys said. He tilted his head, mouth agape. "…Why is there *a dragon* in the doorway?"

Okay, Leyandra mouthed. She followed his gaze, then turned and took his hand. "Love. That's a tabby." To Cailean, "You should see this one to sleep. He clearly needs some rest." Her eyes narrowed—she was lingering on a thought.

"Dawn," Cailean said. "In case you were wondering.

Leyandra nodded. "I'm coming too. For old time's sake."

Theailys giggled, then stumbled backward over his feet and onto the floor.

"All right." Cailean stood from his stool and hoisted the younger man up. "Come on you miserable sack. Let's get you in a bed before you do something stupid." He looked back, giving Leyandra a knowing wink. "See you tomorrow."

6

YSSA

"I've always liked cliffs, especially these," Fiel said as they sat and watched the clouds. Below them spanned the whole of the Frostlands, rocks, trees, and rivers mere dots and lines from this far up. "Makes me feel bigger than the world when I need to be. Gives me perspective when my ego runs amok."

Serece smiled. "I agree." She closed her eyes, basking in the chill breeze, letting it ease her mind, allowing her body to relax. "Mother always hated them." Artemae had hated many things. "Do you think she will ever forgive me for what I did?"

Fiel wrapped an arm around her niece's shoulders. "Hard to say." Her eyes narrowed slightly, a small smile tugging at the corner of her mouth. "She wasn't always so...—she was different once. Years before you came to be. Before Rejya, even. I suppose her character now is the consequence of past failures. A free-flowing river turned to ice."

Serece tilted her head. "What do you mean?"

"Before your mother loved Undrensil she loved another," Fiel said. "Phantaxis."

Serece felt numb. She had an inkling as to where this conversation was headed and she did not like it, not one bit. "Sorin called me the royal bastard the other day." Fiel's grip tightened on her shoulders. Serece inhaled, then sighed shakily. "Phantaxis was my father, wasn't he?"

Fiel nodded. "By blood, yes. But Undrensil is the man who raised you, the man who loved you unconditionally even after Artemae betrayed his faith. Phantaxis..." Her body tensed. "Phantaxis betrayed us all."

"Is that why she hates me?" Serece asked. "Because I remind her of *him*?"

"I suppose," Fiel said. "But Artemae is the only one who can say for sure."

Serece gazed out at the world below, chest tight, tears at bay, anger nonexistent. She felt only sorrow—for her mother. Logic screamed she feel otherwise but she could not bring herself to do so. There was no point. Dwelling in misery would accomplish nothing and anger would only feed Yssa. Instead Serece focused on Undrensil and her memories of the man who'd been there for her every step of the way, even after she'd gone berserk and killed both Rejya and Taür. *Keep doing that,* she told herself. *When everything feels dark, focus on the light.*

"Where are we going?" she asked of her aunt. They'd been traveling half a day.

"To commune with Yssa," Fiel said. "To see if we can't soothe her soul."

Serece cocked an eyebrow. "*Her* soul? I thought Yssa was just energy."

Fiel stood and pulled Serece to her feet. "Our people are ignorant of much. If you could all understand her, know her as I have come to over the years, there might be hope for some change."

Change would be welcome. The very mention of it, the way her aunt suggested the possibility of it made Serece swear she could almost feel the warmth the plague had deprived the phantaxians of so long ago.

"Lead the way."

THE TEMPLE SAT atop a plateau a couple hours' climb from the cliff Serece and Fiel had rested at. It stood at the other side of a bridge, built into the rock and ice. From its roof ascended the effigy of a woman, perhaps two or three hundred feet in height. Instinct suggested to Serece that this was Yssa, or at least one of her many manifestations.

Fiel strode toward and across the bridge with certainty and purpose, but Serece found herself hesitant now that they were finally here. There seemed a strange aura to this place, perhaps because Serece had only *just* learned of its existence. How long had it stood? When had it been built, and by whom? It wasn't mentioned at all in the phantaxian archives, not as far as she was aware, nor had her father ever spoken of it. If *he* was ignorant of its existence Serece was sure the rest of her people were.

Serece hurried after her aunt, the wind whipping snow

and ice. She pulled her hood a bit further past her face and crossed her arms to her chest as if the cold were, for once, not welcome. "What do you know of this temple's history?"

"Little," Fiel said. "Only as much as Yssa relays."

"Who built it? When?"

"*Not* the phantaxians," Fiel said. "A race called the Reshapers, and several *thousand* years ago. To what end I haven't a clue."

Serece had never heard of the Reshapers, but the fact these mountains had at one time been occupied by a race other than the phantaxians was certainly intriguing and perhaps explained the existence of Te Vétur Thae, which her people had stumbled upon and occupied even before their exile from Ariath.

The temple interior smelled of wet wind and rock. Illuminated wisps swam lazily through the air, casting pale yellow light about the anteroom. It was homely, welcoming in a way Serece had never thought a temple could be. The floor bore the inlay of a giant bird, its feathers fluctuating black to white to blue beneath the wispy light.

"Their god, I think," Fiel said. "The Reshapers, I mean. I've seen this inlay in another temple elsewhere in the mountains." She led Serece further in, down a hallway that fell into a descending, corkscrew stairway. The bottom leveled out into a dome-ceilinged room lit also by the wisps, at the far end of which stood a life-sized effigy of a woman, on whose shoulder perched a bird and beside whom stood a wolf. The rest of the room was decorated by a variety of childlike statues in motion, running through trees carved of stone. "This is where we first spoke."

Serece approached the effigy, her steps measured as she gazed curiously about the sanctum. To think such a place as this existed within the rock and ice... She stopped a foot or two before Yssa's statue, completely white save her eyes, which had been painted the color of spring. *Keepers, who are you?* It was an odd feeling to believe *this* was the source of bestial fury.

Serece twitched at a sudden tingling in the center of her mind, like something sifting through her thoughts. She looked back at Fiel, who smiled and gestured she kneel. Serece did so, instinctively closing her eyes so she might somehow look upon whatever or whomever had entered her mind. All she saw though was the blackness of closed lids. She sensed her aunt kneeling beside her, felt her take her hand, and relaxed a bit.

NOT WANT TO HURT, said a voice in Serece's mind, soft and loud all at once. *NOT WANT TO HURT. BUT NO MORE I CAN DO. NO MORE I CAN DO. NOT WANT TO HURT.* Frantic, almost childish in a way.

Are...are you Yssa? Serece asked.

NOT WANT TO HURT, came the reply. *NO MORE I CAN DO.*

Serece tensed her jaw. *Did you hurt someone? Did someone or something hurt you?*

The sound of crying filled her mind. Sobbing, like that of a woman who'd just lost her child. Serece gritted her teeth; Fiel gripped her hand tighter and gave it a couple of reassuring squeezes.

NOT...WANT. NOT...I do NOT... The sobbing faded to sniffling. *No more. No...more.* A face manifested: the spring-eyed woman depicted in the effigy. *I am sorry. I am sorry. I…* She closed her eyes, tears squeezing between her lids and down her white cheeks. *I hate when they hurt, for their hate makes me hurt. You—* She reached out to Serece, and Serece started at the sensation of a soft hand caressing her cheek. *Dear child of Phantaxis, I have hurt you so.* Her expression darkened and she glanced away from Serece.

Serece swallowed. She imagined herself reaching out to this…spirit? *Yssa.* The woman responded to the name, wet eyes fixed on Serece, mouth slightly agape. *Yssa, it hurts me to see you so sad. Is there something I can do? Is there a way I can help you?*

Fiel manifested in Serece's mind. Yssa looked at her, then back at Serece. *Fiel said you were kind, that you would offer me aid.* Yssa approached, eyes wide, desperate. *Please. You have to come. You have to free me from this awful place lest I destroy you and your people. Please!*

Serece breathed shakily, adrenaline racing. She took Yssa's trembling hands. *All right. But…where? Free you from where?*

Lea Mort, Yssa replied, her corporeality waning. *The In Between. Please! Before it's too late!* She shrieked and Serece tumbled from the darkness of her own mind.

Serece looked to Fiel, the two back in the chamber they'd started in. "What just happened? What in Perdition is Lea Mort and The In Between?"

"The realm from which Yssa comes," Fiel said. "A place of memories and spirits."

Serece gawked at her aunt. "And you expect us to get there how, exactly?"

Fiel grimaced and pulled a dagger from her belt. "You aren't going to like it."

VARÉSH—VARE as he preferred these days—sighed. It was a pain in the ass being trapped here in The In Between and having to constantly masquerade as Yssa was beginning to take its toll, though he supposed he deserved it. All the blubbering and screaming, his accidental massacring of nearly half the phantaxian people—that woman Serece would *not* be remotely pleased when she learned his attempts to communicate had made her gut her sisters like swine—...it made him ache for a drink in the way a eunuch ached for his—

"You think I can't smell you?"

Shit. Vare stumbled through the murk of this cave in Lea Mort. If he could flee this awful place and make it to the door at the lake, he might *just* be able to evade Phantaxis' abominable spirit. *Why did I ever think taking a nap this long would be a good idea, let alone in such a forsaken place as this?* Lea Mort, The In Between land of the dead. There was already a middle ground somewhere in the Phantaxis Mountains, so why did The In Between need one of its own?

Vare grumbled as he sprinted through the darkness, half out of breath already. *When I finally leave this place the first thing I'm going to do is go for a run. Celestials, but I'm horribly out of shape.* Hiding left little time for exertion.

Vare leapt toward the dot of light at the end of the cave. He tripped, then tumbled out of the darkness, met by a sky of ever-shifting colors and stars. At least it was pretty here. He couldn't fathom being trapped in a place as horrible as this if it also looked like that shithole city Harbanan. *Garden of Souls. Bah!*

The lake shimmered in the distance. Vare looked back at the cave, at the tiny white dots he figured to be Phantaxis' eyes, then at the valley below. *Please,* he prayed, running, *let my horribly out of shape spirit make it to the lake before he can eat me.* The fate of the world kind of depended on it.

"WHY THE HELL WOULD YOU STAB ME?" Serece took a swing at her aunt, anger and frenzy be damned. "You could have killed me!"

"But I didn't," Fiel said as they stood in a fog-ridden street. "In the physical world our bodies lie just outside the temple, buried in snow." Snow provided the phantaxians with their wretched form of immortality.

Serece glared. "So, the only way to enter The In Between is to be stabbed into unconsciousness?"

Fiel nodded slowly. "Or meditation."

Serece's nostrils flared and her eyes went wide. She pointed an accusatory finger at her aunt. "I could gut you right now. You could have warned me!"

"I said you probably weren't going to like it," Fiel defended.

"Who in their right mind likes getting stabbed?" Serece snapped.

"I could think of a few people," Fiel mused with a smirk.

"All right, all right." She held her hands up. "I should have warned you. I just thought...well, like you said: who likes getting stabbed?"

Serece exhaled slowly. "Where are we anyway? Why is it so foggy?" She did a double take at Fiel, then looked down at her own hands and arms. "No plagued flesh." Just smooth, sunset-purple skin. She looked at Fiel. "How...?"

"A memory, mine to be exact. The Helveden of centuries past," Fiel said and the fog began to thin.

Serece frowned. "How am I in *your* memory? I don't understand."

"Illumancy," Fiel said. "To bind our minds."

"Right." Serece had yet to comprehend just how exactly illumancy worked, let alone the fact her aunt was somehow able to practice it. So far as she knew there had only ever been one phantaxian able to wield illum, and he'd been dead a long time. "How do we find Yssa if we are all the way back here?"

"We look for signs," Fiel said. "Yssa was with us even here, so far from the mountains." She started down the street, gleaming spires rising through the fog, glinting like jagged jewels in the strange gray light. "All we need find are the old phantaxian enclaves."

Serece trailed her aunt, the street gradually filling with people, with mirth. The scent of freshly baked goods, the perfume of flowers, and the metallic tang of... *Illum. Of course.* Her lip curled as she took note of the Illumurgist at the end of the block. Dark brown hair, stubbled jaw, purple eyes, pale skin: common amongst Ariathans to be sure. It was the thin, almost indiscernible threads of shadow twisting around his fingers though that marked him different than the rest.

Was this Faro Fatego, the infamous Betrayer of Ariath, the human lieutenant whom Te Mirkvahíl had tasked with laying siege to Helveden?

She slowed as she neared him, but her presence went unnoticed. She seemed a ghost here, as much a memory to these people as they were to her. How long ago had this taken place, how soon before the phantaxians' exile? It was hard to tell from the look of things. Serece had heard stories of Helveden but she had never spent much time here; her mother had scoffed at the idea of living in enclaves. Enclaves, according to Artemae, were for cultural heretics like Fiel, "Who are blind to the prejudices constantly shown us by the Ariathans." As a result, Te Vétur Thae was the only home Serece had ever truly known.

She frowned, lost in thought as she hurried after Fiel. Te Vétur Thae…there was much Serece loved about the city: her father, the way the trees shimmered in the light like tiny stars, the… She chewed her lip. Was that really all she could find endearing? Her father and trees? *Pick something*, she urged herself. *Pick anything. Anything at all!*

After a moment's thought the answer became apparent: passion. The desire to walk and never stop. There were a handful of phantaxians who believed the immortality their plague had bestowed upon them was more of a boon than not, but Serece—and thankfully the majority of her people—thought otherwise. Yes, barring catastrophe their lives would go on and they'd watch the world around them evolve, all while tethered to the mountains their god Phantaxis—her *father*—had doomed them to. *That* was no boon; it was a life sentence. Freedom was illusory. The moment you left the mountains, the moment you grew out of range of the snow the clock would start ticking and the rot would set in.

Anger roused in Serece. Her skin prickled with the heat of frustration, so she lashed out at the wall of the building to her left. Her fist met stone with a crack and she hissed as the force of the blow traveled up her arm and into her shoulder. She rubbed her knuckles gingerly. It was only when the rage began to subside that Serece realized Fiel was nowhere to be seen. *Great.* She stopped to survey her surroundings: a fountain in the city square just ahead; what she presumed was a church to her left, though the red, white, and black color scheme was a bit jarring; shops all around, people bustling to and fro, walking through Serece like the ghost she was, and—

The man she assumed to be the Betrayer, making a beeline toward her position. Serece tensed as he neared, and he stopped just several feet from where she stood. She tilted her head and he smiled. "Fiel. My love, where have you been?"

Serece blinked. Had he said what she thought he had? She glanced down at her skin, now a warm gold, then felt her hair, a collection of thin braids tied together. *What in Perdition...* Her ears twitched and she rubbed her arm, forcing herself to smile. "Faro," came the automatic response. "My niece, she was ill."

Faro Fatego approached, taking her hand. "Is she well, now?"

Serece—Fiel?—nodded. "Nearly." She coughed. "...Something strange is in the air."

Faro tilted his head. "Strange how?"

"I am not sure," Serece said. "But..." She held her palm out, upturned, and winced. "Yssa fluctuates frequently."

"I see." Faro stared over her shoulder, then returned his gaze, his pupils dilated. Serece glanced behind her but saw nothing. "The Keepers' Wrath is nearly complete, Fiel. Tonight. If things go according to plan our hope to defeat Te Mirkvahíl will have finally come to fruition." He leaned in to kiss her; Serece accepted it with a cringe, reminding herself *she* had not kissed the Betrayer, but actually her aunt.

But why? Aunt Fiel and Faro Fatego? For a brief moment it made hardly a lick of sense, but then it did. Fiel was a "cultural heretic" of the best kind in that she refused to resign herself to the mountain realm her sister so fiercely swore by. Fiel had always seen there was more to life than the blood in her veins; there was an entire world she wanted to know.

"I will come by the Hall later tonight," Serece said, squeezing Faro's hand.

He grinned. "I look forward to it."

He stepped past her, though not quickly enough to conceal the fear in his eyes. Serece watched him disappear into the square. *Strange, this memory.* Faro Fatego and what Serece was almost entirely sure was the start of the phantaxian plague. But how did they all fit? Furthermore, how was *any of this* relevant to her locating Yssa? How was she supposed to escape a memory and enter Lea Mort?

"There you are."

Serece yelped, starting at a hand on her shoulder. "Aunt Fiel? What—?"

"Illumancy is a fascinating practice, don't you think?" Fiel asked. "Sometimes a doorway to the past, and others a glimpse of things yet to come."

"Terrifying, actually," Serece said. She was quite comfortable to let the past and the future remain as such. No sense in worrying about things she couldn't go back and change or those that might not actually come to pass. "I was you and..." She shuddered. "You kissed Faro Fatego and *I* had to relive it through your eyes. How does all of this work? How do we get to Lea Mort? What if Yssa is already dead?"

"We finish the memory," Fiel said. "The In Between is a means for confronting the past, either remembered or not."

"And this? This was something you repressed," Serece guessed, and Fiel nodded sadly. "But why?"

"This was the night the world as I knew it ceased to exist," Fiel said, and the memory started to shift. Fog encroached, and when it finally withdrew Fiel had disappeared once again and Serece found herself standing in a garden. What she presumed to be the Hall of Illumurgists reared up before her in all of its pretentious glory, the figures depicted in the stained-glass windows excessively bright, though Serece thought it pretty.

She started through the garden, blood eased, mind soothed by the perfume of the various colored flowers that lined her stone path. There were trees, too, all of which were in bloom, their blossoms scattered about the grass, some drifting through the air on a breeze. Serece couldn't help smiling and was unsure whether or not it was a smile of her own or that of Fiel's in this moment in time. She supposed it mattered little either way. As she neared the Hall, she felt a tickle in her throat, one that quickly turned to a burning itch. Her body tensed, her fingers curling, back arching as the sensation shot through her body.

This was the night the plague came, she realized. Somehow

Serece had forgotten the pain of this night, had repressed it, and it seemed that Fiel had as well, not that she blamed her. Presently it subsided and Serece made her way into the Hall and down the winding corridors, illuminated by wisps of pale light not unlike those she and Fiel had seen in Yssa's temple. She sensed herself growing nearer to the chambers Faro had been working in, but as she continued on, delving deeper, descending stairways and turning corner after corner, the Hall grew less immaculate by the step. White walls of polished stone grew cracked, a strange membrane-like substance leaking out, and the tiled floors, once swirls of red, white, and gray were almost entirely black with mirkúr.

Shrieks ripped through the Hall and Serece hurried toward them, the agony growing louder and louder by the second, the corridors more infested with mirkúr. Ahead a door stood ajar, tendrils of smoke seeping out. Serece—Fiel—ran toward the door without a moment's hesitation. She reached out mentally to Yssa, and a moment later she felt her senses heighten, her body twitching reactively to the darkness around her. *I thank you for this gift, Yssa,* she thought. Gratitude where it was deserved.

A wall of mirkúr rushed toward Serece as she pushed into the room. The door slammed shut behind her, and Serece crashed into the door, skull cracking as her head ricocheted off the surface. The wisp light in the chamber flickered erratically, making apparent the myriad corpses strewn about the floor, desecrated to varying degrees. Some were limbless, others lacked heads, and some were so horribly massacred it was nearly impossible to tell whether or not they had actually once been anything resembling a human, dissident, or phantaxian. In the center of the chamber knelt a figure wreathed in white, save the smoke trailing from his shoulders like a tattered cloak. In his hand he held a small glowing sphere, and into the sphere went threads of illumination, drawn from the bodies around him.

Their souls! Serece groaned as she dropped to the floor, screamed as she felt her leg break from the impact. "F-Faro…?" she whimpered, and the figure in white responded to her voice. He looked upon her, eyes stark white, mirkúr webbing through his pale flesh. Serece felt the tears on her cheeks. "Oh *Keepers*… Faro, what have you done?" She felt a tug at the center of her chest, light at first, then violent as if something was trying to rip her flesh from bone. She shrieked as glowing strands of her soul leaked through her flesh and streamed toward The Keepers' Wrath, held in Faro's outstretched hand. She struggled against it. Her soul was hers and hers alone, but the effort was fruitless, and she could hardly move with her broken leg, not that there was anywhere to escape to.

Her sight waned, though she kept her eyes fixed to Faro Fatego, the man she had loved the last two years of her life. The people of Helveden had always cursed him a pawn of Te Mirkvahíl for having been able to wield mirkúr, a sign of demonry, profound demonry at that when considering Faro was human and only the dissident should have been able to wield the demon smoke. But Fiel had loved him nonetheless, had believed, had *known* there was more to people than the blood with which they were born. Choice before blood as the Faithbringer Khar Am had said.

What happened to you? she wondered as her world went black and her insides burned.

Burned like the flames of Perdition itself.

Burned like the summer sun.

Burned as her beloved's touch ripped her soul from her flesh. She drifted through the air, weightless, free of pain, drawn to the sphere in the distance, glowing bright as the moon did on nights when the stars refused to shine. She looked back at her body, crumpled by the door and wilting under entropy's touch.

I will keep you safe, a distorted voice whispered in her thoughts. *My dear Fiel...*

The chamber exploded with light, and the light swallowed all. Only silence remained.

VARE DROPPED TO HIS KNEES, panting. He had shirked Phantaxis for the time being, thank Celestials for that, and now found himself on the shore of the lake. The astral sky reflected off its surface and Vare couldn't help admiring its prismatic beauty, made more so by the trees encompassing the lake. He settled back onto his rear and rested his arms on his knees. *Any moment now,* he hoped. Any moment the lake would shimmer and glow with a light bright as the sun and then he might be free of this wretched place. Lea Mort was part of The In Between, yes, but it existed separately, sealed away behind a myriad different doorways and gates. Doorways and gates that Varésh Lúm-Talé—presently known as

Vare Tal-úlm—had been stupid enough to wander through in order to find a peaceful place for a nap.

Serves you right, you idiot, what he assumed to be his conscience snarled.

Indeed, Vare thought. *Though you have to admit, I've done things far stupider than this.*

His conscience snorted. *Is that supposed to make this better? We've been stuck here for Celestials know how many years, in your attempt to gain freedom you accidentally massacred half the phantaxian people, and now you've drawn the wrath of their corrupted god. Pray tell, what could be stupider than this?*

Vare chewed his thumbnail, then spat it into the grass. *Well, um...* Index finger next. Chewing nails, he found, helped him sort through thoughts and memories. *Ah.* This was a good one, a stupid one. *That time I decided to make a planet. Really worked out well for all parties involved, eh? The Reshapers are dead, the world's gone to shit, and who knows what the fuck else.*

The middle finger, first thrust at the sky, then chewed on for peace. Vare sighed. *I would could I go back and fix things, but we all know that to be impossible.* In Vare's experience temporal alteration did little to rectify wrongs and instead seemed only to fuck things up further.

Ring finger. *What do I do when leave this place?*

What you decided to do long ago, his conscience said in a tone that suggested Vare was an idiot for having even asked.

Vare groaned. Pinkie finger to ponder his options. *Or,* he thought, *we could leave this place to implode by itself.*

You're a moron, his conscience said. *But if your goal is to accrue as much guilt as you possibly can then by all means, leave your planet to die.*

That *did* seem like a shit thing to do. Vare frowned. *What do you suggest, besides the obvious?*

The only thing I'm going to suggest is *the obvious,* his conscience said. *And the sooner you understand this, the sooner you can go about rectifying your fuck-ups, and Celestials burn me but there is a* shitload *of those.*

Vare clapped his hands together and stared at the lake. *Right. The obvious.* Restore balance. Temper Entropy while attempting to lift up Law. Do so before it was too late, and everything went to shit again. Vare sighed and leaned back in the grass, gazing up at the swirls of color and stars. Te Mirkvahíl and Ouran'an, Phantaxis and Te Vétur Thae. *From here on out, no more immortals,* Vare decided. One way or another they all somehow became corrupt, though not necessarily by any fault of their own.

Just mine. Celestials but I think I take the cake for the planet's worst parent.

His memories drifted back to Ouran'an, to the last time he had walked the fallen city. What he would give to know the identity of Te Mirkvahíl. He had an inkling, a horrible suspicion, and he hoped he was wrong. He thought of the specter he'd encountered in those plague-infested ruins and prayed it hadn't grown to become Te Mirkvahíl, that the words in the tattered journal he'd found hadn't been some desperate manifesto.

Hope to quell the plague that entropy had wrought. Back then there had been a handful of Reshapers who'd believed the plague to have come from the mortals. Given the lokyn wars

Te Mirkvahíl had launched against Ariath over time, given the demon's twisting of the mirkúr-wielding human Faro Fatego, it was easy to speculate the plague, to Te Mirkvahíl, was actually the mortals themselves. And that was a dangerous thought.

Vare settled into the grass. All he could do now was wait.

———

IT WAS dusk and the air smelled of vanilla and smoke. Serece blinked slowly, first listening to the buzzing of voices, then holding her hands up to her eyes. The skin was cracked and flaking, bruised with darkness that veined its way up her arms. It burned like Perdition and itched twice as much. She sat up, pushed away the blanket and closed her eyes at the sight. *The plague.* She had been right about Fiel's memory, which she was apparently still experiencing. The last thing she recalled was a voice as her aunt's soul drifted toward The Keepers' Wrath. Who had it been? How had Fiel escaped the city alive?

A man approached, a soft smile drawn across his lips. He had a rather hawkish face, with eyes the color of spring and dark hair pulled back behind his ears. It was the feathered wings wrapped around his frame that really drew Serece's gaze. The color of midnight, they shimmered in the fading light, and Serece felt an immediate sense of peace as her questions and worries faded to nothing—for the moment at least.

"How are you feeling?" the man asked. He unfurled his wings and took at seat beside her bedroll. The dark feathers fluctuated midnight to moonlight and back again. It was hypnotizing, and Serece realized the discomfort the plague had caused her had subsided almost completely. She felt the occasional tickle but nothing more, nor did her insides feel like they were tearing themselves apart. The man took her hand in his, caressing it. "Not up to speaking?"

Serece looked around for the first time. They were in a building wrought from stone and wood, and every person here was phantaxian. *This must be one of the enclaves.* Though craning her neck for a better view out the window, Serece realized they were not in Helveden. A sea of tress spanned before her.

"Where…how?" Serece managed. "Who are you?"

He chuckled softly. "The answer is complicated. I have many names and I am many things to many people. For now, you may call me Dren."

Serece looked at Dren. The word was a phantaxian epithet, but it also meant father, and father sometimes referred to a god. "Is that you, Phantaxis?"

Dren smiled sadly, caressing her hand. "Phantaxis is dead."

Serece stammered. "…*Dead.*"

"Things do not end well for those who try to bargain with Te Mirkvahíl, especially not with those monsters the Origin at his beck and call." Dren bowed his head, sighing heavily. "The fool. I've no idea what he did but the consequences are clear." He raised his eyes and they fell on Serece's skin. "I cannot reverse this plague, but the snow that now falls on the Phantaxis Mountains will keep it at bay. There your people can continue to live."

Tears streamed down Serece's cheeks, but she could not feel

their warmth. Just as the plague had taken their flesh and taken their ability to roam the world as the phantaxians saw fit, it too had taken their ability to comprehend warmth. She sobbed into her hands, harder yet as Faro's white-eyed stare found its way back to the forefront of her thoughts. How had this happened?

She closed her eyes, feeling for the peace and serenity Dren's wings had first brought her. What she found was something else, something intimately familiar: the bestial frenzy and rage of the energy Yssa. Serece's eyes snapped open and she pointed a finger at Dren. "Are you—"

There was no sound as Dren mouthed the name Yssa. Fog swathed the forest enclave, withdrawing as fast as it had come. When all was clear Serece found herself beside Fiel in a field of tall grass. Before them stood a portal of brilliant blue light. Above them was a vast expanse of swirling colors and stars.

"How could you have repressed such a thing?" Serece asked.

"Shock, I suppose," said Fiel. "And sorrow. So much happening in such a short time, I think I struggled to process it all. Phantaxis' betrayal, the start of the plague, and Faro's madness all in one night..." She closed her eyes and Serece could see her aunt was trembling at the thought. "No matter. We are here now."

They held hands and started toward the portal. As they neared, a slender figure of shadow and tattered wings mani-fested to impede their progress. Tall and hooded, it extended a warning hand.

"You are Equilibrium," Fiel said. "I have met you on my

previous journeys to The In Between. Will you not let us pass? We have come to save a spirit named Yssa. She is trapped in Lea Mort."

Equilibrium scrutinized them with a faceless stare. Then it relaxed and stepped to the side. "If Yssa is what you seek then you may pass." The portal whirled and shifted color sporadically, quickly enough that Serece had to look away for fear of a seizure. "But know that Lea Mort is a dangerous place, especially for those who are not dead."

"Thank you," Fiel said, and she led Serece through.

VARE COULD HEAR PHANTAXIS' shrieks in the distance. The deranged god was growing nearer and Fiel and Serece had yet to arrive. He stood, fingertips aglow, and began to vigorously trace the air. Fiel possessed the ability to wield illum and he hoped her keen enough to discern what he was leaving behind. Vare yearned to be free of this wretched place, especially with all he had come to learn from watching the world pass him by, but it seemed his time had not yet arrived. He wiped the air clean then did what he had been doing for years—he ran.

SERECE AND FIEL arrived on the shore of a lake. It shone bright as the moon and the air smelled of rain. Fiel narrowed her eyes and paced, muttering to herself as she brushed her fingers through the air. Serece looked on. "Aunt Fiel, what are you—"

"Hush!" Fiel continued to brush. She stopped and stood with her hands clasped behind her, head slightly inclined, eyes darting back and forth. Her expression soured as her eyes grew level with the lake. She took Serece by the hand and suddenly Serece could see words in the air, written in light.

You will find my body in and beneath the cities and towns of my name, the first line read, and Serece recognized the phantaxian symbols for Vare, Tal, and Ulm, named for the old phantaxian Illumurgist Vare Tal-úlm. *Make me whole as once I was and from this wretched place can I escape.*

Yssa is dead at the hands of Phantaxis, the second line read. *His spirit hunts me even now and I fear history has begun to repeat. The weapon of old will soon be made whole and the world will know the Keepers' wrath.*

Serece eyed the third line and her heart nearly stopped. *Te Mirkvahíl yet remains.*

She looked at her aunt, who bore a grim expression. "Is any of this true?"

Fiel said nothing, and that was all Serece needed to know.

BEHTRÉAL SAT in the farmland grass, gazing at the moon, at the city Helveden in silhouette. It reminded him of Ouran'an, of home. Of home in all its shining, architecturally impressive glory, the whole of which he'd looked upon from spires so tall they kissed the clouds. Of home, where erudition had been born. Of home, where the plague had come and claimed his people for its own—mother, father, brother, son, and wife, turned to ash and lost to time.

Behtréal closed his eyes, affording himself the opportunity to weep and lament the life he had lost. *You could have quelled the pestilence,* he thought of his brother, who had been the smartest of them all. *You could have kept our people safe.* He clenched his fists and the tang of iron found his nose. *But you forsook us, abandoned blood and history for a mortal woman brittle as the sun is bright. Because of you I'm all that's left.*

Three millennia wandering the world. Three millennia with little more than memories, nightmares, and the hope for reclamation to keep him pressing on. It'd been lonely save for a period of time little less than half a millennium ago. He'd lived in a small house, in a small city, in a small kingdom, and he had loved it there. Somehow, it'd been enough. Simple folk by worldly standards. A kind, hard-working people who had welcomed him with open arms, only to eventually be slaughtered by the invading Ariathan Empire bent on conquering anything that breathed.

Behtréal recalled that night, coming back to a necropolis of snow and flesh after a month or two away. So many dead, preserved by winter's touch as if to taunt him on his way, to show him where his journey led.

The bold may wisely cage a wolf that wields the power to raise an army, Behtréal thought, *but it is the arrogant, the ignorant who reach between the bars to slay the wolf's cubs.* Emendation, a goal once small in scope, had grown broader by the year. Where once he'd sought simply to traverse the Temporal Sea, he now also strove to bring the Ariathan Empire to its knees.

Vengeance for the sake of retribution. Vengeance for the sake of reclamation. It'd been by twistedly delicious chance that Ariath's Illumurgists were the key to his success.

Behtréal sighed at the prospect of his enterprise. He had earned the right to catch his breath, to mourn what and whom he had lost, for soon the endgame would arrive. A month or two was all he had to wait—and that was but a blink to one who'd soon possess the means to rewrite time.

7

WHISPERS

"*Y*ou seem at ease, my Flesh," Faro whispered. "*Is it the snow, perhaps? Or freedom from that cage you call a city; solace from your sister's secret sins, your wife's defiled tomb?*" Faro trailed a wispy finger down Theailys' cheek, then brushed his chin. "*Something else, perchance? Something…primal?*"

Theailys glanced up from his notes on The Keepers' Wrath. He frowned at Faro as he adjusted his spectacles, then stored his notes away in his bag. "You really do ask questions at the most inopportune times." A grin spread across the silhouette's face to reveal teeth like knives. Theailys rolled his eyes. "Do you really want an answer or are you trying to get me to drop my guard so you can run amok and maim whatever it is you think is lurking out there in the night?"

Faro frowned. A whimper escaped as he coiled his wispy self around Theailys like a snake. "*My Flesh, you wound me! Do you really think I would do something like that?*" Theailys offered an arched eyebrow and the tilt of his head in response. Faro chuckled. *"Keen to my games, I see."* He paused, frowning, and it was one of the strangest things Theailys had seen. *"Indulge, if you would, my genuine curiosity: why* are *you so at ease?"*

Theailys shrugged. "I don't know."

"Is it the red-head with the chest?" Faro asked. Theailys glared. *"The one-eyed Warden?"*

"Neither," Theailys said, and he rubbed his thumb and index finger together to renew the wisp of light that he'd been reading by. Faro hissed and Theailys smirked. Sometimes it was the smallest victories that meant the most, and the smallest victories usually involved bestowing irritation upon Faro in the simplest of ways, such as wisps of illum or a happy thought. "Do you really want to know?"

"Oh yes." Faro tapped his fingers together eagerly.

"If you must know," Theailys said. "I've figured out a way to make you go away. It came to me in Ulm."

Faro arched an eyebrow, then withdrew from Theailys, cackling all the while.

Theailys looked on as the silhouette wheezed and howled. He snapped his fingers and the wisp of illum bloomed, brighter than it ever had before, strong enough to bathe the tent in warm blue light that drew a guttural shriek from Faro as he disintegrated into absence.

Theailys grinned. He produced a matchbook and pipe from his bag, packed it with smoke, and lit the source of Faro's demise. The stuff was stronger than what he and Mistress Khal had smoked a couple nights prior, stronger yet than what he'd smoked atop the ramparts overlooking Ulm. It was a temporary solution to the demons in his mind, but a solution nonetheless. If he could find the balance between intoxication and sobriety Theailys felt there was a decent chance the rest of this journey might proceed without a hitch, especially since the high not only rid his mind of Faro's nattering, but also amplified his joy. And with an elevated mood Theailys could once again properly channel illum, something he hadn't been able to do since Anayela's death. He looked at the wisp of light, curled his fingers, and called it home with but a thought. To his great relief the wisp obeyed, and he drew its illum back into his hand, watching the pale blue luminescence permeate his veins.

Feeling both bold and warm Theailys rose to his feet and withdrew from the tent to find Leyandra and Cailean having a drink and meal by the fire. The two shaghounds lay at their sides, one asleep and the other gazing intently at the piece of meat Cailean meant to shove into his mouth.

"About time you joined us," Leyandra said. "This one's nearly drunk himself out of the conversation."

Cailean grumbled indiscernibly as he chewed, nearly choked, then swallowed his food. "Booze makes for better warmth than a blanket, my dear."

"That so?" Leyandra said. "Why you shakin' like a pup that's pissed himself then, eh?"

"Hmm." Cailean gave his crotch a pat. "Well. Probably 'cause I pissed myself." He took a swig from his flask, which Theailys guessed he'd filled while in Ulm. "Oh, don't give me those judgy stares. I'm quite warm and I'll change my pants when I'm done if you want."

"Nothin's changed much, I see," said Leyandra. Cailean gave her the finger and she blew him a kiss.

"You mean he was always so charming?" Theailys inquired, pulling his flask from the folds of his cloak. "I never would have guessed."

Leyandra smiled softly and leaned against the log at her back. "It's a facade."

"I know," Theailys said, soft enough only Leyandra could hear. "That much is easy to tell, especially having worn masks of my own." He took a breath. "I've never been to war, but... Keepers, I can only imagine what something so violent does to one's mind." Searyn flashed across his own. He hoped she was all right, that Khoren and the Faithbringers hadn't subjected her to some violent form of interrogation. "My sister is a general and..."

Leyandra placed her hand on his arm. "Cailean told me what happened to her the other night. He thinks about her a lot."

"Searyn always spoke highly of him," Theailys said. "Said he was one of the best she'd ever commanded."

"Hard to believe at first glance," Leyandra said. "What with the cynicism and persistent stench of booze. Sometimes you get him talkin' after a couple o' drinks...and history flows like a river in spring. Takes the proper questions, you see? The proper alcohol too. Nice bit of wine and he sings like a jay."

Theailys frowned. "The wine I gave him must have been piss because the conversation ended before it really began."

Leyandra nodded. "Was it a red or a white?"

"Red. I think?" Theailys wrinkled his nose.

"There's your problem, then," Leyandra said. "You want the man to speak his mind, you have to white wine and dine the one-eyed fuck." She rested her chin on her fist, gaze still fixed on Cailean, who had taken to snuggling against the shaghounds for warmth. "He was a such a different man the first time we met. And now, havin' seen him for the first time in five years…"

Theailys placed a gentle hand on hers. "I remember the day Searyn came back from the front. It felt like talking to someone wearing her skin." Again, he recalled his incarcerated twin, wondering what hell she was going through, wishing he could do something to help. "It was awful, and the only thing I could do was sit back and wait for things to *maybe* be as they were before this whole mess of a war began."

"I suppose that's sort of what this feels like, then," Leyandra said. "And it makes me glad I only served as long as I did."

Theailys looked at her. "You fought?"

"For a time, after the onset," she said. "I went far to the west when I was discharged. To Harbanan."

"Why?" Theailys asked. "Why were you discharged?"

A melancholy smile spread across her lips. "Not much use for an Illumurgist robbed of her light." She yanked her collar down to reveal a web of darkened, risen flesh. Claw marks. "Lokyn bastards nearly killed me. Some days I wish they had." She rolled up her sleeves and each wrist bore a criss-cross of scars. "Ariath isn't too fond of the dissident to begin with, and it's even worse for those of us who can't wield the light."

Theailys stared, feeling cold, disgusted. Leyandra was one of his own. She had fought in the war, nearly died so that others could live, and *this* was how she'd been repaid. He grabbed a fistful of snow and squeezed as hard as he could, feeling it melt in his hand and his rage along with it.

"I'm dissident too," he said.

"I know. The surname gave it away," Leyandra said. All dissident had one-syllable surnames. "But I appreciate you tellin' me anyway. Nice to be travelin' with more than one person to talk to, you know?"

Theailys nodded, settling back against the log.

"I should probably change my pants," Cailean said. "I think I may have done more than just piss."

Leyandra groaned.

Theailys closed his eyes and laughed.

THEAILYS STOOD *beneath the oak tree. To his right was Varésh, not a bird this time but a man with great feathered wings the color of midnight. To Theailys' left was Anayela, garbed in a soft white gown that came to rest an inch below her knees. Her dark brown hair tossed gently in the breeze and her green eyes twinkled in the sun.*

"'Tis been a while since your dreams were so serene," said Varésh, and his wings began to glow.

"Longer yet since I was more than smoke and ash," said Anayela, and she smiled. "Have you finally learned to cage the beast, my love, or is this mental peace a lie?" She approached, stopping little less than a foot from where he stood, then raised a finger and tapped the air. Waves of energy rippled outward and Anayela's smile fell. "I had a feeling."

Theailys tried to speak. He felt himself saying the words though he could hear no sound. He reached for Anayela's hand and the barrier pulsed, throwing him back through the air. He hit the ground and rolled through the grass, coming to rest on his back, the sky the color of dawn, day, and dusk all at once. Was that simply the nature of this dream or was his mind trying to tell him something?

He pushed himself to his feet and strode to the barrier, stopping just short of where he thought it began. Anayela gazed back, still as a doll. Varésh approached, hands clasped behind his back, wings furled like a cloak. He cocked his head, blinking like a bird in thought, like the bird he was in his heart, then tapped the barrier just as Anayela had. It shimmered with resistance. Varésh tapped it second time and the waves froze; the barrier fell away as if it were mist in the wind. Anayela remained as she was, and Varésh extended his hand to Theailys.

"What is the point of this dream," he inquired, "if you refuse to let down your guard? You longed so badly to gaze upon your wife, yet here she is, and you erect a wall?" Varésh unfurled his wings and pulled Theailys into a gentle embrace. "Why, dear friend, do you allow yourself to live in such pain?"

Tears fell from Theailys' eyes. "I ripped her soul from her chest when she was alive"— he sucked in a ragged breath, then the truth came tumbling free—"and I was afraid if I let myself get close to my memory of what she once was I would destroy the only thing of her that I had left." His body shook as he sobbed into Varésh's chest. "I miss her, Varésh. I miss her so much."

Varésh wrapped his wings around them, permeating Theailys with warmth. "Then allow yourself to relive your time together every night when you close your eyes," he said. "The pain of absence will weigh a little less when you wake if you allow yourself to find peace in your dreams."

Theailys looked up at Varésh. "How can you be so sure?"

"Because," said Varésh, "we have had this conversation many times before and it always seems to work."

Theailys blinked and he was alone in the grass. Varésh and Anayela were gone. Night had come and the oak tree loomed, moonlight dancing off its leaves. Theailys sighed and approached the old thing at a measured pace, wondering when his friend and his wife might appear. As he neared the tree, he discerned something he never had before: a city in the distance, a city first like ice and rock, then choked in flames, and then at rest as though the ruin never had come. What did that mean?

"In your heart you know," said a voice not unlike his own.

"That sometimes dreams are more than dreams," a second said.

Theailys turned to acknowledge whatever had come. Before him, to his right, stood a figure of shadow. On the left, one of brilliant light. Mirkúr and illum. "My dreams are naught but wartime fears," he said. "Anxiety and sorrow made manifest."

"Think that, if you wish," said Mirkúr. "But beware the triptych."

"Dream your dreams," Illum said. "But heed the signs."

"Truth from madness," Theailys said, and he narrowed his eyes. Another of Khar Am's tenets.

"Indeed," the figures said, and then they fell away to radiant mist and smoke and Theailys was alone.

He turned to look at the oak tree, but it was gone, and in its place remained a stump and…

He took a seat in the grass and crossed his legs, gazing out into the vast peculiarity of his dream. The tree stump, beneath a sky of night; beyond that, a sapling in the cloudy dawn; further yet, the oak tree, stout and green beneath the azure sky and shining sun. A triptych.

What, *he wondered,* is its truth?

SERECE AWOKE BURIED up to her chin in the snow. It was night, the moon was full, and Fiel sat at her side.

"How do you feel?" her aunt asked.

Serece pushed herself to sit up, shedding snow as she did. She blinked, allowing her eyes to adjust after having been out for… Keepers, how long *had* it been? "Light. Airy." She stood up from the snow. "Almost weightless."

"Something to consider the next time you feel a bit sluggish," Fiel said. "Extended sleeps in the snow do wonders for our plagued bodies." She stood, gazing out into the night at nothing in particular. "Do you remember what you saw?"

"Your memory of Faro Fatego," Serece said. "Vare Talúlm's message."

"Then you know what must happen next," Fiel said, turning to look her niece in the eyes. "We must return to Te Vétur Thae and impart what we've learned upon our people, regardless of whether or not they see us as pariahs."

Serece nodded slowly. She could just imagine her mother's reaction to all of this, to her return, to *Aunt Fiel's* return after Keepers knew how many years she'd been gone, proclaimed dead. "Father will believe us," she said. "He always thought Te Mirkvahíl might still exist and what we saw in The In Between proves he was right." She paused, chewing her lip. "If Yssa is dead…"

"Then we need not worry about tempering rage," Fiel said, "though it would serve us well not to let such practices fall by the wayside. Who knows what comes next? Something more primal than Yssa, perhaps?"

Serece was not keen on the possibility of such a thing and so let the thought dissolve. "We should be on our way."

"Yes," Fiel said, and she dropped to all fours.

Serece gawked, withholding a scream as her aunt snarled and writhed. Bones snapped. Flesh and muscle tore only to reknit themselves beneath tufts of thick white fur. Serece blinked and pinched her cheek as hard as she could. The great wolf—her aunt—remained, large as a horse with azure eyes. Fiel snorted, dropping down so Serece could climb onto her back.

Serece did so, body trembling, though whether with fear, awe, or some combination of the two she wasn't exactly sure. She had seen beasts such as this several times in her life— High Wolves, they were called—and here her aunt was one of them! But how?

The question lingered as they took off into the night.

———

THEAILYS INHALED THE SMOKE, letting it sit for a moment before he breathed it out through his mouth and nose. His body tingled, and he felt the weight of the questions his dream had invoked lessen a bit, though they refused to completely leave his thoughts. And why should they? With everything that had happened these last few days maybe it was time to consider the notion his dreams *might actually be something more.* But if that were the case then what were they hinting at, what were the various triptych manifestations trying to say?

The tree, he recalled. *The city.* Had there been anything else? He frowned as they rode the shaghounds up the mountain path, dawn light creeping out from behind the clouds. The idea that had come to him was as much insane as it was plausible. *Me?* He had been standing in that field with illum and mirkúr—was he supposed to represent some sort of middle ground, some sort of balance? Or might it all have something to do with the calendar? The first third of the year was Dawn Year, the second was Mid Year, and the last was Black Year.

"You look like you're thinkin' a bit too hard," Leyandra said, eyeing Theailys from the back of Cailean's shaghound.

"Weird dream." He fell back into thought and the madness swarmed like house cats toward milk. Dawn Year, sapling, illum; Mid Year, oak tree, balance; Black Year, stump, mirkúr. Where the hell did the city fit into this? A city in frost, a city in flames, a city at rest—what did it all mean?

They crested the incline, coming to a collection of boulders dusted with snow, beyond which stood a length of trees that ran for miles in all directions. "It'll take us a while to pass through," Theailys said. "After that it shouldn't be more than an hour to the phantaxian city."

Cailean snorted. "Paleskins sure like their privacy."

"Yes, and they also like beheading the mouthy fucks dumb enough to sling slurs," Theailys snapped. "Remember what I said in Helveden, Cailean—country over person. I'm not afraid to let them have their way with you so long as I get the argentium I came for."

Cailean waved him off, muttering indiscernibly, and they continued into the trees.

They rode for a time in silence, listening to the birds and the breeze.

"Do you hate them, Cailean?" Leyandra asked. "The phantaxians."

"Why would I?"

"Because you call them paleskins," Theailys said. "Not exactly the friendliest of terms."

Cailean chewed the thumb of his glove, then brushed his hand through his hair. "I don't hate 'em, but I'm not fond of 'em either, you see? Something unnatural about 'em. 'S almost like..." He grimaced. "Like they're *dead*. I s'pose I don't really trust them. If something looks dead then damn it all it should *be dead,* not walking around."

Theailys arched an eyebrow. "That's got to be one of the stupidest excuses I've ever heard."

"Yeah, well, if you'd seen some of the shit I have then maybe you'd understand a bit more," Cailean said. "You ever heard of rusalks?" Theailys shook his head. "They're feral, born of violent deaths. They exist only to enact vengeance on the ones who wronged them," Cailean said. "Phantaxians look a hell of a lot like 'em and are twice as mean, so..."

"I suppose that makes a little more sense," Theailys said, rolling his eyes, "but the phantaxians are *people*, not the undead. They've come under enough scrutiny already so why fan the flames? Why not give them the respect they ask for? That's really all they've ever wanted."

Cailean frowned. "They've killed people I—"

"People you know?" Theailys said. "Cailean, they slaughtered my requisitions team—a team I personally put together. And we've slaughtered them! Ariath treated them horribly when they lived in the enclaves. Ariath cut down those who remained after the onset of the plague. The barbarism goes both ways."

Cailean remained silent for a time, brooding as they broke, as they mounted up and continued through the trees. "You're right," he said finally.

Theailys nodded. Leyandra gave Cailean's arm a squeeze.

Twigs snapped and the sound echoed. Theailys looked about, listening; Leyandra and Cailean each had a hand on the hilt of their blades. They hadn't encountered any hostility three days into their ascent, but Theailys supposed things were subject to change. A snarl followed the snaps, and a chorus of shrieks superseded the snarl. Shrieks that sounded almost like cackling.

"*Fuck*," Cailean hissed. "Lokyns."

He squeezed his shaghound into a gallop, Theailys quickly following. "If it's lokyns," Theailys yelled over the sound of paws pounding snow and earth, "then why the hell are we running *toward* them? And what about whatever that snarl came from?" Neither of his companions offered a reply. *Great.* Theailys tensed his jaw and sighed. He focused, drawing from his internal well of illum to conjure an orb. He wasn't sure if Cailean—a Warden—would be able draw power from it like he was supposed to, but it was better to be safe than sorry.

They erupted into a clearing in the trees. In the center was a *massive* white wolf, beneath the wolf the unconscious body of a woman, and around them a dozen or so lokyns. Theailys cringed, lips drawn back in a rictus of disgust. Lokyns came in various shapes, though they were primarily humanoid, but these looked like several corpses amalgamated and held together with mirkúr. Some had heads where hands should have been, others heads in the center of their torsos with limbs protruding from wherever the hell they saw fit.

"Can't take them all," Cailean growled.

"No shit," Theailys said, wincing at the demons' grating cackling.

"Dear Flesh..." Faro offered a wispy chuckle. *"Might I come out to play?"*

Fuck it. Theailys slipped from off from atop his shaghound, landing in the snow with a crunch. Mirkúr streamed from his fingers, cold as the snow beneath his boots. Theailys closed his eyes and Faro grinned back from the void.

SERECE AWOKE in her bedroom in the citadel of Te Vétur Thae. Her body ached horribly, and she could recall little if any of how she had arrived here, let alone what had transpired in the time between now and when she and Fiel had been ambushed in the forest by lokyns. She sat up and, wincing, stood from her bed and crossed the room to the window, looking out into the dusk.

Presently there was a knock at her door. She bid them entry and in stepped Undrensil. Serece ran to him and threw her arms around his neck, hugging him tight. He returned the gesture with a firm embrace.

"I was worried about you," he said. "You were in horrible shape when they brought you home."

They? Serece furrowed her brow. "Who? Is Aunt Fiel all right? Where is she?"

Undrensil rubbed her back gently. "Fiel is all right. She is resting. The others, the Ariathans…"

"Ariathans *again*?" Serece spat, pulling away from her father. "Did they not learn their lesson after the last time?"

"They saved your life," Undrensil said, tone measured as ever. "That is cause enough for me to permit them entry into our realm. That and the fact the Illumurgist at their head is a friend."

Serece narrowed an eye, studying the momentary twinkle in her father's eye. The way he had said the word 'friend,' especially about an Ariathan Illumurgist… "No. *No.* You have *got* to be kidding me!" Her eyes went wide and struggled against her father's superior strength as he held her against him. "Please tell me it's not Theailys An. Father, please!"

Undrensil chuckled at her aggravation and it was all Serece could do to keep herself from thumping his chest. "One day the pair of you will learn to get on," he said. "But until such a day comes, I expect you to be civil, Serece. They will not be staying long, I think. Argentium is most likely the reason for this visit, but…" He frowned and faraway look entered his eyes.

"Father?" Serece said. "But what…?"

"Curiosities," he said after a moment, and Serece's memories of what she had seen in The In Between came rushing to the front of her mind.

"Might I accompany you, then?" she asked, and with a begrudging sigh added, "I promise not to offend your little Illumurgist. Not *too* much, at least."

"I suppose," Undrensil agreed. "You had best get properly dressed. I was on my way to meet with him before I stopped to check on you."

"He can wait just a moment," Serece said, and she ushered her father out the door so she could change.

THEAILYS SAT in Undrensil's study. The phantaxian king had yet to appear, but Theailys found he didn't mind too much at the moment. He was busy trying to recollect what had happened between their arrival at Te Vétur Thae and their encounter with the lokyns in the woods.

I don't suppose you might care to indulge me, would you? So much for banishing Faro. At least he had the strength of will to dictate when the stupid voice could take possession of his body.

"*I had fun, my Flesh,*" said Faro almost instantly. "*Fun, just as you willed.*"

Are Cailean and Leyandra all right?

"*As well as can be, considering…*" Faro snickered.

Considering what?

"*You put on quite a show,*" Faro said. "*One of these days I'm going to let you watch.*" The door opened and in stepped

Undrensil and a young woman Theailys thought he recognized. *"Until next time, my Flesh,"*

Theailys' mind went quiet, allowing him to focus on the other individuals in the room. He eyed the woman up and down and she glared. *Probably thinks I'm trying to pass judgment on her skin— Oh. Perdition.* Theailys bowed his head. "Great King." He glanced up, stare lingering on the woman. "Serece."

"You look shorter than I remember, Theailys An," Serece said, taking a seat at the long table opposite her father. "Older too. A bit fatter as well."

Theailys tensed his jaw. *Breathe. Just. Fucking. Breathe.* "Yes, well…war tends to perpetuate stress, thank you for noticing. And thank you, Undrensil, for agreeing to meet with me in light of recent events. I offer my sincerest apologies for whatever offense my previous requisitions team made; I should have come myself from the onset, but…" He shook his head. "War, ending a war takes time, time I am afraid I simply could not afford, not with the clock I am on."

Undrensil bowed his head in response, his platinum locks bouncing. He was a bit more hawkish in the face than Theailys remembered. "Apologies accepted, Theailys An. I hope no offense was taken by our course of action? A covenant broken yields brutal consequence, you understand."

"None," Theailys lied with a tight-lipped smile.

"You're an awful liar," Serece said. "You always have been, byaun." Byaun—fool. It had been her favorite thing to call him for as long as he could recall. "What did your people say, hmm? Did they call for phantaxian blood?" She drew a dagger and twirled it airily as she looked him in the eyes.

"Serece…" Undrensil glared, though Theailys could detect a hint of amusement in his eyes. The phantaxian king cleared his throat. "Politics aside—you are here for argentium. I am inclined to bestow it upon you. It has been a while and you played a part in both saving my daughter's life and driving the lokyns away, but I wonder what purpose you seek it for."

"A weapon," Theailys said. It was best to be transparent here. "The Keepers' Wrath."

"You're forging…*that*?" Serece asked before her father could speak. Was that fear in her eyes? "*Why?* Do you know what Faro Fatego did with that thing?"

"Yes," Theailys said. "I do."

"Why, then?" Undrensil asked. "Why forge the weapon that almost brought your country to its knees?"

Faro had said nearly the exact same thing. "There is a barrier of energy around the Heart of Mirkúr," Theailys explained. "I am the only one capable of doing away with it, but to do so I need to amplify my ability to reap. If the Heart isn't destroyed the lokyns will only keep coming, regardless of the fact Te Mirkvahíl is dead by my sister's blade."

"I believe that *you* believe your words to be true, Theailys An," Undrensil said, "but my experience begs to wonder if your war-mongering country has once more been struck blind by ignorance." He stood from his seat and closed the gap between them with three long steps. "Te Mirkvahíl is cunning. The Demon Prime is a force of nature, a wind that starts as but a whisper and evolves into a storm of madness you cannot comprehend." He ran his fingers along Theailys' cheek. "You wield *mirkúr*, dear friend, but you are also naïve."

90

Theailys kept his tongue, eyes shifting to Serece. He wondered if it was the cold that made him shiver or the look Undrensil had bestowed upon him.

"I pity the ignorance of your country, the arrogance with which you all speak," the phantaxian king said in a tone Theailys was not used to hearing. It was almost…hateful. "It blinds you. You believe Te Mirkvahíl to have perished in your last assault on the Heart of Mirkúr, but what proof do you have? What attestation did your generals bring to give this proclamation credence?" He returned to his seat. "I have seen much in my existence but *never* have I seen or heard of proof attesting to the downfall of Te Mirkvahíl."

Theailys nodded slowly. "I see," was all he could muster. He eyed Serece again, who looked torn between whether or not to keep silent or speak whatever barb was on her mind. "Did you have a thought?"

"Te Mirkvahíl is alive," she said, and Theailys couldn't help rolling his eyes. "You might think us mad, Theailys An, but if I speak a single truth to you this day then let it be this."

Theailys propped his chin up on his fist. "My sister felled Te Mirkvahíl. Her word, as far as I'm concerned, is proof enough."

Serece closed her eyes. "Then you're a fool."

"I am inclined to agree," Undrensil said. "I will bestow you with the ore you require for The Keepers' Wrath and I will pray this weapon of yours destroys the Heart of Mirkúr once and for all; I will pray for your safety. You may rest here in Te Vétur Thae tonight to build your strength and replenish your supplies, but I command you leave at dawn tomorrow."

Theailys nodded. "Thank you kindly for your hospitality, Great King Undrensil."

He bowed deeply then withdrew, breathing a sigh of relief once he was out of sight.

UNDRENSIL LOOKED to his daughter once Theailys An had withdrawn. "You saw something during your time away, I am certain of it."

"Aunt Fiel, too," Serece said, and she relayed to her father what she had learned in The In Between. "What should we do?"

Undrensil sat, gazing out the study window, hands clasped together on the table. "Assemble the council to start, to see if we might be able to sway them to our side. We are both stronger and weaker without Yssa's influence and because of that we will need help if we are to defend Te Vétur Thae and defeat Te Mirkvahíl."

Serece offered her father a skeptical frown. "With what army? Te Mirkvahíl and the lokyns outnumber us horribly—"

"Which is why we need to retrieve Vare Tal-úlm from The In Between," Undrensil said. "But to do so we need the council's vote. Vare is, *was*...eccentric, chaos made manifest and Keepers know how much your mother despises him."

"She despises everyone," Serece muttered. "Do you think you can sway her? She has the council in the palm of her hand and if she sees reason with what we say then the others are more likely to follow."

"I will try as best I can," Undrensil said. "But it will likely take time."

"Right." Serece glanced out the window, just in time to spy Theailys An walking through the courtyard. "For now, time is really all that I have. If you'll excuse me, father…" She kissed his cheek, then stood and withdrew.

"Care to join me for a walk, half-blood?"

Theailys turned to the source of the barb. It was all he could do to keep himself from retaliating with "Sure thing, paleskin." He sighed. "Are you going to try and knife me like the last several times I was here?"

Serece rolled her eyes. "No. Surprisingly, I'm just here to talk."

"Fine. Lead the way."

They walked in step down a tree-lined street, hoarfrost clinging to the bark, snow falling from the silver leaves and onto the cobblestones. "I saw things," Serece said.

"Have you been smoking anything?" Theailys asked. "That usually tends to bring the phantoms out to play."

"No, byaun," Serece said. "I—Keepers, why the hell am I about to tell you all of this? I don't even like you."

Theailys gestured to the intersection ahead. "Good place to duck out then, yes?"

"It would be if I actually felt like doing so," Serece said. "But despite my distaste for your country, I'm still going to let myself yammer away. I'm trying to keep you safe, Theailys An."

He snorted as they turned down the path to the right. *"You,* save *me*? You do recall the first time we met, right? You tried to kill me, and my wife subdued you."

"How is the mirkúr-wielding bitch?" Serece asked.

Theailys tensed his jaw, swallowing. *Breathe.* He looked Serece in the eyes. "Dead."

Serece's ears twitched, her cheeks went red, and she looked away. "Sorry to hear." At that she turned and started back the way she'd come.

Theailys kept on; this way led to where he, Leyandra, and Cailean were staying anyway. He thought of Serece as he walked, of their history. They had first met when he was nineteen or twenty years of age and for whatever reason she had not taken well to him at all. They always seemed to bring out the childish anger in each other and Theailys could not understand why to save his life. Had he offended her at some point in their previous interactions over the years?

He batted away a snowflake as it fell, mood souring further with every step he took.

FOR THE SECOND time in four days Serece found herself atop the highest spire in Te Vétur Thae. This time it was Fiel who found her brooding in the night, and it was Fiel who had come with a flask. Situationally useful, those things. Serece took it from her aunt without hesitation and knocked back the liquid inside.

Water. She glared at her aunt. "You can't hand someone a flask with *water*. It's criminal."

Fiel chuckled. "Serece, the last thing you need is a drink."

"Why are you here?" Serece asked. She paused, hating herself for her words. "I'm sorry. How are you feeling?"

"I should be asking the same of you," Fiel said.

"Well enough for having been savaged by demons," Serece said. "Just a mild concussion; nothing a night in the snow can't cure."

"So, what brings you here?" Fiel leaned against the balustrade, gazing off into the night.

"Regret," Serece said. "Regret and shame for having spoken to and treated Theailys An as I did, as I *always do*." She slid down the wall and sat with her knees pulled to her chest. "Why, Aunt Fiel—I don't understand why I treat him so…so…"

Fiel raised an eyebrow. "Poorly?"

"*Yes!*"

"I could posit a theory based on what we saw in The In Between," Fiel said, hesitating.

"You could," Serece said, "but Theailys An wasn't in The In Between."

"Not directly," Fiel said. "Did you notice he's nearly identical to Faro Fatego?"

———

"YOU'RE NOT DEAD!" Cailean took a swig from his flask.

"You're not sober," Theailys said, taking a seat at the table. Leyandra sat across from him, arms crossed as she glared at Cailean. Theailys frowned, just now noticing the black eye and fat lip that Cailean was sporting. "Do I want to know?"

"The better question is: will those sentries mention the exchange to Undrensil?" Leyandra said. "This idiot and his drunken, slur-slinging mouth nearly got us killed while you were away. 'Paleskin bastards'—did you *have to*? Even *after they apologized*?"

"Better pray to the Keepers they don't," Theailys said. "Undrensil already promised me the argentium. We can ill afford a change of heart." He shot a scathing look at Cailean. "You said, you *promised me* you would hold your tongue. You apologized on the ride up!"

Cailean waved his hand dismissively and took another shot. "You worry too much."

"*You don't worry enough*," Theailys snarled, summoning every ounce of strength he had to hoist the older man out of his seat and shove him away from the table. "Go lie down. Go to sleep."

Cailean wiped a trail of alcohol from his cheek, his expression darkening. "You fancy touching me like that again, boy?" He neared Theailys, jabbing him in the chest with a finger. "'Cause you won't like what comes of it."

Leyandra leapt from her seat, pushing Cailean away from Theailys. "Both of you, knock it the fuck off. The last thing we need to be doin' is fightin'." Then, to Cailean, "Lie down. Sleep. You're makin' a fool of yourself."

"Fine." Cailean glared over Leyandra's shoulder, good hand tapping the dagger sheathed at his waist. "Touch me again…"

"Cailean…" Leyandra growled.

"And you'll what—knife the one person who can destroy the

Heart?" Theailys asked. "Because that would be the stupidest thing you could do in this moment, which is saying a lot considering you could have fractured our already delicate relations with the phantaxians just by opening your mouth!" He swallowed and sucked in a ragged breath, trying to keep the mirkúr at bay before Faro could rouse. "Just…go the fuck to sleep."

Cailean gave him the finger, then started toward a couch at the far side of the room. He managed half the distance before tripping over his own feet and landing with a thud. He grumbled profanities and curled himself into a ball, falling asleep where he lay.

"Perdition," Theailys muttered, taking a seat at the table. "Sorry, Leyandra. Rough day."

"No apology necessary. A giant fool, sometimes, especially when he gets drunk. …So. The argentium," Leyandra said, shifting the topic of conversation. "Undrensil said he was going to give it to us?"

"Yes, and hopefully he still will," Theailys said, and he proceeded to relay the phantaxian king's skepticism about Te Mirkvahíl's demise.

"He does raise a valid point, love," Leyandra said. "I've fought my fair share of demons, went up against things straight outta nightmares when I lived in Harbanan and ran with the Galrun Muir. Their rule of thumb? Unless you have proof, it's not dead."

"Makes sense, but that doesn't mean Undrensil is right." Theailys yawned. He drew his pipe, smoke bag, and matches from his sack. A little joy before sleep to keep Faro at bay. "We should pack it in for the evening. We've a long day ahead of us tomorrow and we're expected to depart at dawn."

DAWN CAME FAR TOO EARLY. Theailys and his companions found themselves at the outskirts of Te Vétur Thae within the hour, shepherded by a half dozen leather-donning, dagger-wielding phantaxians and a pair of gray-robed heralds. Neither Undrensil nor Serece were present.

"Dren Undrensil and Tem Artemae send their regards and wish you well in your travels," the first herald said. She produced a bundle of cloth and passed it to Theailys. "Farewell."

Theailys stowed the bundle away in his pack and watched the phantaxians withdraw. For some reason he had expected the exchange to be a bit more ceremonial, but the fact Undrensil hadn't bothered to see them off personally said more than words ever could, especially considering the previous day's exchange.

Back to Ulm, then straight to Naldunar.

The Church city was a good week or so from the Phantaxis Mountains, but Theailys found himself looking forward to the journey. It would surely be more welcoming than the phantaxians had been. He adjusted his pack, gritted his teeth, and started after his companions, thankful the mountainside would not be thrashed by storms this time around.

SERECE HAD NOT SLEPT a wink and Aunt Fiel was to blame. What she had said about Theailys An, about the possibility Serece loathed him because he looked nearly identical to Faro Fatego…it made sense in more ways than one. It also filled her with a strange feeling of dread, especially when considering the message Vare Tal-úlm had left in The In Between. Was history really on course to repeat? If that were true, what fate would befall her people this time around? Another plague? Complete annihilation?

She started from the cliff she'd been sitting at and made for the trees. It was going to take time to sway the council to their side, but Serece refused to sit idly by as this eldritch shadow fell over her world. What had the Faithbringer Khar Am once said? *Truth from madness.* Something was amiss and Serece was going to find out what. If there was a connection between Theailys An and Faro Fatego, she was going to figure it out.

It was time to return to Helveden.

8

WITNESS

"Relatively quiet these last couple days," Cailean said. It was night and they had made camp in the Gray Meadow east of the Phantaxis Mountains. A fire burned in the center of a collection of rocks. He prodded the kindling with a stick, then tossed it into the flames. "Peaceful, here. Away from the snow."

"Away from the phantaxians, you mean," Theailys said from behind a stack of parchment, spectacled eyes glued to whatever secrets they held. He looked up, setting the parchment aside. He appeared tired, more than he usually did, though it could have been a trick of the light.

"No," Cailean said, taking a breath. "Just the snow." He sat up straight, his good eye fixed unblinkingly on Theailys. "Sorry about that whole thing. Sorry about my mouth and thoughts. I'm just…"

"Sorry," Theailys finished, nodding. "Me too. Just…caught

up in the moment I suppose. My meeting with Undrensil didn't go as well as I'd hoped. His daughter was there and…and…" He removed the spectacles, brow furrowed, jaw tensed. "You said something to me the night we rode to Ulm, about guarding my heart, about things not always being what they seem."

"I did," Cailean said slowly. "What are you getting at?"

"Undrensil and his daughter, Serece, are convinced Te Mirkvahíl is still out there," Theailys said. "Leyandra more or less agrees."

Cailean nodded. "Course she does. The ways of the Galrun Muir die hard."

"So, what do *you* think?" Theailys asked.

"I think you're afraid," Cailean said, "and rightfully so. I think your fear is causing your mind to run amok. I think that's why you haven't slept for a day, because you're busy wondering whether or not Searyn actually felled Te Mirkvahíl."

The dread in Theailys' eyes was as plain as the night was dark. "I can't stop thinking about it, Cailean. I know she's my sister and I trust her with all I have, but…"

"Things are odd," Cailean said. "The incident with the burial mounds, the claims she wields mirkúr, and now all of this. I get it—I've been wondering the same things. My past forbids me from turning my good eye away." He crawled over to where Theailys sat and dropped down beside him. "I'm not saying your sister lied to everyone, not by a long shot, but there *is* something weird going on."

Cailean pulled a flask from his pocket and took a swig. He passed it to Theailys. "Warm yourself up and knock yourself out. You need some rest, my friend. Long day's ride ahead of us."

"I asked about your shield last week," Theailys said, taking a sip.

Fuck. "You did," Cailean said, supposing it was better than Theailys asking him about the time he'd died, not that the gray-eyed man would be privy to such a thing. But either way... "And here you are asking again."

"Are you going to deflect my question a second time?"

"No," Cailean said. "But only because I know what Leyandra said about me and white wine. The two of you whisper louder than you think." He chuckled, then pulled up his sleeve to reveal the patchwork that had at one point been his functioning left arm. "Beautiful piece of work, this. Wrought from stupidity, now serving as a monument to failure."

"Perdition," Theailys murmured, brushing his fingers along the flayed skin, through the angry red fissures. "Your shield did *this*?"

"Thing went off like a bomb," Cailean recalled. "My fault. We were surrounded, I was in command. Told the Illumurgist to keep channeling into my shield or else the barrier was going to fall. Stupid thing to do. Lost half my contingent, Illumurgist included, and nearly lost my arm." He chuckled again, wryly this time. "Might have been better if I had. Hell, might have been better off if the blast had taken my life."

"You think so? If you were dead, who the hell would be making sure I get to where I need to be?" Theailys said. "You're a prick sometimes, Cailean, but so am I. My point is, you're here for a reason."

Cailean knew damn well why he was here, and it wasn't because the queen or Searyn had asked him to go—because they hadn't. It was much more than simply playing body-guard for Theailys An. "Redemption," he murmured. "Deliverance. So many things have gone to shit in my life, and I thought if I could see you to the end of this war, to the destruction of the Heart, it might free me from an endless cycle of failure and make me feel as though my life wasn't a complete waste." He paused. "That, and I knew it'd break Searyn's heart if anything happened to you."

"Thanks." Theailys sniffled, then took a drink.

"You're welcome." Cailean produced a second flask and clanked it against Theailys'. "Spiced rum from Egan. Cheers" —he felt Theailys' drowsy weight against his arm— "and may your dreams be sweet."

It was strange to be standing in Helveden after all these years. Stranger yet to be standing alone, horribly out of place in phantaxian garb, hood pulled well past her eyes. In a perfect world Aunt Fiel would have stayed with Serece to help her sleuth. Then again, in a perfect world none of this would actually have been necessary. Fiel's reasoning for not staying was sound: she would need to corroborate Undrensil's claims if they hoped to free Vare from The In Between. They would need to full support of the council if they were to retrieve the parts of Vare's corpse from beneath the Ariathan towns and cities of his name. *Not that the council will believe either of them,* Serece grumbled to herself. Most if not all of the council members thought her father mad and the majority of Te Vétur Thae viewed Fiel as a pariah. They had an uphill battle ahead.

Which is why you'd best not focus on the things you can't control. She looked at the city before her, rising up in silhouette like some monstrous thing from the void. Was there any distinction between the two? Perhaps not, considering what the Ariathans had done after the onset of the plague—the butchery, the forceful exile, the brief conflict in the Phantaxis Mountains.

Serece rubbed the crystal vial hanging around her neck, feeling the cold of the snow encased within. She had several more in her bag, lifelines, the means to temporarily halt biological rot whilst away from the sanctuary of her mountain home. She was hopeful if things went smoothly enough she wouldn't need to use them all.

So where now? What now? It was late and much of the city was asleep. Surely there was somewhere she could go and collect her thoughts and come up with a plan of action. She spied a tower in the distance—the Bastion, home of the Ariathan queen. *Perfect.* She started north and had not gone far before she heard the clank of armored footsteps closing in from all directions.

"Hey, girl! Over here!"

In the shadow of two buildings stood a figure. Not eager for a meeting with the Faithbringers undoubtedly coming to arrest or cut her down—the latter was highly probable considering the gift the phantaxians had sent back less than a week ago—she darted toward the figure and followed them at a sprint into the darkness of the side street. When they were well enough away, they stopped for a breather and the figure conjured a wisp of light.

"A phantaxian in Helveden," he said. He looked to be in his mid-years, face stubbled and scarred, graying blond hair pulled back behind his ears. "Been a while since I seen your kind hereabouts." His eyes were hypnotically silver and Serece found herself having a hard time focusing on anything but. "Y'okay, girl?"

Serece blinked. "I...yes, thanks."

"Name's Fenrin," he said.

"Serece."

"Dangerous for you to be walkin' around so out of place," Fenrin said. "Especially now. Though I'm guessin' 'now' is what's brought you all the way here."

Serece eyed Fenrin. "I...suppose? What do you know about 'now'?"

"Little," Fenrin said, looking past her shoulder. "But enough to know that things ain't what they seem if you catch my drift."

"I think so," Serece said. "If you mean to say Te Mirkvahíl is alive."

Fenrin tapped his nose and winked. "Indeed. Common knowledge among my kind, as was your appearance this night. Foretold."

Aunt Fiel had said something vaguely similar. "So, now what?"

Fenrin grinned wolfishly. "Follow me."

Serece crossed her arms, narrowing her eyes. "Where?"

"Somewhere safe," said Fenrin, offering his hand. "I promise. I've no reason to maim or cut you down, you see?"

Serece hesitated and Fenrin sighed. "Does it help to know your aunt Fiel and I were the best of friends at one point in our lives? She was a great help to me and my people, the drenarians."

"I've never heard of the drenarians," Serece said.

"Children of Dren to others," Fenrin said.

Serece tilted her head. "Dren? The winged man?"

"Indeed," Fenrin confirmed. "You know him?"

"Saw him," Serece said. "In a memory not my own. Is he your god? Your creator?" Fenrin nodded and Serece found herself a bit more at ease. If Fenrin was of Dren's making, she supposed he meant her no harm. She took his hand. "Lead the way."

"*My Flesh, you've not said word these last few hours,*" Faro whispered

Theailys ignored the voice, instead focusing on the copse looming in the distance, on the golden grass of the meadow, radiant in the early morning light. Going on four days removed from their time in the Phantaxis Mountains they were on schedule to arrive in Naldunar a day or two early, which was a great relief to Theailys as it meant they would return to Helveden that much quicker. His thoughts drifted once more to Searyn. It was impossible not to think of her, especially not after the conversation he'd had with Cailean the previous night.

"*My Flesh?*" Faro tried again. "*Can you hear me?*"

Unfortunately, Theailys replied.

"*Your thoughts are loud,*" Faro said. "*You ache for your sister's safety, for an inkling as to what's transpired in your absence.*"

Can you blame me? Theailys thought.

"*No,*" Faro said, and there seemed to be genuine sympathy in his tone. "*Not with miscreants like General Khoren in charge of policing the city. Do you know his ancestors were very much the same? Zealous, phobic individuals obsessed with maintaining the purity of home.*"

That doesn't surprise me, Theailys thought. *Khoren's never been one to adhere to the tenets of Khar Am. Hell, it seems like hardly any of the Faithbringers do these days.*

"*Orders are easily corrupted when power falls to individuals like Khoren,*" Faro hissed. "*I've little doubt he framed her—his motives for doing so are myriad. A dissident trying to quell news of the gift the phantaxians sent? Why, it would depict your sister in the darkest light, as a demon traitor to the crown.*"

It made sense, and it was no secret General Khoren saw Searyn's promotion to Second General as a slight against his person. There was little, if anything Theailys could do, but he found a modicum of hope knowing Searyn held favor with the queen. That had to count for something.

"*Smell the salt in the air, my Flesh,*" said Faro, manifesting on Theailys' shoulder as a white-eyed bird. "*Have you ever sailed the sea?*"

Once, Theailys thought. *To Thaleorn.*

Faro clucked approvingly, settling in for what Theailys guessed to be a nap.

"If you look hard enough," Cailean called from behind, "you can see Tal beyond the trees."

"Ever been?" Theailys asked, slowing his shaghound to ride in step beside Cailean and Leyandra.

Cailean grinned. "Several times. Had a couple of wild nights with the innkeepers' twins."

"What is it with you and the innkeepers' children?" Leyandra sighed. "Every fuckin' city or town…"

Cailean shrugged, grin persisting. "If you keep an animal locked away that long…well, the beast is bound to come out at some point." He chuckled, and it faded to a reminiscent sigh. "Good times. Simpler times."

"Times best kept to yourself," Leyandra said, jabbing him in the back. "Sometimes I wonder why I decided to follow you on this journey of yours."

Theailys scratched his nose. "Why did you?"

"You can only bartend for so long before the old itch creeps back in," Leyandra said. "I suppose…I suppose it's unfinished business. The need to prove to myself I'm *not useless* without illum. My time in Harbanan showed me I wasn't, but sometimes, when the world around you starts goin' to shit and people you love go with it, it's hard to remember." Her gaze fell east, past Theailys' shoulder and he could see the sea reflected in her eyes. "I want the darkness to end, if not for me then for everyone else."

"Well said," Cailean murmured, giving her a pat on the knee.

They passed silently into the trees.

"*They are noble,*" Faro offered, rousing from his brief sleep. "*Tragically so. The death they have known, the things they must have seen…*" He shuddered. "*How terrible.*"

Theailys nodded. *How terrible indeed.*

SERECE HAD NOT SLEPT since arriving in Helveden. Fenrin had given her much to chew on over the last day, though she was a little unsure as to whether or not the information was pertinent to her undertaking. The winged god Dren was dead and had been for centuries; he had gone mad shortly after his creation of the drenarians. More interesting was how he'd come to be. He was what Fenrin referred to as a temporal paradox, a figure coexisting with another version of himself in the same timeline.

"Doing so has severe consequences," Fenrin had said. "I saw Dren's memories shortly before he went mad. He meant to rewrite history, to prevent Te Mirkvahíl's conception."

But some things were written in stone. She stood atop the Bastion, gazing out over Helveden like the bird she sometimes wished she was. *Temporal paradox.* The phrase still sounded ludicrous. How did one go about traversing time, rewriting history? Serece tried her best not to focus on the mechanics lest her mind decide to implode out of confusion. Instead she ran through what she had learned in the last several days, her focus drifting to the physical similarities between Faro Fatego and Theailys An. Was time the culprit there? Serece's gut told her there was a connection whether or not it was momentarily obvious.

She scratched an itch under her jaw, flakes of dried skin falling away. Her time away from the Phantaxis Mountains was already starting to take its toll. *Just focus. Truth from madness.* Temporal paradoxes, the possibility of history repeating... She furrowed her brow. Who was to say these current events hadn't already played out? It was a maddening thought, but the world itself was growing madder by the day.

She closed her eyes, the darkness welcome, soothing. *What if...* Her brewing theory made her shiver. *What if Theailys An is older than he appears? What if Faro Fatego wasn't actually human?* What if they were one and the same? What if Faro Fatego was a temporal paradox? The possibilities made Serece feel colder than she already did. Like Te Mirkvahíl's conception, some things were written in stone. She just prayed Theailys An going mad wasn't one such thing.

"Surprisingly easy to get up here," Fenrin said, causing Serece to start. "Sorry, didn't mean to scare you."

"Don't worry," Serece said, "I've scared myself just fine." She conveyed her thoughts, Fenrin nodding all the while.

"Interestin'," he offered when she was done. "But there's a flaw in the logic, that bein' Faro Fatego *was* actually human. Still..." He stroked his chin. "Perhaps existin' as a paradox does somethin' to the body, alters the genetic makeup, you see? Then it might be conceivable your Theailys An and Faro Fatego are twins of a sort."

"Have you learned anything more of Te Mirkvahíl?" Serece asked. "If the Demon Prime still lives, where is it lurking?"

"I've got a hunch," Fenrin said. "Saw...*somethin'* in an illum dream. But we'll 'ave to wait 'til night so as to not get nicked by the false Faithbringers." He nodded north. "Somewhere there. We'll 'ave a sleep, then see what secrets the dark reveals."

Night.

Stars blooming through…smoke?

Theailys sniffed. Fresh smoke. The orange glow against the sides of buildings said as much. And were those screams? Distant at first, then grating, like a knife on glass.

Fuck. Theailys sat up, looking about. *Where am I? What the hell happened?*

He swallowed, his throat dry, itching like Perdition. It was sore, as if he had screamed himself hoarse; his breath came raggedly. He swallowed a second time, realizing his hands were slick with… *Not blood.* Something black and oily, membrane-like. And around him were myriad bodies, the flesh rotting from their bones. The odor of decay manifested like a storm. Theailys retched to the side, not sure if the sudden urge had been triggered by the smell or sight of the corpses.

He pushed himself to his feet, staggering slightly before he found his balance. His clothing, too, was stained with the black substance. He pressed himself to remember but his mind was foggy. The last thing he recalled was emerging from the trees before Tal just after dusk.

And an argument with Faro.

Fuck. Should have smoked more; he'd been lenient the last couple days what with Faro having…what was the proper phrase? Reined himself in? He supposed it didn't matter right now.

And where were Leyandra and Cailean?

Theailys started through the ruin of wherever he was,

visibility hampered considerably by the flames and smoke. He clenched his jaw as the screams continued, doing his best to push them away. His efforts, though, were fruitless.

"Cailean? Leyandra?"

Theailys continued blindly. His foot caught and he tumbled forward, yelping, wrist and chin smacking the cobblestones. He groaned, spitting blood; thankfully his teeth were still intact. He rubbed his wrist and looked behind to see what had obstructed his path.

A body, but there was something different about this one —it was fresh. Flesh and garb were torn, the belly was ripped open, the arms and legs were splayed wildly, streaked with blood and the same oily black substance Theailys' hands were slicked with.

He shivered. *Had he done this?*

Theailys stood and backed away. He turned and broke into a run, unsure of where he was going, the screaming growing louder all the while. But where was it coming from? He stumbled through the massacre of missing limbs and face-less skulls; of severed torsos with their entrails trailing sadly.

Finally, through the smoke, he discerned the outline of a fountain and a church—

Voices.

"Cailean?" Theailys called. "Leyandra?"

A burst of luminescence set the smoke ablaze and turned the black-gray mass to warming light. It dispersed as quickly as it'd come, and from the smoke emerged Leyandra, Cailean a few seconds after.

"Thank the *Keepers*," Cailean said. "Been searching Tal for hours. Why'd you run off like that?"

"Didn't necessarily have a choice," Theailys said, mentally cursing Faro. That explained some of the bodies and the mild amnesia. The rest of this, though? "What happened here?"

"Lokyns," Leyandra said darkly, brow furrowed. "Hell of a lot by the look of things."

"Sometime before we arrived," Cailean said, sword gripped tightly in his good hand. "All dead this side of Tal so far as we can tell. Town near two-thousand at its peak… Bastards must've gotten off right hard with this one." He paused, alert to something moving in the smoke: metal clanking on stone, the sound of cloth flapping.

Five figures stepped forth: a Warden, two Faithbringers, and two Illumurgists by the look of things, the latter wielding illum staves that hummed and radiated warmth.

"I am Marshal Iel Nor," the first figure said. She was dark-haired with a pair of scars running beneath her left eye. "This is Warden Neyma and Faithbringer Brehm."

She gestured to a young woman with dark red hair and golden eyes, then to a sandy-haired older man who looked strikingly similar to Cailean. If there was any relation between the two men, neither acknowledged it, though their quick glances and narrowed eyes suggested they knew each other.

"We are Ronomar and Raelza," the pale-skinned Illumurgist twins announced in unison. Theailys had studied with them at the Hall years ago. "If it pleases you then call us Dual."

"Who are you three? What are you doing here in Tal?" the marshal inquired.

"Could ask you the same thing," Cailean said hotly.

"We're traveling to Naldunar," Theailys said, and he relayed their names.

"Catil," Marshal Nor mused, looking at Cailean. "Knew you looked familiar." She looked to Theailys. "The Seraph is expecting *you* in Naldunar. Once we've finished here, we'll escort you to the city."

"Great," Cailean said, "but what are *you* doing here?"

"We've been on patrol for the better part of a week," Marshal Nor said. "With reports of lokyn activity in from Ulm, Helveden, and the towns and villages neighboring Naldunar, the Seraph deemed our action necessary. Our company strafes the Gray Meadows even now. We broke away when we saw the smoke rising from Tal just a couple of miles out." She looked from Cailean to the church. "You're aware of the reliquary Tal houses, yes?"

Cailean nodded. "Of course."

"Reliquary?" Theailys asked. The notion of such a thing had never come up in his previous visits to the slaughtered town.

"Nothing more you need to know," the marshal said, starting toward the church, her companions at her heels. "But if you feel like being useful you are more than welcome to help us inspect the interior. We're to collect the reliquary and return it to Naldunar for safe keeping."

They followed the newcomers. A sense of dread wound through Theailys as they neared the church, the screams persisting. They stepped inside, Theailys and Dual conjuring illum wisps that bathed the room in pale blue luminescence and revealed the blood-smeared walls and faceless dead, the latter garbed in white and scarlet robes denoting them as Naldunarian priests.

Theailys clutched his ears, crying out as the shrieking in his head grew louder. "Keepers, I can hear them," he uttered, half to himself, half to the others. "The dead. I can hear their spirits shrieking in my head."

Marshal Nor gave him an odd look. "Then we had best procure our quarry and retreat. Be on your guard."

They continued through the nave and chancel, passing through a pair of heavy oaken doors beyond which stood the rear of the church. At length they halted at an argentium door inlaid with glyphs. Marshal Nor placed her right hand on the surface of the door, beads of illum dripping from the fingertips of her gauntlet and into the narrow grooves of the glyphs, drawn from the pendants around her neck. There was a tiny burst of light and the door swung inward with a groan, revealing a small chamber. In the center, on a pedestal, sat the reliquary: a simple black box, about four feet in length.

The church shook. Not violently, but enough to make Theailys' teeth rattle. It was over almost as quickly as it had started.

The screams, Theailys thought. *They're almost silent.* He could still hear them, though they were little more than whispers, than the wind tickling his ear. "What was that?"

"A mass ascension." Marshal Nor drew her blade. "Hopefully."

"Hopefully? You don't sound too confident," Cailean said, his own blade clutched tightly in his right hand.

"Best not to be," the marshal said.

She took a deep breath as Dual began to channel. She

extended the long, hungry blade in a slicing motion, and a spear of white illum javelined from the chamber and down the hallway. It made no audible impact as it pierced a cloud of mirkúr forming in the nave.

Cackling echoed through the church, and before Theailys had a chance to blink the faceless priests were rushing toward them, strengthened by the mirkúr of their phantom puppeteer. Brehm, Nor, and Cailean lunged, their blades taking the dead priests with ease, severing them at the waist. The halves flopped pathetically as blood and black fluid sprayed the walls and floor.

More came; Theailys hadn't realized how many there were. Their numbers seemed endless, as was their dark resolve. Legless torsos clawed their way up the sullied hall, snarling, hissing, cackling as they swiped feebly at their prey.

Theailys kicked one in the face. He brought his boot down, the skull crunching loudly under the weight. He retreated further into the reliquary chamber, Leyandra with him, putting herself between Theailys and the priests. He felt useless. He hadn't trained nearly enough with a blade, and he dared not try to channel, not after waking up in the middle of a necropolis.

He shifted focus from Nor to Cailean, who even with a useless left arm was still plenty capable with a blade; from Cailean to Dual, lingering on the twins, so graceful, so fluid in their movements as they danced and ducked around the priests' reckless swipes, their mauve eyes bright.

Theailys crashed to his knees, writhing. Something else had come, something wreathed in shadows, something birthed from chaos. He felt its shrieking laughter in his head, sure his skull would split at any moment from the agony. Faro erupted into laughter of his own, as if in direct competition with the encroaching threat.

"Oh *fuck!* Reaver!" Cailean bellowed. "REAVER!"

The hall and chamber were enveloped in a cloak of shadows. Metal raked against stone and a flash of luminescence forced the darkness back, pushing the mirkúr toward its source. An illum barrier stood between them and the aggressor, pulsing every time it was struck by mirkúr. Dual channeled continually into Neyma as she worked to keep their safeguard strong, the black power surging hungrily.

Theailys rose to his feet, eyes fixed on the massive shape looming at the end of the hall. He could see no visible limbs or head, but at the center of the smoky mass were a pair of white almond-shaped eyes. Somewhere in there was undoubtedly a mouth, stretched to form a monstrous grin.

What are you doing? Theailys thought at Faro as his laughter persisted. *Stop!* His breathing labored and he realized he had no control over his actions. No control, and yet he was conscious.

Theailys' hands shot forward, fingers splayed as he first drew the illum from the barrier, then the mirkúr it'd been keeping at bay. The two contrasting forces rushed toward him in a spiral of luminescent smoke. They slammed into the center of his chest, nearly knocking Theailys from his feet. He remained standing though, pressing past the others amid shouts, toward the menace situated in the chancel.

"*My dear Flesh,*" Faro hissed. "*I told you one day I would let you watch. Behold!*"

The mirkúr crashed against him a second time, and

Theailys felt something rupture inside of him. Physical or spiritual, he was not sure. A plume of hot illum erupted outward from the center of his chest, connecting with the Reaver, growing brighter, brighter yet as it devoured the monster. Theailys' own scream braided with the demon's roar and he discerned a wiry humanoid shape beyond the light.

Faro hissed and Theailys surrendered wholly to his will, the hallway fading into blackness as the screams around him fell to silence.

THEAILYS SMELLED smoke on the air, felt the heat of fire. He sat up far too fast, overcome with dizziness, but was able to discern his general surroundings despite the blurred vision. He was in a camp; the smoke was from a fire several feet away. The flames were gentle, the heat welcoming.

"How are you feeling?" Neyma came into focus, kneeling at his side. "Lost your voice, did you? Shall I fetch more soup and tea? Been spoon-feeding you the last few hours or so."

"I feel...like I've just roused from the worst hangover of my life," Theailys said. He recalled mirkúr and illum surging toward him, siphoned hungrily by the voice in his head. There were the faceless priests as well, and the Reaver, veiled in shadow. "What happened? After I blacked out, I mean."

"You destroyed the Reaver, sure as anything. Impressive, certainly," Neyma said. "But your actions have dug you one hell of a grave. Reaping the souls of Naldunarian priests?" She sighed heavily. "A capital offense. What you did deprived our holy brethren of the Second Life. I cannot say for certain what consequences you will face, but mark my words, they will be profound."

Theailys shook, brow knitting in disbelief. "I...*reaped their souls?*" He massaged his temples. "You must be mistaken. I didn't—I couldn't have."

But in his heart Theailys knew her words were true. The solemnity of her expression said as much; the ethereal chuckle in the depths of his mind only gave further credence to this.

Keepers, what have I done?

Theailys looked about the encampment, at the various silhouettes and half-illuminated figures. His companions were nowhere to be seen. He glanced at Neyma. "Leyandra and Cailean...?"

"They are fine," she said. "Shaken, and save for a few cuts and bruises, relatively unscathed." Neyma touched Theailys' arm, her expression softening. "I do not blame you for Tal, but my word means little in the eyes of the Church, of the Seraph."

Neyma stood. "Rest. Try to keep your mind clear."

She withdrew, and Theailys snorted at her words. He flopped back down onto his bedroll and gazed up at the stars draped across the black-blue canvas of night. What consequences would his actions bear? It was impossible not to come up with wild guesses. Maybe they would imprison him or force a complete and total burnout of his illum and mirkúr, leaving him with absolutely nothing.

Or maybe they would sentence him to death. And would that really be so bad? He tried to brush the thought from his mind, but it lingered, festering as the seconds passed.

Just breathe, he urged himself. He filled his lungs with crisp air and held that breath for a seven-count before exhaling slowly. He did so four more times before he finally felt the weight begin to lift. It still remained, but it was light enough to bear, to continue on without too much trepidation.

Footsteps neared.

Theailys sat up—slowly this time—to see Cailean and the twins approaching, bundled in cloaks. They took seats in the grass beside him, the twins wearing expressions of curiosity and Cailean one suggesting he was either drunk or nearly so.

"Feeling better, I hope." Ronomar said. "That was quite the display. Darkly bedazzling." They sniffed Theailys' face and he recoiled, glaring. Ronomar rolled their eyes. "I was merely curious."

"Yes, well, maybe instead of sniffing me you might *ask me* whatever questions are on your mind," Theailys grumbled, feeling very weary.

"That mirkúr of yours has gotten stronger since last we met," Raelza said. "We trained together at the Hall for a year, do you remember? You were always so..." They looked at their sibling, eyes narrowed, wrinkling their mouth and nose. "Haughty."

"*Haughty?* I was never haughty," Theailys said coolly. "Not my fault I excelled where so many of my fellow apprentices did not."

The twins giggled. "Nothing's changed."

Theailys clenched his jaw. "I'm feeling a bit better, thank you."

Raelza clapped. "Oh, fantastic!"

Cailean thrust a flask toward Theailys. "Look like you

could use a drink. Go on. Get some warmth in your bones." He shot a quick glare at the twins. "At least take a swig to silence these mouthy mirror image fucks."

"Cailean Catil, ever the poet," Ronomar said. "A pity you can't lead as well as you brood. If you could then perhaps things might have turned out differently." They rubbed their left arm ever so slightly.

Cailean swallowed hard. "Keep the flask. Was yours to begin with," he muttered to Theailys. Then, to the twins: "Bastards." He stood and stalked off.

"A bit much, don't you think?" Theailys snapped at Ronomar.

"Cailean was impolite. Would you have me coddle him with silence?" Ronomar crossed their arms. "It would teach him nothing."

Raelza eyed their twin and cleared their throat.

Ronomar sighed. "I *suppose* I was a bit harsh. As Mistress Khal once said, people can and will be cruel, but their taunts are simple, meaningless words. I suppose I can't be too annoyed with Cailean. That's how he's always been, even before..." They rubbed their left arm again. "He's just a tad snappier now, and understandably so. It's probably wise to ignore him as necessary."

Silence. Dual looked at Theailys, the fire dancing in their round, mauve eyes. He could tell they were hesitating.

"Indulge our curiosity if you would," Ronomar said. "What's it like to harbor such a primal force?"

"Maddening. Taxing." And that was without the added weight of his dreams, especially those of late. Theailys narrowed his eyes, a small lump forming in his throat.

"Lonely. I never asked for this, I don't walk the streets brandishing the mirkúr like a sword, and yet the people curse my name. Some call me Te Mirkvahíl…" He trailed off. It stung even coming from his own mouth. He looked at Dual. "Not the answer you were hoping for, was it?"

"No. But it's the one we expected. We empathize with you," Raelza said. "People think us strange and usually not in a kind way. We ignore it as best we can. It's like Mistress Khal said."

Theailys nodded. He yawned wide.

"You should rest.," Ronomar said. "We ride for Naldunar at dawn and the marshal is intent on reaching the city as quickly as possible."

The twins rose to their feet. "Dream well, Theailys An."

9

MASKS

Behtréal walked the old foyer with measured steps, breathing in the dirt and dust and darkness of this house he'd once called home. This wasn't the first time he'd returned. He'd been here several times before, half to feel the anguish lingering in the floorboards, walls, and air, and half to reminisce about the memories he'd made. They *were* good memories and he knew he'd be a fool to refute that.

The furniture was broken. Shattered glass and shards of splintered wood lay strewn across the floor. They'd not moved an inch in three years' time. He held his hand out to the air, palm upturned, and called the mirkúr with his mind. Threads of shadow, cold as ice came streaming through the cracks and Behtréal caressed them, shaped them to a sphere of smoke he then imbued with what little light he could. That was getting harder these days, his ability to wield illum, but that would change once he had obtained The Keepers' Wrath.

Dear Faro, he thought. *I will see your ingenuity to its full potential.* His memories drifted through the years, to Ouran'an before its fall, to his beloved Aveline and Jor, his wife and toddler son; they had been among the first to perish when the plague returned. He squeezed his eyes shut, throat tight as tears dripped between his lids and down his cheeks.

"*Your eyes are wet once more,*" the darkness hissed. It called itself Te Mirkvahíl.

Indeed, they are, Behtréal thought. *This is a thing that happens when I think of all I've lost.*

"*It is a weakness,*" said Te Mirkvahíl. "*An affliction of the heart.*"

Without my heart I would be nothing, Behtréal thought. He could feel his freedom waning as the darkness fought to wrest control. *Without my heart this undertaking to restore my people would have never come to be.*

"*Without your heart,*" Te Mirkvahíl hissed, "*you would have killed your wretched brother when you had the chance.*"

That was cause for consideration. His brother, because of whom the plague had spread and reaped their city of its life. His brother, who had turned his back on Ouran'an to aid the mortals when the plague had come.

What good would have come from that? Behtréal had despised his brother, but he had never sought to kill him, not even in their final moments.

Te Mirkvahíl remained silent, relenting its urge to possess. Behtréal took this as a sign and continued through the house. He came upon a mirror hanging in the hallway and stared into his own emerald eyes, half concealed behind a mane of dark hair, remembering the night he'd sown the first of many seeds imperative to the deliverance of his people.

"Such hope I saw," he whispered, thinking of the gray-eyed man for whom he'd masqueraded as a wife. "They will know your name, Theailys An. I will tell them of the man who made their reclamation possible and they will pray to you like once they did to Varésh Lúm-talé, their god."

"*I sense remorse,*" Te Mirkvahíl hissed.

Indeed, you do, Behtréal thought. *It is a thing I feel for knowing I will one day have to kill a man I loved.*

"Theailys An is a martyr for a cause," said Te Mirkvahíl. "A means to an end."

Indeed. The darkness wreathed itself around Behtréal. *But one can still love a tool.*

THE AIR WAS strange this night. Heavy, almost suffocating, more so the further north through Helveden Serece and Fenrin went. Her ears twitched at every sound and shadow, at everyone they passed. *Madness,* she thought. *Madness in the air.*

They crouched in the gloom of the prison ramparts, the towers rearing up like jagged teeth, wisps of illum bright like eyes. Faithbringers, Wardens, and Illumurgists patrolled the grounds in trios, every step, every movement mechanical. Serece shivered; there was something about this place that made her sick. *And to think, you're going to walk inside to find out why.* She looked at Fenrin. "What now?"

"We wait." He tapped his forehead lightly. "All part of the game."

Serece arched an eyebrow, whispering, "Have you...*seen* what's going to happen?"

"I've seen the two of us in there. Nothing more, nothing less," Fenrin said. "The vision is always clouded, like whatever's in there doesn't want us peekin', you see? Ever since the Ariathan forces made their grand return three months ago my ability to divine has been limited. I've only been able to see bits and pieces."

"So, we're more or less going in blind," Serece said, taking a deep breath.

"One way of lookin' at it." Fenrin stood, pulling Serece behind him. "Here we go."

THE PRISON WAS EMPTY. Every wing, every nook and cranny, completely devoid of inmates, guards, and staff. Serece and Fenrin stood in the center of the moonlit anteroom. "Where the hell is everyone?" Serece asked, gazing about. "Did you foresee this?"

"No." Fenrin held his hand to the air, palm upturned, and frowned. "Odd."

"What is it?" Serece asked. "Fenrin?"

"Somethin' here. Somethin' powerful, but..." He tilted his head. "Benevolent."

Serece eyed the darkness around them, ears twitching madly. "Are you sure?"

"Positive." He knelt, motioning for Serece to do the same. "We're in the presence of a deity."

"Enough with the formalities," a voice said. "Up off your knees."

They obeyed, and a dark-haired, amber-eyed woman in robes emerged from the darkness. She had a hawkish face and Serece was certain she had seen this woman before. She narrowed her eyes, searching for the answer, and it dawned. "Master Illumurgist Khal?" Serece was pretty sure that was her name.

"Changed your name again," said Fenrin. "Shame. I was fond of Mistress Lorésh."

Khal snorted. "Haven't gone by that in *years*. Not that it ever did me any good."

"You knew we would come?" Serece asked. She was still ignorant of illumancy's many intricacies.

Khal nodded. "Didn't know who it would be, but I saw you coming here in a dream. Lucky. This place is infected. I'm surprised you made it past the patrols."

"Thank you for interferin', then," Fenrin said. "I can't imagine doin' so was easy."

"It wasn't," Khal said. "For the exact same reason I can't lay a finger on Te Mirkvahíl, let alone discern where it's at."

"Which is…?" Serece said.

"This world is not of my making," Khal explained, "and thus the capacity and frequency with which I can intervene in certain events is severely limited. Such is the rule of my people, the world builders, the Celestials. I am little more than a teacher here, a font of wisdom for Illumurgists of varying rank."

"What happens if you break that rule?" Serece asked.

"It depends," Khal said, "on the magnitude of the event in

which I overstep my bounds. Worst case scenario, I die. Best case…who knows? For now, let's move on to the task at hand, yes?"

"Yes," Fenrin said. "If you came to save us from our blind stupidity you're aware of what we seek."

"I am," Khal said, motioning for them to follow. "And while I am unable to divine the Demon Prime's location, I *can* divine where it is not, and I am reasonably sure Te Mirkvahíl is not here."

"Then why are we?" Serece asked. "I thought we were here to discern the demon's identity."

Khal snorted. "My dear daughter of the mountain, what makes you think either you or Fenrin would have stood a chance at surviving if you had come face to face with Te Mirkvahíl tonight?"

"We weren't going to engage," Serece said as they started down a spiraling stairway lit by wisps of blue light. "We aren't fools."

"You would have been made regardless of your intent," Khal said. "And whatever you saw, whatever you learned you would only have done so because Te Mirkvahíl allowed you to."

Serece's ears twitched. "You may have a point. Where are you taking us?"

"To see the woman who claimed to have slain Te Mirkvahíl," Khal said.

"Searyn An. I saw her brother only a few days ago," Serece said. "You surely know he seeks to forge the weapon that nearly destroyed your city centuries ago."

Khal was silent a moment as they continued their descent.

"I do. But like I said, there are certain events in which I cannot intervene—this is one of them. I can offer my opinions, but I cannot physically assist with or attempt to thwart the creation of The Keepers' Wrath."

Serece grumbled to herself as the stairway leveled out into a long passageway of white and black polished stone. "Can you tell me whether or not there's a connection between Theailys An and Faro Fatego? If you weren't already aware they look nearly identical."

"I'd seen that too," Fenrin offered. "In a...dream, I think. There was a tree, if I recall. A tree in a meadow and..." He furrowed his brow. "Three iterations of Theailys An. Dren was there as well. Or someone who looked an awful lot like him. The sky shifted; the meadow and the tree did too. Three moments in time, all seen at once."

"A triptych," Khal said. "An omen. Did you see anything else in the dream?"

"No. Funny thing is..." Fenrin said. "I don't think it was *my* dream."

Serece arched an eyebrow as they continued on, passing empty cell after empty cell. "Do you think it was Theailys An's?"

"It could have been," Khal mused. "Or it could have been foresight. Either way it's oddly specific, considering how repressed our ability to divine has been as of late."

Serece's ears twitched. All of this felt off. It felt too easy, easier than their initial infiltration of the prison had been. The fact that a so-called deity had foreseen their coming and had arrived in time to mask their intrusion from whatever lay in wait seemed far too convenient. She kept one hand wrapped securely around a dagger and the other resting at her side, comforted slightly by the knowledge Yssa no longer forced her to keep her rage at bay should she need to tap into it.

They stopped before an argentium door inlaid with glyphs. Fingertip aglow, Khal reached forward to imbue the glyphs with illum. There was a clicking sound and the door swung inward several inches, revealing the darkness beyond. "When I drop my illusion—the barrier that's kept us all unde-tected—I'm going to lock us all inside to avoid arousing suspicion."

Serece and Fenrin stepped inside; the door clicked shut behind them and a faint glow emerged.

Serece clapped her hand to her mouth and Fenrin closed his eyes, muttering a prayer.

Searyn An was dead, left sprawled on the floor in a threadbare burlap gown. She bore myriad scabbed tattoos of names and faces from the waist up, and the flesh around her chest was veined black, as though it'd been touched by mirkúr, as though her soul had been reaped. Serece allowed herself to shed tears. Despite her dislike of Theailys An she had never wished something so horrible as this upon him. First his wife, now his sister. Keepers, she knew how this felt, and she was reasonably sure Theailys had been close with Searyn.

"Didn't see this comin'," Fenrin murmured.

Serece cocked an eyebrow.

"Nor I," Khal whispered after a moment. "But I can make a reasonable assumption as to who's responsible for this trea-sonous butchery." She knelt, caressing Searyn's blackened flesh. "General Khoren had Searyn arrested for desecrating the burial mounds with mirkúr, but I think it's safe to say he was doing so to cover his own actions."

"Do you think this General Khoren is Te Mirkvahíl?" Serece asked.

"A lieutenant at the very least," Khal said, brushing her hand over Searyn's wide eyes to close the lids. "The poor woman had probably outgrown her use."

"Which would have been what?" Serece asked.

"Any number of things," Khal said. "A font of information, a host body for a lieutenant, or…"

"A voice in Theailys An's ear," Fenrin offered.

"Whispering what?" Serece asked, mentally reciting a prayer of her own.

"Whatever twisted words would push him toward forgin' The Keepers' Wrath," Fenrin said. "His wife's death was already a drivin' force; you think his sister's death won't push him to complete it quicker? Think on what you know of this weapon. Te Mirkvahíl tried to steal it once before, who's to say the bastard's not attemptin' to again?"

"For what reason?" Khal asked.

"You tell me," Fenrin said. "World builder and all, you sayin' you haven't a clue as to why Te Mirkvahíl would want a weapon as powerful as The Keepers' Wrath? C'mon, Khal —think!"

Khal shook her head, frustrated. "I…I don't know. To free the Origin from their prison, maybe? It could be any number of things—things my mind has not yet seen; things in which I cannot interfere."

Serece looked at Searyn's corpse. "We can't just leave her here."

"I know, and I'll make sure she's taken care of." Khal put a hand on her shoulder. "She was my friend. Now come. Let me take you from this wretched place."

IT HAD BEEN years since Behtréal had inhabited his own body. So many, in fact, he could not recall his true face or form. No matter, he found his ability to inhabit different bodies liberating. It meant he could be anyone he chose, whether it was the wife, sister, or mentor of the man who soon would forge the key to the reclamation of his people.

"*Such tears will he shed,*" Te Mirkvahíl moaned. "*Such sorrow will he bleed.*"

Yes, Behtréal thought. *He will be consumed with anguish once reality comes to light.* And reality would be as cruel as snow was white. Behtréal could hardly imagine the pain of knowing Searyn An and Eisley Khal were dead and had been for a while. He supposed though it would pale in comparison to the pain of Theailys' learning Anayela was a lie and always had been. This was how you broke someone. Barring death, this was how you destroyed their ability to trust. It was cruel, but such was life.

"Will you tell Theailys An?" Serece inquired.

"Not until he returns," Behtréal said. "But Queen Ahnil will undoubtedly command I send news of Searyn's death to the Seraph in Naldunar, and I find it highly unlikely Theailys An is not informed." He looked at Fenrin. "What will you two do now?"

"Don't know," Fenrin said. "I suppose this General

Khoren is a bit of a lead. Perhaps I'll sniff him out on the morrow."

"Why not end them now?" Te Mirkvahíl said. *"The diviner and the child of rage before your very eyes, Te Luminíl!"*

Behtréal pushed against the darkness raging. *Their ignorance is useful if not entertaining.* Useful because he wondered what the underlying cause of Theailys' triptych dreams might be. It was a variable he had not accounted for. Entertaining because he was well aware of the connection between Theailys An and Faro Fatego, having born the former from the latter's soul little less than five hundred years ago.

They arrived at the egress from the prison grounds. Behtréal gave Serece and Fenrin the customary salute of an Ariathan soldier—right fist to left shoulder—then bid them goodnight. There was still much to tend to.

"You look like you're thinkin' hard about somethin'," Fenrin said. They had gone back to his room at a seedy inn to lodge for the night.

Serece glanced up from her hands, then stood from the chair she'd been sitting in. "Did none of that feel odd to you? Premeditated?"

"Felt strange is all," Fenrin said. "Always does when my foresight is blocked."

"Maybe if you relied less on your foresight and more on your instincts you would have noticed *nothing* in that prison was right," Serece said, crossing her arms. "A deity appeared out of nowhere and led us to Searyn's corpse in the middle of a mission to discern Te Mirkvahíl's identity."

Fenrin cocked his head. "You think *Khal* is Te Mirkvahíl? Seems likelier than not it's this Khoren bastard."

Serece sighed. "I don't know what I think. Maybe General Khoren is Te Mirkvahíl or a lieutenant of some rank. Either way, I don't think Khal was entirely straight with us. That bit about us learning and seeing what Te Mirkvahíl wanted us to…it seemed like a warning and an obvious one at that."

"A warnin' to what, stop meddlin' in the affairs of demons?" Fenrin chuckled, but his amusement quickly faded to a narrow-eyed frown. "Now that I think about it, Khal *did* seem different. Didn't notice it at first."

"Notice what?"

"Her eyes," Fenrin said. "She's a world builder, a Celestial. Their kind, for whatever reason, aren't able to change the color of their eyes."

"She's a shapeshifter?" Serece asked.

"Sort of," Fenrin said, "but that's not the point. They can't change the color of their eyes, and Khal's were always red. Tonight, though, they were amber."

"And you think that's a sign she's been compromised?" Serece asked.

"You said to trust my instincts," Fenrin said, "so that's what I'm doin'. And I'm tellin' you whoever we met tonight in the prison *was not* Khal."

"Te Mirkvahíl?" Serece said, feeling colder, more confused. "Something else?"

"Somethin', all right," Fenrin murmured. "Somethin'."

Serece sat back down in the chair and looked out into the

night. Khal was not Khal, Searyn An was dead—who could they trust? She glanced at Fenrin—could she even trust *him*?

Don't think like that—just don't! This city's out to get your kind enough as it is, so don't shun the only person who seems to give a shit about you.

She sighed, closing her eyes. Little less than two days in Helveden had been enough to make her skin crawl and itch more than it usually did. Stealing a horse or shaghound sounded like a pretty damn good idea right about now.

———

BEHTRÉAL APPROACHED the queen's throne. Dawn light showered the crystalline room and he winced; the crystal of fallen stars were particularly painful to him in such close proximity. It was one of the reasons—the biggest, perhaps—why he himself could not forge The Keepers' Wrath, could not hold the power focus in his hand until it was encased in the argentium Theailys An had gone to collect from the phantaxians.

"My queen." He dropped to his knee—dropped *Khal* to *her* knee—and offered the formal salute. "I come bearing ill information." Queen Ahnil rose to her feet at this. Forcing the tears to fall, Behtréal said, "Searyn An is *dead*."

"It was Khoren and his men," Ahnil guessed, tensing her jaw, a dangerous glint in her yellow eyes.

"Yes," Behtréal said. "And there is proof left on her flesh." He stood, producing a small box from his robes, and held it out to Ahnil.

The queen took the box. She removed the lid, nostrils flaring, the corners of her mouth twitching. "Tattooed flesh."

"Just as he had threatened," Behtréal said, feigning tempered rage. "This is treason. General An had yet to stand trial."

"Send word to the Seraph in Naldunar. Inform them of what's transpired," Ahnil commanded, just as Behtréal had anticipated. "And once that is done, dispose of General Khoren—discretely."

Discretion was Behtréal's middle name and chaos was his favorite game. "Of course." He bowed his head then turned and started on his way, Te Mirkvahíl a grinning white-eyed countenance in his mind.

10

JUDGMENT

Historians called Naldunar the Hand of the War Mother for the simple fact the city sat atop a massive island shaped like a hand with its palm upturned. Theailys marveled at the crystalline metropolis as the shaghounds thundered across a great stone bridge wide enough twenty or so of the beasts could easily stand abreast.

"Never less impressive," Cailean opined. "Not much a fan of the Church or the Faithbringers these days but Naldunar's still something to behold." He gave Theailys a light pat on the shoulder. "How you feeling?"

"Uncertain, I suppose," Theailys said. The last couple of days had been relatively quiet on all fronts. No Faro, no dreams, no ruin. Nothing. A nothingness that had given way to endless thoughts about what might happen here in Naldunar. Would the Seraph present him with the crystal he had petitioned for and been promised months ago? And what of Tal, what of the consequences? Theailys took a deep breath, blinking slowly as to allow his eyes to adjust to the brightness of Naldunar.

"I don't blame you," Cailean said. "The Church is strict about that Second Life nonsense and whatnot. If that's what you're worried about, I mean." Theailys nodded. "Right. Well...maybe the Seraph will show a bit of leniency. Not like you can control being possessed, right?"

"Honestly," Theailys said, "I'm more worried about being refused the crystal. Without that there's no Keepers' Wrath. And without that..."

"The Heart of Mirkúr yet remains," Cailean said darkly.

"I don't think the Seraph is stupid enough to ignore that," Leyandra offered from behind Cailean. "My guess? If you're to be tried for what transpired in Tal, it'll be *after* the Heart has been destroyed. It would be hypocritical for the Church to condemn you for the reapin' of souls when they would effectively be sentencin' the rest of Ariath to the same fate. Hundreds of thousands of people, all deprived of the Second Life."

"She has a point," Cailean said.

"I hope you're right." *Otherwise,* Theailys thought, *those hundreds of thousands of souls will all be on my conscience.* He knew it was a stupid belief, an outlandish one at that, yet still he couldn't escape the guilt that'd been festering these last couple of days. It wasn't his fault, not directly at least. *But Faro is still a part of me, and it was with my body that he reaped those souls.*

They continued their ascent of the tiered city, crossing through the Palm with its shops and parks until they came to a switchback at the base of the Ring Finger. Lined with trees and built into the rock, it offered a shaded view of the fjord in which the island sat. It took little less than five minutes for the shaghounds to crest the Ring Finger, atop which sat the cathedral, a four-story, crystalline pillar of intimidation. Its spires jutted upward like talons, and the figures depicted in the stained-glass windows judged their approach, judged *Theailys'* approach. The sun put radiant fire in their eyes and turned them into remnants of the fallen, from an age long passed.

The quarter-mile promenade yawned into a quartered semi-circular courtyard. At the center of each triangular quarter stood an effigy of one of the four Keepers. Encircling the effigies, kneeling with their heads bowed and right hands touched to their left shoulders, were throngs of prayer givers.

The riders passed the praying by, dismounting in the center of the courtyard, several yards away from a wideset stairway. An oak-lined cloister spanned the perimeter of the cathedral grounds; Theailys watched as a quartet of handlers emerged from the north, greeting them with the traditional salute. The handlers took the shaghounds and led them away by the reins, disappearing beyond the cloister wall to care for the dogs.

From the south came a quintet of acolytes, adorned in the scarlet robes of their order. They gave silent salutes in the traditional style then ushered Theailys and his companions away. Marshal Nor walked in step beside him.

"I don't know how long it will take for the Seraph to summon you," she said. "They will of course need to deliberate." She wrinkled her nose as if to soothe an itch, then her expression softened a bit. "How are you feeling after...you know?"

"Reaping souls?" Theailys muttered, glancing at the marshal.

"I didn't mean it like that." Marshal Nor tensed her jaw as the acolytes led them around the corner and into the shade of an apple grove. "I was simply curious about your health. About..." She paused, lowering her voice. "About what you transformed into in the church just before you destroyed the Reaver."

Theailys' eyes widened. *"Transformed?"*

"Unless my eyes deceived me, and I doubt they did," the marshal whispered, "you were smoke and shadow come to life."

"So, I was one of *them*." A lokyn. Theailys felt cold; he wanted to scream.

Marshal Nor shook her head and pulled Theailys to the side as the guest quarters came into view. "I've been fighting in this war since it began. I've seen some real shit. Never saw whatever it is you were the other night, of that I'm damn sure."

"But you said smoke and shadow—"

"There's a difference. I'm surprised you of all people don't know that," Marshal Nor said. She put her hands on Theailys' shoulders. "The lokyns, they're just parasites, dark souls wearing corpses. You, though? There was form, there were facial features. There was an aura, one I've never felt in my life. A searing light beyond the madness, one powerful enough to obliterate the Reaver with little effort."

We're going to have a talk, Theailys thought at Faro. To Marshal Nor: "What do you think I am?"

She shrugged. "Don't know." Then, starting off: "I will vouch for you where I am able, but my words have little sway when it comes to the Seraph's decisions. Get some rest."

Theailys watched her disappear around the corner. *Why,* he thought, *do things always see fit to complicate themselves at the worst possible moment?* Killing lokyns while under Faro's possession didn't bother Theailys as much as it once had; at this point it was starting to feel routine. What did bother him was the fact he was apparently transforming when this happened, and that Faro had neglected to mention it. Not that he was surprised by the latter. Theailys supposed if their roles were reversed, he might do the exact same thing. Keeping the body you longed to wholly possess ignorant of such drastic alterations seemed a good way to keep them malleable, if not a bit accepting.

Head threatening to explode, Theailys started for the guest quarters, wondering what fate the Seraph had in store for him.

NIGHT CAME FAR TOO QUICKLY for Theailys' liking. He had heard nothing all day and it was making him antsy, itchy in the way one gets when they haven't eaten in hours. He glanced at Leyandra and Cailean, seated at the end of the table, drinks in hand whilst they mumbled back and forth.

"Marshal Nor said I transformed in the church."

Leyandra and Cailean looked at one another with hesitant

expressions. "We, um…weren't sure what to say." Leyandra stood, then took the seat beside Theailys, putting her hand on his. "Tal was a shit show. We didn't want to burden you after what you went through."

Theailys averted their eyes. "I transformed. Into…"

"Something," Cailean said. "I'm guessing it's not the first time either, right?"

"Probably not." Faro had yet to actually confirm this, but his silence was telling. "Suppose it would explain how and why I always seem to wake up next to massacred corpses after I blackout. After I'm possessed."

"Maybe it's not a bad thing," Cailean said, and both Theailys and Leyandra raised eyebrows. "That power, that control you had—"

Theailys snorted indignantly. "What *control* do you think I had, Cailean?" He stood, banging a fist on the table. "I was possessed! I felt everything, I heard souls screaming as I reaped them"—he hadn't remembered that until now—"and I *liked* it. It imbued me, the thing possessing me, with strength. I saw it all, watched myself destroy the Reaver without actually being able to move." He shook his head, eyes wet. "That…that's not control. That's imprisonment, torture in its highest form. Imagine if this darkness inside of me, this *thing* decided it wanted to kill more than just lokyns. Imagine if I had to watch myself kill Anayela again, or Searyn. Imagine being powerless to prevent yourself from slaughtering those you love."

Cailean narrowed his eyes and downed the rest of his drink. "I don't need to," he said. "I've been there before."

"What do you mean?" Theailys asked.

"Galska Nuul," Leyandra murmured. She looked at Cailean, confusion drawn across her face. "I thought—"

"I lied." Cailean sniffled, then heaved a sigh. He fixed his eye on Theailys. "When I lived and worked in Harbanan I loved a man named Bar. We were married. We were going to start a family." He tensed his jaw to keep his lips from trembling. "But he died, and I was alone." He let a watery chuckle escape. "Except...except Bar wasn't actually dead, you see? This monster, this thing called Galska Nuul that'd been terrorizing Harbanan for *years*? Turned out he and Bar were one and the same. He came back to me in the end; for a moment it was just the two of us, like old times..."

Cailean trailed off, trembling.

"He possessed you, didn't he?" Leyandra asked. "Oh, Cailean..."

"I couldn't do anything," Cailean murmured. "So, I watched, powerless to stop myself from driving my blade through Bar's heart."

Silence hung over the room.

"I'm sorry," Theailys said finally. "That's—fuck. I'm sorry."

"'S why I told you what I told you on our way to Ulm," Cailean said. "You let the devil in, you better be ready for the inevitable pain." He sighed. "Fucking entropy. Fucking coin bullshit."

"What are you talkin' about?" Leyandra asked.

"Something Bar told me the day I drove my dagger through his heart," Cailean said. "I understand it now, I think, and fuck all if it's not twisted." He poured himself another drink and took a sip, swishing the liquid around in his mouth before swallowing. "Think of the world as a coin. On one side, entropy; on the other, law. When the coin favors entropy then shit like this"—he held his arms out wide—"happens. When it favors law, we have decades, centuries of peace."

"And if it favors neither, then we have balance," Leyandra guessed. "From chaos comes law, from law comes chaos."

"Right," Cailean said. "Galska Nuul's reign of terror was about restoring balance in some really sick and twisted way—"

"You think this war with Te Mirkvahíl is about restoring balance?" Theailys scratched his nose. "I suppose that makes a bit of sense. Without chaos law becomes tainted, thus we look to horribly entropic events to draw law back to its true purpose."

"Exactly." Cailean took another drink. "Interesting philosophy. Fucked, too ."

Theailys motioned for Cailean to pour him a drink. As he caught the glass Cailean slid across the table a thought occurred: chaos, law, and balance, another triptych. It felt appropriately applicable to the dream he'd had several nights ago, the dream in which the idea of the triptych had first manifested. Faro was surely entropy or chaos, so what was Theailys: law or balance?

There came a knock at the door, and in stepped an acolyte with a folded piece of parchment in hand. The acolyte beckoned to Theailys; he stood and accepted the parchment curiously, the acolyte withdrawing.

"What's that you have?" Cailean asked.

Theailys opened it, scanning. Smudged ink, written hastily it seemed. General Khoren charged with treason for…

Theailys blinked. He had surely misread that. Trembling, adrenaline rushing through him, he reread the letter in its entirety.

"Theailys?" Cailean stood and approached. "You all right?"

Theailys said nothing, only held the letter out to Cailean, who read it, cursed, then picked up a chair and hurled it across the room, screaming.

Searyn was dead.

FIRST MAR. THEN ANAYELA. *Now Searyn.* Theailys sucked his flask dry. He stood at the edge of the Thumb, looking north as the moonlit sea crashed against the rocks below. *Some triptych. Some…* He hiccuped, then leaned over the stone banister and retched, tears trickling down his cheeks to amalgamate with his disgust. *Khoren had better be alive when I return. I'm going to kill that fucker myself.*

"Together we will reap the general of his soul, my Flesh," said Faro, finally rousing after two days of sleep. Theailys welcomed the company of chaos, regardless of what had transpired in Tal. "I will help you avenge your sister. I am sorry she is gone."

I didn't even get to say goodbye before I left, Theailys thought. *They just showed up and whisked her away.* He recalled that moment clear as day. The fear in Searyn's eyes, the confusion. Theailys reared his head back but no scream, no howl of anguish came. Just a sob as he dropped to his knees, the flask clanking several feet away.

"*There now, my Flesh,*" Faro whispered, manifesting at Theailys' side. He put a hand on his shoulder. "*There now.*"

Theailys looked up at Faro. For the first time he saw not a white-eyed shadow, but a gentle face composed of smoke. *Why do you look like me?*

"*Do you really not know, my Flesh?*" Faro asked. "*I would have thought it obvious. We are the same, you and I.*"

Theailys tilted his head. *How?*

"*Think, my Flesh. That day when the Faithbringers confronted you in the woods.*"

Theailys recalled being collared in the woods, questioned about the bodies. He also recalled their ignorance of Faro as the shadow had toyed with and mocked them. How he was the only who could see Faro.

I'm…phrenzic, aren't I?

Faro nodded. "*To admit an illness such as this is not easy, my Flesh.*" He dissolved, withdrawing to Theailys' mind. "*But it is a good first step toward achieving balance.*"

Theailys snorted. *Funny coming from you, you know? Chaos preaching balance.*

"*No one is perfect, my Flesh.*"

Why'd you do it? Tal. Why'd you make me watch, make me feel? Theailys pushed himself to stand, leaning against the banister for support. *Shit, why'd you cede control?*

"*It is truly remarkable, my Flesh, how many questions you seek answers to when you already have them floating in your head,*" Faro chuckled. "*If we are to fix* this, *this situation of ours, then law must come to light. Without law there is no balance.*"

Theailys heaved a second time. *Are you…saying…?*

"Yes. Another voice," Faro said. *"And the fact I sound less crazy than usual suggests my efforts to invoke him haven't been for naught."*

Theailys vomited again. *What…the hell…is wrong with my head?* The night swam in and out of focus, the volume of the crashing sea waxing and waning. Theailys staggered back from the banister, tripping over his own feet. The back of his skull smacked the flagstones and darkness embraced him.

"MIRKÚR."

"Illum. It has been a long time," Faro said. Before him stood a figure of…well, illum.

"You say that as if my absence was self-imposed," Illum said, crossing his arms. "So many years of repression, of being subdued by your bloodlust and madness—why seek me now?"

Faro narrowed his eyes. "You know why."

"Balance," Illum said. "We suffered the loss of our parents, our brother, and our wife. Now our sister, too, it seems. So why now, after all this time, after all this pain *you* caused us?"

"Because," Faro said, "the world is going mad. I can sense that, and I am quite sure you can too. Something is horribly amiss whether our waking self cares to admit so or not."

"Why not do as you always do, then, hmm?" Illum snapped. "Reap. Annihilate."

"I would not have to if you were here to temper my insanity," Faro hissed, mirkúr blades forming in his hands. "Without law, chaos, or had you forgotten?"

A brilliant longsword took shape in Illum's hand. "I would be able to temper your insanity if you had not banished me in the first place!"

"I AM DEPRESSION!" Faro lunged and swung. Illum danced out of reach. "BANISHING YOU IS WHAT I AM MEANT TO DO, YOU FOOL!"

Illum extended his blade, threads of luminescence shooting forth and encapsulating Faro. "This is true, yes." Illum flicked his wrist and the encapsulation shrunk, reducing Faro to a shrieking orb of smoke. "But I am Euphoria, and *I* am meant to banish *you*." Illum extended his free hand, palm upturned, and drew the orb in. "Your time is at its end."

"*BALANCE!*" Faro raged. "*BALANCE!*"

Illum shook his head, then crushed the orb. Balance simply would not do. Balance meant that chaos always had a chance to supersede. If things were as mad as mirkúr claimed them to be then law and only law could rule this fragile husk of what had once been a happy man.

Illum dismissed his blade and held his arms out wide, allowing himself to dissolve, his brilliant essence beginning to permeate the blackness of this thing that was Theailys' mind.

I will see this world absolved of darkness. I will see myself absolved of fury and despair. The outside world blinked in and out. Theailys An was starting to wake. *I will do what must be done.*

Another blink, and Illum was blinded by the brilliance of the waking world.

THEY CALLED the Seraph's chamber the Seat of Divinity. Before Theailys stood an effigy perhaps a hundred feet tall. Embedded in the massive statue were seven podiums and seats: one for each upturned palm; one for each of the four unfurled wings; and one for the faceless hood. At each podium stood a figure shrouded in white and wearing a helm with an eyeless visor; fixed atop each helm was a circlet.

Theailys bowed his head to these figures, waiting to be addressed. His gaze wandered, admiring the architecture and design of the Seat. The white of the floors bled into the walls, ascending in threads that gradually faded to shades of gray the closer toward the ceiling they grew. The ceiling itself was like an ascending stairway, the stairs replaced with stained glass that cast threads of white and red light onto the chamber floor.

"Theailys An," the Seraph's Head finally addressed. "Welcome."

"Thank you." Theailys took a breath to push away the modicum of anxiety. Weirdly enough he felt better, more at ease than he had in weeks, and that was even after last night learning of Searyn's death. He recalled momentarily vomiting off the Thumb, then shook away the memory and scanned the Seat. "I have come to collect the star crystal for which I petitioned and was granted access to months ago. In light of recent of events, however, I understand if the Seraph sees need for further deliberation, though I would implore that any punishment you see fit to bestow upon me comes after we have destroyed the Heart of Mirkúr once and for all."

Theailys clasped his hands behind his back, taking a second steadying breath. That had sounded well enough. Formal, responsible, devoid of desperation. He only hoped the Seraph would see reason.

"The transpirations in Tal were most troubling indeed," the Head said, voice doubled and distorted by its visor.

"How many souls was it?" the First Right Wing inquired. "Marshal Nor offered only an estimation."

Theailys swallowed. "I…" He shook his head, casting his eyes toward the floor in shame.

"Too many to count, presumably," the Second Left Wing said. "Surely such a beast as this cannot be left to run amok."

"Beast?" The Left Hand chuckled. "How boldly excessive. I see no beast, but a man at war against himself, against the demons in his mind."

"Indeed," the Right Hand offered. "There is a darkness in Theailys An. Call it chaos, call it entropy, whatever you desire, but know this man might be our only hope to raze the Heart for good." The Right Hand turned to acknowledge the Wings and Head. "We all have darkness in us. Let us not forget that some here are dissident too."

"The Hands present valid observations," said the Head, "but let us not forget when last The Keepers' Wrath was wrought."

Theailys tilted his head. "I am not some clone of Faro Fatego if that is what you are insinuating. I am not some puppet of Te Mirkvahíl. If I believed there was even a chance

The Keepers' Wrath would fail do you think I would be here? Do you think I would have pushed myself to see this weapon to fruition if I thought history was trying to repeat?"

"If *you* thought history was trying to repeat," the Head said. "Therein lies the key: *you.* But what about what the rest of Ariath thinks? Pray tell, what might the *phantaxians* think?" The Head leaned over the podium. "We have eyes all around, Theailys An. Did you think the Seraph unaware of the time you spent in Te Vétur Thae?"

Theailys tensed his jaw. "King Undrensil and his daughter believe Te Mirkvahíl to be lying in wait."

"A belief that contradicts your fallen sister's claim of having slain the beast," the Second Left Wing said.

"What to think?" the First Right Wing mused. "What to think?"

"Respectfully, you have my condolences," the Left Hand said.

"Childish behavior, shaming a fallen general before her kin," the Right Hand scolded, looking up at the Head and Wings.

"Childish indeed," the Second Right Wing agreed. "You align yourselves with General Khoren's school of thought with such flagrant disrespect."

"If we are all done arguing amongst ourselves," the First Left Wing interjected, "might we proceed with judgment?"

The head sighed. "As you wish. Those in favor of officially granting the petition?"

Four hands. Theailys felt a rush of relief and heaved a sigh.

"Those in favor of trial upon destruction of the Heart?"

Raised hands from the Head and Wings. A bit of weight returned to Theailys' shoulders, but it was nothing he hadn't anticipated. In fact, he found he more or less agreed with being tried, which felt a big departure from his previous mindset. *From chaos, law,* he thought. And from both, balance. Maybe this was a first step toward restoring balance to his country, to his world.

What do you think? he asked of Faro.

"*A trial is fair,*" the voice replied. It was different, more measured and soft-spoken. "*A trial is law, after all.*"

Are you the other voice? Theailys asked.

"*Call me Remy, if you wish,*" the voice replied.

Where's Faro?

"*Is that what he had taken to calling himself? How ironic,*" Remy mused. "*Mirkúr is asleep. The coin has flipped.*"

Which would explain why Theailys had felt so light the entire day despite the shitstorm that had been the previous night. He supposed he was all right with this, though being unable to feel Faro's presence was strange. It made Theailys feel naked in a way, vulnerable, even.

"We will have the crystal prepared and delivered to your quarters," the Head said.

Theailys nodded, bowing to each of the seven in turn, offering prolonged gratitude to each of the Hands. "Thank you, Seraph. I will take my leave." He offered the formal salute, then turned and started from the Seat, feeling an amalgamation of discomfort, confusion, and relief.

Wars were not won with one broad stroke. Victory required strategy, and strategy required patience, the former being something Behtréal had always excelled at, the latter being something he'd acquired through the years. He'd had failures, yes, but from failure blossomed wisdom. His father and brother had always been fond of that saying.

This will work, he assured the monster in his thoughts. *I have seen it. I have learned from past mistakes.*

Faro Fatego had been a pawn encircled by knights, empowered by a king and queen, and Behtréal had made the mistake of trying to take Helveden and The Keepers' Wrath by force. But not this time. No, he was keen to play the waiting game, the slow burn as some might say. He would clear the board then strike with unbounded fury. Vengeance for the sake of vengeance. Vengeance for the sake of reclamation.

He looked at the box atop his desk, at the mirkúr-tinged face residing within. "Oh, General Khoren." The man had been quite alarmed to see Searyn An's naked corpse come staggering at him with a blade, not that Behtréal blamed him. It had made defacing him all the more worthwhile. Tender flesh was easier to flay and my—how the general had screamed!

"His soul shrieks even now," Te Mirkvahíl groaned. *"May I, Te Luminíl?"*

Yes, Behtréal thought. *Devour what little of it remains. We are low on illum.*

He felt a surge of a power moments later and Te Mirkvahíl sighed contentedly within his mind.

Behtréal reread the letter he had composed, then scrawled

the queen's signature at the bottom. He placed it in the box with Khoren's face and tied it all together with a piece of string. *What do you think?* he asked of Te Mirkvahíl.

"*There will be chaos,*" the voice replied. "*And from chaos, death. From death, deliverance.*"

I thought as much, Behtréal agreed. He stood from his chair, parcel in hand, and started from Mistress Khal's office to send word to the Seraph. They were going to panic, then retaliate with a force of Faithbringers when they learned that Queen Ahnil had murdered General Khoren and devoured his soul.

Like I said, Behtréal thought. *Wipe the board.*

INTERLUDE

THE LAUGHING HEART

"Once marked, always marked."
—*Galska Nuul*

THE TRAUMA

There was only darkness in this place.

So far as Cailean could tell, that was all there ever *had* been, immeasurable and smothering. A frigid swaddling that forced him into endless introspection, endless recollection of the trauma that had brought him to this void. A trauma that had woken with a yawn, then risen to a scream within his mind as he relived the cold and horrible desolation of his world, of all that he had loved.

This is death. The thought was riddled with uncertainty. Cailean had never put much stock in Rapture, in the Second Life, or whatever the hell came after death. But now? He touched the spot on his chest where in life the dagger had found its mark. It was smooth, unsullied by the trauma of his end; the entirety of his flesh was soft as silk. The longer he lingered on the spot, the deeper into memory he fell. The cathedral. The bodies. The betrayal and a voice like buzzing flies.

"Once marked, always marked," it whispered. A terrible grin stretched wide and stark across the void. It yawned and a serpent's tongue of starlight flicked his way.

Cailean struggled not as it took him in a cold but tender embrace. Tears dripped down his cheeks and along his jaw. What a fool he'd been. What an ignorant, fucking fool.

He closed his eyes to the monstrous maw, once again enveloped by the memory of his end. Spellbound by the cosmic gaze of Galska Nuul, tantalized by his touch as the fallen angel's dagger sheathed itself in Cailean's heart.

MISERY

B ar was dead and there was nothing Cailean could do to bring his husband back.

It'd been a month, but the agony of his loss had made it feel a year. Thirty days without Bar's touch, without his scent, without his laughter and his words. Thirty long, inebriated days of snarling, tears, and guilt. Of self-inflicted wounds and sleepless nights. Would that he could, Cailean liked to think he'd slaughter time as retribution for the misery games it played.

He leaned against the balustrade of the tavern balcony, gazing out at the moonlit sea. Across it lay the Ariathan realm, the origin of his blood. And across it he had come,

159

dishonorably discharged for having lain his weapons down. Treason, Ariath had said. Exile, they'd enjoined. All for having had the spine to lay down arms in protest of preemptive village culls. Fighting demons did things to the mind. It imbued the xenophobes with zeal. Sucked sanity from the sane. Made monsters out of men and cast humanity aside.

"Thought I might find you here."

"Leyandra," Cailean said, still gazing at the sea. While he adored the young woman, he wished she'd leave him be. She meant well, but sometimes solitude was better left untouched. "You need something?" His words were sharper than he'd meant. "Sorry. Just..."

Leyandra touched his shoulder gently and they watched the sea. Listened to the distant crooning of the waves and the late-night squawks of fishing gulls. It was enough to ease his mind, and he recalled the many times that he and Bar had stood here just the same, basking in each other's warmth, spellbound by the beauty of that shimmering expanse and all that lay beyond.

"We were going to adopt," Cailean murmured finally. "When things were right."

Leyandra leaned against him. "He would have been a brilliant father."

Bar had been a constant presence at the orphanages. Cailean's heart sunk further, wondering if they knew. They had loved Bar as much as he had them. Cailean's shoulders rose, then a ragged sigh escaped his lips.

"Head to the Beacon," he said. "I'll meet you when I'm done."

· · ·

CAILEAN WAS A MASOCHIST AT HEART—WANDERING alone so late in the Forjét Mahn Athuul. The Forest of Dark Remembrances. A rough translation in the indices of the Galrun Muir. One of countless many kept and archived in that buttressed manor that they called their home. The land on which Harbanan stood was old; there was much to learn, much the spirit of this eldritch realm had left untold.

But also much that she'd revealed. And right now, Cailean sought what none save the crypt of Lúm Duu'Mahl could give—the illusion of euphoria, a walk through memories of yesteryears. A momentary respite from the misery bedeviling his soul, devouring him from the inside out. Agony to alleviate the anguish.

Masochism in its purest form.

The night wept as Cailean neared the crypt. Drops of rain like faerie lips upon his cheeks; soft and forlorn all at once. He thought of Bar, of his touch, his kisses, and his eyes, all lost to memory, and let the pain constrict his heart. This was what he'd come for, after all. Yet this was foreplay in comparison to the crypt.

Or so the indices relayed.

He came to a gate in a glade, on either side of which stood effigies of the angel Lúm Duu'Mahl. She beckoned with an upturned palm, and her feathered wings curved in such a way that Cailean felt a modicum of warmth, a bead that started in his chest and emanated outward, growing more profound for every second that he held the statues' gaze. The first of things remembered in this wood of yore. He hadn't felt this warm in months.

Cailean pushed the gate ajar and stepped inside. Before

him lay a maw of weathered stone, and around it, daffodils. Beautiful, yes, but as woebegotten as the Forjét Mahn Athuul, for the only time the flowers grew was when a person died. Cailean wondered if there might be one for Bar.

He hoped there was.

Whispers grazed his ears, and Cailean started toward the crypt. Light bloomed within, brighter yet for every downward step he took, tempering to a pale and soothing blue as the stairway leveled out. The room was small and saturated with a scent like dust and earth. Save the casket and the effigy of Lúm Duu'Mahl it was rather plain.

"Once more you grace this place my bones call home." The voice was soft and unsurprised.

Cailean knelt and bowed his head. He closed his eyes, trying to picture Lúm Duu'Mahl in a sea of grass. The very same he'd seen in dreams. The golden field in which he'd married Bar. The angel came, lithe, composed of feathered wings and light, a hood drawn past her eyes. As had her effigies, she beckoned with an upturned palm and Cailean obeyed, allowing her to pull him close and swathe him gently in her wings.

"Once more that summer dusk," the angel said. *"Is this what your heart desires most?"*

It was, in the way an addict craves their fix. Cailean clung to Lúm Duu'Mahl. "Yes."

"Then I will make it so," the angel said. *"And I will pray you someday flee this tomb of memory."*

An unrequited prayer if ever there had been.

He blinked, and Lúm Duu'Mahl was gone. Where once she'd been stood Bar, boring into Cailean with those sunset eyes; Keepers knew how many times he'd gotten lost in them. They were hand in hand, smiling like fools. Of all the stupid things they'd done…

"Makes the day-to-day feel tame," said Cailean, and he hoped he'd been profound.

Bar rolled his eyes. "You going to keep on blathering, man, or have you strength enough to hold your tongue and kiss me lest I leave you here unwed?"

Cailean flashed a rueful grin. He wrapped his arms around Bar's waist and pulled him close, capturing his lips. They stayed like that a while. Bar ran his hands through Cailean's hair, his touch electric, sending shivers down his spine.

At last, Bar pulled away.

Cailean gazed upon him fondly. "What now?"

Bar offered a melancholy smile.

Then, he fell to ash, just as he had a month ago in the dark of night.

IT WAS black as pitch when Cailean emerged from the Forjét Mahn Athuul. Nary a star to paint the sky, not that he cared. What would they do save twinkle as souls were devoured, as children were flayed, as mothers and babes were boiled alive?

As Bar fell to ash in the wind?

Cailean cursed the stars, then Galska Nuul, and finally himself. He should have been quicker. He should have been closer. He should have known they were walking into a trap.

But he wasn't, and he hadn't.

He balled his hands into fists, tensed his jaw as he entered the grounds of the Galrun Muir, the Beacon looming, spired and pretentious. Windows were betrayed by dots of light, the entryway by azure flames from lanterns hanging on the walls. Cailean stalked his way to the courtyard, past others in long coats emblazoned with roses and ravens the color of snow. The family crest of Gabriel Muir, the man for whom the Order was named.

The courtyard was abuzz, and it was only when he reached the double doors of the manor that Cailean learned why.

Leyandra met his gaze. Her brow was etched with worry, but something hungry flashed inside her eyes. "Made it just in time for the briefing."

Cailean's heart was pounding in his chest. Instinct whispered this was something big. "Tell me."

Leyandra pushed the doors ajar, then gave a backward glance. "Galska Nuul."

MEDICATION

THEN—THE MONTH OF CEMB, BLACK YEAR 1154
TWO DAYS BEFORE THE END

Waiting was the worst.

Cailean ached to drive a blade between the fallen angel's eyes. Galska Nuul would die a slow and painful death, and Cailean would drag his dagger through the monster's flesh for every soul consumed, for every life extinguished by the madness he had wrought. He would carve the deepest mark for Bar.

But first he had to wait.

Snow fell. Cailean walked the Beacon courtyard with his collar up and hands shoved deep inside his pockets. It was a hollow dawn; the world was little more than shades of gray above a gelid shroud. In a way it reminded him of home.

"Ariath," he whispered, thoughts falling to the demon war that raged beyond the eastern sea. He'd heard little in the last two years. Though considering the reasons why he'd left, why he'd been dishonorably discharged, he wasn't sure he cared. Not for the architects of bloodshed and the means by which they'd sown their xenophobic zeal. Not for a king who lacked a spine, whose fears infected Ariath like a plague and strung him as a puppet for the Church. They could burn for all he cared. Preemptive culling had a way of souring one's concern while tarnishing their faith.

He met Leyandra at the northmost edge of the courtyard. She'd sent a message—there was whiskey to collect and daggers to be dipped. Cailean hoped these tasks would be enough to occupy his mind lest thoughts of vengeance drive him mad or into recklessness.

THIS WAS NOT your mother's whiskey.

This was not the piss that taverns served for sipping in the eve.

This was something else. Something old, wrought by masters with the aid and blessing of the angel Nor Vaa'Dahn. Consecrated by her blood to imbue consumers with her strength and amplify intrinsic capabilities. This was the drink of a conservator, of a man that met the night with blades in hand and fire in his eyes.

This was the whiskey of the Galrun Muir.

Cailean turned the spigot handle and the flow of liquid ceased. He corked the vial and set it to the side, allowing himself a moment's worth of rest. He'd been at this for an hour and his hands were sore; there were plenty more to fill.

He leaned against the column at his back, inhaling fumes of consecration. Smooth and smoky like a fire in the night. Whiskey, weaponized yet soothing all at once. It eased his mind and Cailean heaved a sigh.

"We're going to cut that bastard down," Leyandra said. She mimicked Cailean's posture and brushed a strand of hair behind her ear. "We're going to end this, just you wait."

Cailean smiled wryly. He produced a knife from the inner pocket of his coat and tossed it, watching it flip. It descended and he caught it by the hilt. Wait—his favorite thing to do. Wait, while the world dissolved. While chaos reigned supreme. He tossed the knife a second time. It arced above his head, finding purchase in the post. He left it there and paced the room. "Waiting. The irony…"

"How do you mean?" Leyandra asked.

"In Ariath, abandon pushed forbearance off a cliff," said Cailean. "We slaughtered thousands out of fear; we forsook our mantles as custodians for those of injudicious zealots. And here? The Galrun Muir have grown reserved where they should not."

"It was a war," Leyandra said of Ariath. "Against chameleon antagonists."

Cailean wheeled around. "*Demons*. It was a war against *demons*, yet how many towns and villages were we made to cull? How many lives were lost to the madness of preemptive strikes, to the Seraph's bigotry and our sovereign's fear?" He closed his eyes to the memories. "How can you defend them after what they did, what they made us do, what they *did* and *tried to do* to *you*?"

Leyandra was silent. Cailean opened his eyes and met her gaze. She looked irked, forlorn. There was shame there too. She scratched at her wrists; each bore a crisscross of scars. Like Cailean, she too had been dishonorably discharged. Unlike Cailean, Leyandra wasn't human; she'd descended from the demons Ariath fought. Her expulsion had been purely prejudiced and the scars she bore betrayed that fact.

"They branded you when you no longer met their needs." Cailean approached, took Leyandra's hands in his. "Ley, they tried to kill you in the dark of night, to pass it off as self-defense…" A man and woman they had served with, had considered friends.

Cailean had decapitated both.

"Because," she finally answered, "I understand their fear."

Cailean frowned. He understood as well, but to systematically annihilate entire towns and villages, to be enveloped wholly in one's paranoia? He shook his head. "Still, it's no excuse. No excuse for targeting a certain race because of what their predecessors were. You and the rest of the dissident are the opposite of monsters, Ley. Your people are a sentient attestation to that fact."

Cailean pulled her into his arms. She returned the embrace with a ragged sigh.

"Hard to see that sometimes." Her jaw tensed against his chest. "Scars have a nasty way of fixing things in place."

Cailean pulled away, produced a flask from the inner pocket of his coat. He shook it mischievously and grinned.

"True, but drinking has a way of soothing aches." He took a sip, then passed the flask to Ley. "Go on. Put some fire in your blood."

CAILEAN LOOKED at the numerous blades and vials, adrenaline surging as he thought of knifing Galska Nuul, of what it'd feel like when his monstrous reign was finally quelled. Of restoring peace to a city bent by fear.

"Bar told me something once," Leyandra said. "'Memory is medication.'"

Cailean lingered on the phrase, a tiny smile playing on his lips. Bar had always been a man of words. More often than not he'd had his nose in a book; their home had seemed an archive, what with sheaves and pages strewn about the countertops and floor.

"What do you think he meant?" Leyandra asked.

Cailean shrugged. "Knowing Bar?" He chewed his thumbnail pensively. "A lot. You?"

"I always took it literally," Leyandra said. "I like to think good memories can soothe a broken heart. That they can ease a troubled mind." She frowned. "I suppose it works the other way as well. A dark memory can trigger rage."

Cailean thought of marrying Bar in that golden sea of grass. He thought of Bar becoming ash the night he died. He closed his eyes, immersed in agony and bliss. He could almost hear Bar whispering in his ear. *"Make your medicine, my sweet."*

He opened his eyes and blinked.

They started from the room.

"You all right?" Leyandra asked.

Cailean nodded. "Just…making medicine."

MENDACITY

C ity of Masques.

Garden of Souls.

Befitting epithets for a city intimate with festivals and death. For a city where the two were often times entwined. That Harbanan stood was not by chance, but by the dark benevolence of Galska Nuul. One soul, one month, in perpetuity. Habitual reaping. An equivalent exchange of lives, at least in the fallen angel's eyes.

Eyes like ghosts these last four months. Four masques. Four offerings unclaimed. It troubled Cailean—where had the monster been?

His stomach churned as he paced the snow-swathed

Beacon courtyard, hands behind his back. He felt hot despite the cold. More tense than he had ever been. Sweat slicked his brow. His left eye twitched.

Breathe.

Easier said than done. Just like ending Galska Nuul. How many times had the bastard shirked the Galrun Muir? How many lives had been lost?

And how much blood is on your hands?

It a question that'd been stalking him for years. His intro-spection rounded back to Bar and Cailean heaved a sigh, his dejection clouding in the frosty night.

In the distance rang a bell. Cailean turned and started toward the Beacon doors.

The time of masques and souls had come.

THEY CALLED Drahl Muuz cathedral the Crown of Spires. Folklore claimed it once had been the diadem of the serpent god Dragúl. History told it'd been erected by the ancestors of Gabriel Muir. Apostates thought it fashioned by the raven god Alerion. Whatever the origin, it was widely accepted Drahl Muuz had sheathed itself in the earth a millennium prior to the birth of Harbanan.

The grounds were a cacophonous swirl of vibrancy and mirth. Harbanan lived for its monthly masque. A part of Cailean understood, loathe as he was to see good in a festival that most times ended in death. It brought comfort in a time of fear. The comfort of routine. A comfort *bred* by fear, but a comfort nonetheless.

"Ig tahn na'tuul," he murmured. May you rest. For the

people of this godsforsaken city, there was nothing Cailean longed for more. A decade's worth of terror at the hands of Galska Nuul was a torment none deserved.

He tensed his jaw, once more entranced by the fantasy of ending Galska Nuul, of slaughtering the monster in his husband's name.

I failed you, Bar, but I'll not fail the city you loved. You mark my words, you pretty shit—it ends tonight. Even if it means my life, I'm going to punch my dagger through that fucker's heart.

He started for the oaken doors.

"*A COIN FLIPS, and the world transforms.*"

Cailean gasped.

Slaughter bloomed like waking stars; costumed corpses caked the chamber floor. Blood shimmered in the dying light. He stood amidst the butchery, body tingling, mind empty save the memory of oaken doors. What the hell was this? How had he gotten here, so deep in Drahl Muuz? A ragged breath escaped his lips, clouding in the frigid air.

"*So long I dreamt of you, O Galrun Muir.*" The voice was *wrong*; soft like summer wind, cacophonous like a thousand buzzing flies. It gave a resounding, drawn-out moan. "*Craved you like the styrgé thirst for gore...*" A reverberant chuckle, hungering yet coy. As ethereal as its host.

Cailean started at a breath against his neck, a whisper in his ear.

"*Cailean Catil, I've missed you so.*"

He pulled away, half stumbling as he drew his blade. He wheeled around but there was nothing there.

Incorporeal amusement.

"Come out!" he snarled. "You fallen fuck—reveal yourself!"

The illumination waned. Bodies rose with fire in their eyes and screeches in their lungs. Needled-toothed and ravenous, they came. Cailean sheathed his blade and bolted for the rearward doors.

Fucking styrgé. A nasty vampire breed. He could handle one or two, but this? They'd flay him head to toe and drink him dry.

But not before I cut your master down. The beasts could have him after that. A Bar-less life was unappealing and acutely masochistic.

Cailean barreled into the hall beyond the doors. He had distance on the risen dead; newborn styrgé shambled instead of running. He kept on at a desperate sprint, following the laughter as it goaded him to tears. How could anything so divine as angels bend to sociopathy so profound? What had bled this creature of its sanity and heart?

Cailean ran until weariness betrayed him. He pressed into the vestibule, steps hampered by a stitch. There were corpses here but they were still. He neared them with his dagger drawn and paled. They were men and women of the Galrun Muir.

"Ig tahn na'tuul," he whispered, swallowing a lump. He hoped Leyandra was all right; thankfully she wasn't *here.*

"*The irony amuses me.*" In a twist of light came Galska Nuul, pale and lithe with brimstone eyes, wingless and adorned in white. "*A prayer for souls that never were.*" He grinned at Cailean's dismay. *"Homunculi. You were mine since you arrived those years ago."*

Cailean bared his teeth in a rictus of disgust. His stomach churned and his blade arm shook. "You lie."

Galska Nuul approached. *"If only it were so."* His smile fell; his eyes swirled and his flesh began to warm. *"Fiction is the cruelest mistress of them all. That she should greet you here…"*

Time slowed; deaf ears turned words away. Cailean shook, immobilized by dread, by dark bewilderment wrathful as a winter night. He fell to his knees, hand to his mouth, a scream in his throat. It was a lie. He was surely asleep, wrapped in a blanket and dreaming a dream. A horrible dream from which any moment he'd wake. Wake to find Bar in his arms on a warm summer eve. An eve of moonlight, stories, and stars.

"Memory is medication," Galska Nuul intoned, *"and medication makes the memories."*

Cailean retched at the fallen angel's words. Blood and bile smacked the floor.

Yet he pushed himself to stand. By strength of will he rose to meet this *thing*, to meet its sunset stare.

And could not raise his blade—not to him.

Not to Bar.

"The world is a complex thing," said Galska Nuul. *"A coin, if you prefer."*

Cailean ignored the words. The fallen angel looked like Bar, smelled and spoke like him as well. A memory came— Bar had acted strangely in the week before his death. "Would you castigate a man for past mendacity?" he'd asked. The question clung to Cailean like hoarfrost to a fence; the implication made him sick. Had Bar been trying then to tell him what he really was? Or was this all a twisted joke, the fallen angel toying with his memories and thoughts? Had Bar ever actually been *real*?

"If you're really *him*...what was I to you? Did you love me or was I just a pawn—"

Galska Nuul hissed. He closed the gap, wrapped Cailean in his arms, and, in a twist of light, whisked them to the apex of Drahl Muuz. To the highest point in all Harbanan so they might observe the city as it fell to madness and monstrosities beneath a gentle snow.

Cailean pushed himself from the fallen angel. He ached in ways he'd never known. There was cackling in his head, resonant and wry. Black amusement birthed and fostered by each hammer of his heart. His ignorant, shattered, laughing heart.

Harbanan wailed.

"Everything..." Cailean wept, keeping his dagger level with the monster's eyes. "*Why*?"

"*For equilibrium,*" said Galska Nuul, and his words were soft. "*They call me Madness. They call me Lucifer. They call me Entropy, for I am that which raises Law, provokes it to ascend. Each is requisite for symmetry lest Pandemonium drink the world.*"

He closed the gap in a luminescent blink and ripped the blade from Cailean's hand. He punched it through his chest and pulled him close. Held him as the cathedral waned. Held him as he had the night that they'd been wed.

"*You were mine since you arrived those years ago. Mine in more ways than you know,*" whispered Galska Nuul. "*Once you let the devil in your bed there is no letting go. Once marked, always marked.*"

"*B...ar...*" Tears fell from Cailean's eyes; shock kept them wide. Blood trickled from his mouth. Trust from his soul. How could this be? He gazed at Bar, lost in the stare he had loved. Their history danced and died in those pastel eyes that had sold him lies; Cailean clutched the fallen angel's arm.

Then darkness carried him away.

THE VULTURE

THEN—THE MONTH OF OVEM, BLACK YEAR 1154
FIVE WEEKS BEFORE THE END

W ould you castigate a man for past mendacity?"
inquired Bar.

He and Cailean walked the Beacon grounds amidst an evening snow.

Cailean quirked an eyebrow. "Something I should know?"

Bar chuckled softly. "No. Just a question." He sucked his upper lip. "But suppose there was... Suppose my past was marred by fabrications of a most egregious sort."

"I would rather not," said Cailean. "Supposition leads to horrible thoughts and I'd prefer to keep you in as bright a light as I'm allowed."

"As you're allowed?" Bar poked at Cailean's ribs. "Has

my brilliance waned, my sweet?"

Cailean rolled his eyes. "No, but I can see your ego's waxed."

Bar smirked. "That's not the only thing…"

Cailean allowed himself a snort. They continued on in silence for a time, the snowfall ebbing as they neared the shrine of Nor Vaa'Dahn. The effigy greeted them with unfurled wings and open arms; azure torchlight echoed in her eyes.

"Been a while since you prayed," said Cailean. "Something wrong?"

It was less of a question than it was an opening for Bar to speak. He'd been acting strange these last few days. Strange for Bar, at least. Antsier and more abrupt, beset with hypotheticals and ignorant of his work.

"Feeling lost is all," said Bar as he bowed his head. "Out of place."

Cailean took his hand. "You can talk to me about this, Bar. You know that, right?"

Bar smiled. "Your sympathy is endearing. It's what I love about you most." There was a sadness to his words. He let go of Cailean's hand. "Just need a moment to myself. I'll find you when I'm done."

Now—Time Unknown

Bar was monstrous.

And I am dead, thought Cailean as he drifted through the

memory for what could have been the third or thousandth time. The simplicity of this fact feasted on him like a vulture did on flesh. And what could he do but drift and wallow in this void, this retrospective hellscape all his own?

"You were mine since you arrived those years ago."

Cailean lingered on the words, each one a needle tracing patterns in his flesh. Torturing the modicum of trust that still remained. Had anything between them been sincere, or had he simply been a puppet dancing to the movement of his strings?

And what the fuck had Bar meant? Equilibrium, Entropy, and Law—epithets personified and claimed as if they all were gods. Bar was not a god, not so far as Cailean was aware, but that didn't mean he wasn't what he'd said. Keepers knew his actions were indicative enough.

Cailean screamed, and the blackness ate his rage.

He cried, and the emptiness drank his woe.

If this is Hell, he thought, *then let me not exist.* To be unwritten was a better fate than this—reliving agony in a place where sound was dead and light had never been.

He sighed.

And his breath became a fog, luminescent and abrupt; a swaddling, comforting and warm.

A light to ward away the dark.

He javelined through the void. Whispers found his ears, a soundless scream escaped his lungs. Raindrops kissed his cheeks and he slammed his head and back against the ground. The pain was comparable to a hammer to the chest, but even it could not distract him from the majesty that was the nimbus-dusted night.

SUDDEN SKY

I t was an ashen sky.

A waking sky.

A *sudden* sky. One that drew a violent gasp from Cailean as he gulped the rainy air. As shadows of a previous life waltzed across his mind. One of agony and war, purposeless and bleak, yet at the same time harboring hope for something past the wonted madness of the world. Something beautiful and warm, like a summer breeze against one's cheek.

"Or a whisper in one's ear."

Cailean started, bolting upright.

"Find me past the eldritch moon, beneath a hidden sun."

He looked about the pallid glade. All was still; he was utterly alone.

Cailean touched his chest, touched the scar where blade had punched through bone and siphoned trust. *Is this real…?*

Or was he mad, dreaming as the desolate dead were wont to dream? He touched his face with a trembling hand. His skin was rough and unrefined, scarred and dry like parchment left to bake beneath the sun. A far-cry from the silk-flesh he had worn in death. A remnant of the war-sworn life he'd led.

Cailean pushed himself to stand. The glade spun and he staggered like a foal. He retched a bitter, midnight ichor and it burned. With it, bile and blood, pooling at his feet and washed away by rain. He tottered toward the trees. Every breath was short, and every fiber of his being screamed as the atrophy awoke.

He collapsed in a heap, weighted by the steeds of apprehension galloping through his mind. He was *alive*—and he had never felt such dread. Things dead were meant to stay as such, for things returned were never whole, so said the axioms of the Galrun Muir. So said the mind of a man who'd danced with nightmares wrought from borrowed flesh.

The night screeched and an owl landed on the ground. It scrutinized Cailean with a storm-eyed stare and snapped its beak. "Get up." The words were resonant and unexpectedly direct. "Endure the atrophy and rise, O Bane of Nuul. Rise and seek the eldritch moon. Drink her like you would the rye of Muir."

Would that he could, Cailean would have laughed at the absolute absurdity of the owl's words. Bane of Nuul? He was limp as a fucking rag and weaker than a babe, naked who the hell knew where and listening to a bird. These weren't exactly hallmarks of the man who'd vanquish Galska Nuul.

"How..." He paused to catch his breath. "How would... how would you have me rise?"

Fuck, but this was tiring. So many questions, so little verve. Cailean frowned as if to convey this thought and the owl cocked its head. *The Bane of Nuul commands you pick him up,* he thought, and he yearned for a cask of rye. Longed for whatever liquor might temper the inanity of his plight.

"Clearly, gratitude is not your bent," the owl said and it seemed to glare. "Your mind is gallingly cacophonous."

So that was owl's game. Cailean returned the glare. *I've little love for things that wander where they ought not be. Especially nameless birds with a flair for histrionic convocations.* He smirked and the owl screeched.

"I was sent by the spirit of Lúm Duu'Mahl," it hissed. "She has a certain fondness for you, but I wonder now if she was wrong. Perhaps I'll leave you here and tell her you were dead when I arrived."

She'd know you're full of shit, thought Cailean. *Are you going to help me up or not?*

"What makes you sure I can?" the owl asked with such apparent nonchalance it might as well have been a barkeep mopping floors. "With such a *draining* flair for histrionic convocations I have strength for little else, oh woe is me." The owl snapped its beak. "You must have been particularly loathsome to have died the way you did."

Cailean tensed his jaw. Gradually he pushed himself to sit; the exertion was akin to lifting blocks of stone. He took a pained breath and let the raindrops kiss his skin. He licked his lips and they were dry; his throat was sore but he ignored the ache. His mind was glued to Bar and the memory of that night. To those monstrously intoxicating eyes and the beautiful lies that Bar had led.

"Maybe."

Cailean swallowed a sob; tears met rain and streamed along his cheeks. He sat there wondering, sifting through the memories of their lie, searching for a sign, an inkling of an answer to his every why.

The owl hooted softly; there was sympathy in its stare. It flapped its wings and in a twist of light the bird became a man, feather-cloaked and cowled. He offered Cailean a taloned hand and pulled him to his feet, wrapped him in a warm and comforting embrace.

"Truth resides in madness," said the man, "just as madness lurks in truth. Each is requisite for symmetry lest Pandemonium drink the world. 'Tis the utmost principle of our world, O Bane of Nuul; hope endures."

Cailean was silent as he synthesized the words. Was it possible to sunder Bar from Galska Nuul? Had his husband been a complicated fiction or were Bar and Galska Nuul two separate halves of something more? Reservation warred with desperation and he felt his skull might crack beneath the weight of his internal plight.

"How do I find the moon?" he finally asked, and he withdrew from the man's embrace.

The man gestured toward the trees. "Walk and you will know, for she calls to you and you alone." He shed his cloak, gifting it to Cailean's scarred and shivering frame. "This will ward you on your way."

The cloak was soft and light, yet at the same time warm like nothing Cailean had ever worn. He gazed at the man, this statuesque specimen of midnight flesh, of taloned hands and feet and twisting horns that shone with all the splendor of a starry night.

"Thank you," Cailean said. "Who are you?"

"An acolyte," said the man, "but if you wish then you may call me Pan."

There was a fleeting familiarity about the name, but it went as quickly as it came.

"Thank you, Pan."

Pan bowed his head. "Farewell, O Bane of Nuul. May you find the symmetry you seek."

Then, he vanished in a snap of light.

Cailean was alone.

He closed his eyes and breathed the forest air, let the wet and cold awaken whispers in his mind. *"Memory is medication,"* they intoned, *"so make your medicine, my sweet. Make your medicine and drink it deep."*

It tasted of finality and woe. Cailean knew where it would lead.

So he went.

ELDRITCH MOON

A nd so the forest whispered, *"Abandon hope all ye who enter here."*

And the fog sung, *"I am ghost. Forever, I am ghost."*

Cailean clutched his feathered cloak. This wood was old, older even than Drahl Muuz. He could feel it in the earth beneath his feet, the biting wind against his cheeks; could taste it in the air and smell it in the rain.

Yet against the forest's melancholy will he persevered, his atrophy allayed and seemingly entombed within the feathers of his cloak. With every step they shone a pastel blue; with every step his strength returned, until he felt that he could sprint. "Ig tahn na'tuul," he prayed in thanks to Lúm Duu'Mahl and Pan.

Time was boundless as the dark wood dragged him deep. Eventually the forest fell to ruin and a strange necropolis reared its crumbling vine-constricted head. Cailean gripped his cover tighter yet, trying to find a modicum of courage beneath its feathered warmth. Halfway through the boneyard he procured a pair of tattered pants; it was nice to not feel so completely bare.

He crossed through dust and lichen-covered rocks, up perished stairs, and underneath an arch, scrutinized all the while by a host of winged effigies with missing eyes. Had this place at one time been a shrine? Perhaps a temple where the dead were blessed before their bodies met the earth?

Or maybe something worse.

Cailean came to a pool of murky water at the promenade's end. The rain had stopped, he realized, for he could see the moon reflected clearly in the placid gloom. He touched the water and it hissed. Cailean stumbled back.

"What the fuck?"

The surface rippled and a head appeared, inset with full-moon eyes. "Who are you?"

"Cailean Catil." He held his ground and wished he had a blade. "Who are *you*?"

She rose from the water, elegant and lithe, with leather wings and taloned hands, her flesh like marble and her hair stark white. She approached and Cailean felt a pang of dread. "Shy Rii'Vahl," the creature said. "Untethered acolyte and guardian of the eldritch moon."

Cailean stifled his surprise. The Untethered were supposed to be a myth, a supposition of an angel neither fallen nor divine, but rather something in between. It was ironic, then, this thing claimed guardianship of anything other than itself.

"I don't suppose that you might let me drink of her..." said Cailean.

Shy Rii'Vahl bore her teeth. "The eldritch moon has not been drunk in all her countless years."

"And yet she called to me and me alone," said Cailean, holding up his hands. "Just a sip is all I ask—"

His stomach roared and he doubled over onto his knees, once more retching midnight ichor. *No*, a voice inside him moaned. *More than just a sip.* Cailean eyed the pool and thirsted for the moon like styrgé did for gore.

Shy Rii'Vahl snarled and her talons grew in length. "It clings to you like hoarfrost, does the touch of Galska Nuul, and it will claim you for its own. Once marked, always marked. I will end you lest you spread my fallen brother's blight."

Cailean rose and made for Shy Rii'Vahl. His thirst was maddening and it spurred him on. "She called to me and I must drink." The feathers of his mantle shone a violent red. *"You will let me drink."*

Shy Rii'Vahl charged him with a screech.

Cailean caught her by the throat and held her in the air. He squeezed—tight, tighter yet as the Untethered flailed. Her talons raked his arms and chest but Cailean did not relent. The newfound power coursing through him ached to break her neck, to end the irony she called her life. It longed to quench its thirst, to drink the eldritch moon and sate its quickly growing rage.

Shy Rii'Vahl fell limp with a final squeeze, at a muffled snap, and Cailean let her body crumple at his feet.

"Fool," he muttered, and he eyed the eldritch moon, reflecting luringly within the pool.

He knelt before its edge, cupped his hands, and drew the water to his lips.

Sweet, the voice inside him moaned. *So absolutely sweet.*

And Cailean drank.

And drank.

And drank—

THE NIGHT WAS cool and the wind kissed Cailean's flesh.

He was amongst the stars—he was *of* the stars and the world was small. Gossamer threads of cloud curled round his arms and legs and the astral breeze crooned songs like he had never heard. He felt...whole. At peace for the first time in Keepers knew how long.

Cailean declined his head and beheld the moon in all her soft grandeur. Her light was neither warm nor cool, but somewhere perfectly in between. It reminded him of Bar and the countless nights they'd gazed upon the sea.

"*We meet,*" said a voice, and a specter manifested before the moon. "*At last we meet.*"

The specter neared and Cailean sensed no mal intent. The ghost exuded peace and Cailean felt at ease. She was lithe, composed of light like every angel was—and Cailean was sure that's what she was; her gossamer wings betrayed as much.

But she was something more.

"*I am Korska Nuul,*" the angel said. "*And I am finally free, all thanks to you.*" She took his hands and pulled him close, breathed him deep and sighed. "*I see, now. Things have changed —the coin has flipped.*"

Cailean frowned. "What—"

"*Please*," said Korska Nuul, and there was sorrow in her plea, "*set my brother free.*"

"Galska Nuul," Cailean murmured. His heart sunk—he knew what freedom meant and it made him ache. Pained him in the worst of ways. He looked at Korska Nuul. "Is there a chance...? What I mean is...Bar."

"*The devil is not so black as he is painted, Cailean Catil,*" said Korska Nuul, "*but the end is not for us to make, for destiny does as balance wills.*" She kissed his forehead. "*Sleep, now, weary wanderer. Rest, for peace is scarce and the road is long.*"

She cupped his cheeks and the world dissolved.

THE GRAY of dawn was overhead when Cailean finally awoke.

He stood with little ceremony from the empty pool, walking past the corpse of Shy Rii'Vahl. She was mad—the Untethered *all* were likely mad—and the only logical release was death. She was free and Cailean was glad; he envied Shy Rii'Vahl in the most woebegone of ways.

He started from the ruin at a walk, Pan's feathered cowl pulled past his eyes; they were sensitive to light. Cailean wasn't sure what energies of yore resided in that pool, but, for better or for worse, the rumbling in his gut suggested drinking of that placid gloom had been the proper choice; his mantle shone a warming pastel green. He had done as Pan had willed and he had freed a gentle ghost, cleansed his body of whatever hellish thirst his resurrection had instilled.

Cailean lingered on the words of Korska Nuul—had she been real or just a dream?—and they filled his heart with dread, roused sorrow from its sleep. "Destiny does as balance wills." He had never felt so small as when considering what that meant and it made him sick.

He traversed the northern trees and it wasn't long before they thinned and melded with a meadow vast and gold. A sea of reeds beneath the wan light of a hidden sun—*the* hidden sun, for in the distance was a man, the monster Cailean had loved.

Bar had brought him home.

HIDDEN SUN

THEN—THE MONTH OF NUA, DAWN YEAR 1150

Cailean adored Drahl Muuz. Its old grandeur exuded charm in a way that made him think of youth-year tales. From an early age he'd had a wild mind, had dreamt of far off places in a world beyond the war-scarred Ariath he called his home.

Now here he was, in a place with troubles of its own, though he supposed that anywhere was subject to a darkness of a kind. That just seemed to be the way things worked, the way the world was wrought, and what could he do but fight?

"Beautiful creatures, angels."

Cailean started at the voice; he hadn't realized anyone was there. He turned and the face that greeted him was handsome in a bookish way, inset with sunset eyes and framed by locks of scarlet shimmering in the morning light. He had seen this man before—they both were new to the order of the Galrun Muir.

"Indeed," said Cailean. He felt a little hot. He extended his hand. "Name's Cailean."

"Bar," said the man, and he shook Cailean's hand. His grasp was firm, his touch was soft.

Cailean was spellbound.

Now—The Month of Cemb, Black Year 1155

BAR HADN'T AGED A DAY. In fact, he looked more beautiful than he ever had, and Cailean hated him for that. He hated Bar for a great many things, but the fallen angel's elegance only served to magnify his monstrousness—and what a beastly thing he was.

Cailean strode toward Bar and Bar to him. They stopped a couple feet away from one another. *Those eyes,* thought Cailean, and he balled his hand into a fist. *Those fucking sunset eyes.* He struck Bar in the chest and the fallen angel stumbled back a foot. Bar did not react; there was something similar to sorrow in his eyes—weariness, perhaps?

"Here I am," hissed Cailean. "What do you want? What do you *need* you...you..."

Cailean shook his head and gulped the morning air. He was at a loss for words despite the fact he had so many things he longed to say. To scream. To shout. His chest was tight and a cold sweat slicked his brow. He pulled the cowl away so Bar could see his face, could look him squarely in the eyes.

Bar said nothing. And, save the glint of *something* in his eyes, his face betrayed no semblance of emotion. Had he a blade, Cailean liked to think he would have punched it through his monster-husband's chest, just the way that Bar had done to him.

But Cailean knew he never could. It was fantasy of the blackest kind.

Bar reached for his face. Cailean smacked his hand away.

"You *arrogant fuck*," Cailean hissed. "You think that after all this time, after all you put me through, after *murdering me*, you get to touch me as if nothing happened? As if things are just the way they were when they were good?"

Bar lowered his hand.

Still, Cailean's heartache raged, and he was hotter than the day he first met Bar. "You brought me here, the grass where we were wed. Of all the fucking places, Bar...—SAY SOMETHING! Tell me this is just a dream, that we're home, asleep and safe within each other's arms. That I'm feverish and the hell I've been subjected to is...—*fuck*." A sob escaped his lips. "*Keepers damn you, Bar...*"

"You were always pretty when you cried," said Bar and his voice was not the buzzing flies of Galska Nuul, but simply, unequivocally Bar, as soft and warm as it had always been. He reached for Cailean, this time taking both his hands inside his own.

Cailean wanted to pull away. Damn it all, but he wanted to with everything he had.

But he could not. "Fuck you," he said, swallowing the

lump in his throat, and he allowed the fallen angel to pull him close and hold him tight, as tightly as he had the night that they'd been wed, the night the lie that was their future came to be.

"I never wanted this," said Bar. "This agony and madness. But alas, destiny does as balance wills, and balance is the cruelest aspiration of them all. A master unfathomable in its strength." He pulled away from Cailean and his eyes were wet with tears, his wan cheeks streaked with woe.

"You're saying what, then?" Cailean asked. "That you're some sort of...*puppet*?"

Bar nodded. "I suppose. Think of the world as a coin, and think of the coin as balance—on one side Law, the other Entropy. From Entropy, Law. From both, balance. As I said to you before, I am that which provokes Law to ascend.

"But things are different now," said Bar. A cool breeze tossed his hair. "The coin has flipped to favor Law, and on a scale far larger than you know. You drank the eldritch moon, you freed my sister Korska Nuul as I had planned—she is central to a history that's yet to pass. As are you. That's why I brought you back—destiny does as balance wills, and I am but a cog in the machine."

The pervading silence chilled and heated Cailean as he tried to synthesize what Bar had said. The fallen angel was a pawn in a game of unfathomable scale (or so he claimed)—so what was Cailean to him? A simple toy?

"The devil is not so black as he is painted," echoed Korska Nuul inside his mind. *"But the end is not for us to make."*

Destiny did as balance willed.

"I loved you more than anything," said Bar. "Still do...but

things are complicated in the worst of ways; they always were. If the choice was mine, the lie we lived would be our truth. No—it *is* our truth…" Bar was weeping, now. "But every truth has its end. Come to me, my sweet."

Cailean started forward and his steps were not his own. A stronger will pervaded him and it would not relent.

"Pan did well to cloak you, to entreat you drink the moon," said Bar. "My sister is free and your resurrection thirst is dissolved—now, we sing our final song." He took Cailean in his arms, in an embrace that awakened memories of yesteryear, and Cailean returned the touch, held Bar against his chest as the sunlight crept between the clouds.

"I am ghost," Bar sung softly in his ear. "Forever, I am ghost."

He pulled away. For a minute, he was Bar, just as he had been that evening in Drahl Muuz.

For a minute, he was Bar, the Galrun Muir who'd never met a book he didn't like.

Bar, the man whose sunset eyes had captivated Cailean from the day they'd met.

The man with whom he'd shared a beautiful lie.

The truth inside the madness that was Galska Nuul.

For a minute, he was Bar.

Cailean punched the dagger through his chest.

THERE WAS SUNSHINE, and the meadow was ablaze with gentle light. The air was sweet with the scent of myriad perfumes, pungent with the tang of iron. Cailean held Bar's body close. It was still warm despite the blood crying around the dagger impaled in Bar's chest—the dagger with which he'd murdered Cailean in Drahl Muuz.

You fool, Cailean thought, choking back tears. *You fucking beautiful fool.*

In his heart of hearts Cailean knew Bar's death had been for the best. The fallen angel had said so himself in his way. "From Entropy, Law. From both, balance." Peace. Cailean wondered what that might feel like. He'd jumped from one war to the next, though searching for what, he was still unsure. It certainly wasn't this. This was just chaos of a different kind, the chaos brought by Law, and Keepers did it hurt something fierce.

Cailean laid Bar down in the grass and sobbed as uncertainty claimed his world for its own.

THE ALBATROSS

Two Months Later—Bru, Dawn Year 1156

Cailean rode in silence through the moonlit night, Harbanan little more than a silhouette in his wake. He'd been expelled from the Galrun Muir in secret. Things dead were meant to stay as such, but Cailean had returned at the hand of Galska Nuul. He'd been Touched; he was a walking scourge, so said the indices of the Galrun Muir. Once marked, always marked. He hadn't argued; he'd agreed wholeheartedly to leave. Bar was dead and Cailean was lost. There was nothing for him here.

Cailean reached beneath his shirt, fingering the scar above his heart, the place where Bar had sheathed his blade little more than a year before. All in the name of balance, the fallen angel had intoned. An eternal tug of war between the vehicles of Entropy and Law. After all, life was not just ending wars, but igniting them as well.

He thought back to Ariath, to the culling sprees he'd so passionately abhorred. His gut churned, tears of rage filled his eyes, and Cailean cursed himself for finally seeing even a modicum of logic in such savage acts of war. If there was one point Galska Nuul had driven home, it was the fact that things were never as they seemed. That, sometimes, beauty masked the monster underneath—and what a monstrous creature Bar had been.

"Ig tahn na'tuul," he murmured, though to what or whom he wasn't sure. To himself? That seemed unlikely. How could he rest? How could he be at ease with all that he had seen, with all that he had done?

To Harbanan, then. To its people, to its streets and structures. To the memories of simpler times. To the ecstasy of ignorance. To Leyandra and the Galrun Muir, though he knew their work was far from done.

To the Cailean he once had been. The man who'd crossed the sea and died, reborn sans purpose with an albatross upon his soul and a scar along his chest. A blemish to remind him things were never as they seemed. To remind him love was fickle if not masochistically compelling. What was it Bar had said? Once you let the devil in your bed there is no letting go. Once marked, always marked.

"Ig tahn na'tuul." To Bar, the truth inside the madness that was Galska Nuul.

To the world that Cailean had known. To the world that

he had loved. The veil had parted that night in Drahl Muuz, in the fallen angel's arms, a dagger buried in his chest. The coin had flipped upon his resurrection and the truth of things was utter pandemonium. There was only madness.

There was only darkness in this place.

ACT TWO

TRUTH FROM MADNESS

"Time has little meaning to forever people."
—*Unknown*

11

DREAM

"You've been quiet, lately," Cailean said.

Theailys glanced up from his evening meal of bread and meat. "A lot on my mind."

"*Quite the understatement,*" Remy said, manifesting as an inverse silhouette. His almond-shaped black eyes scrutinized Theailys. "*Do you plan to indulge his curiosity with a better explanation?*"

No, Theailys thought. *No need.*

"Figured," Cailean said. He took a sip from his waterskin and sighed contentedly. "If you feel like talking…"

Theailys smiled. "I'll let you know." He bundled away his food, then stood and stretched. "I'm going to go for a walk. Try and clear my head before I sleep."

Cailean nodded, and Theailys withdrew.

"*You are particularly adept at avoiding conversation,*" Remy said. Tall grass passed through his incorporeal frame. "*At least when it comes to the individuals without your mind. In here?*"

He tapped his temple. "*Utter chaos. So much so one might think your head was full of ghosts.*"

From law, chaos, Theailys thought. *Unpack that as you see fit.*

"*You desire General Khoren's head,*" Remy said. "*A life for a life. From law, chaos, and from chaos, law.*" He crossed his wispy arms. "*Or perhaps it's something else. A darkness in your dreams?*"

An apt, if not tame conjecture on Remy's part. Theailys sighed. *It was different the other night, more than fantasy. Almost like a…memory. In Helveden, yet at the same time not. An analog, a reflection of its ruined self.*

Remy stopped. "*Show me.*"

What do you know? Theailys asked, turning to face the silhouette.

"*Little,*" Remy said. "*But enough to guess my presence in your mind is what's responsible for this immigrant dream of yours. After all, from law, chaos.*" He held his hand out toward Theailys. "*I should like to see it, please. If it's kept you silent, occupied your thoughts these last couple of days, then you should have some semblance of an answer as to why.*"

"Maybe dreams *are* sometimes something more," Theailys murmured aloud. With everything going on, he supposed it wise to heed such a notion, no matter how ridiculous it seemed. As Khar Am had once said, truth from madness.

All right. Theailys took Remy's hand and the silhouette dissolved into his flesh. *How do I show you? I can remember little else beyond what I explained.*

"*Take a seat in the grass,*" Remy said, so Theailys did. "*Close your eyes. See your illum swimming toward your mind and allow the energy to wreathe your nebulous recollection in its warmth.*"

Theailys closed his eyes, greeted first by darkness, then a sphere of luminescent energy, threads of which streamed out and upward through the void that was his mind. He took a steadying breath. He could feel Remy's presence, unwavering and warm, searching for the memory of the dream.

"*Beneath the ashy oak, she waits,*" Remy whispered. "*A silhouette wrought by the softness of the moonlight. She beckons, starting from the tree, a spire city looming in the far distance of the world.*"

The illum swelled at Remy's words. "*You call her by a name you can't discern. She does not slow, so you press yourself to sprint, to chase this gentle ghost you swear you've seen before.*"

The illum pulsed. From its nebulous core a doorway came to be, beyond which stood the snow-swathed walls of the spire city Remy had described. "*She implores you follow. Something in the ruin of this place has called you both.*"

The illum surged one final time, the doorway yawning to its full capacity, and Theailys found himself beneath the moon and clouds, the city rising up before him like a monster in the night. He started up the grass-lined road, occasional threads of moonlight revealing the city for the ruin that it was. Every step he took sent shivers up his spine; his skin was gooseflesh underneath his robes. Something tugging from the deepness of his mind suggested he knew why.

Another step. The dreamscape fluctuated briefly to reveal a brilliant city bathed in golden light. It vanished, though, as quickly as it'd come, and Theailys neared the dark necropolis, eyes keen to any movement, ears to any sound as he willed the silhouette to reappear.

In, a voice inside him whispered. *In the city does your gentle quarry wait.*

Theailys crested the incline, stepping into the shadow of the city wall. The entryway portcullis had been ripped away; the path ahead was clear. He crossed the threshold, greeted by a city entombed in ice. Mirkúr webbed its way along the streets; it crept up buildings like vines. Its gossamer threads extended from the myriad rotted corpses strewn about—the black essence had left none untouched. Theailys shivered, pushing down the urge to retch. What had happened here, wherever *here* was?

"This is new." Theailys started at the voice, and Varésh stepped beside him to observe the ruin. "New and terrible. Why this? Why not the meadow and the tree? Why not your Anayela, hmm?"

Theailys eyed the winged man. "I…don't know. Remy said—"

Varésh cocked an eyebrow. "Remy?"

The illum silhouette materialized at the mention of his name, scrutinizing Varésh with a furrowed brow. "Varésh Lúm-talé. How long since last we met? At least a year before my Ana's death, I think."

"Ah." Varésh stroked his chin, nodding slowly. "Now I understand. The coin has flipped. Mirkúr is at rest." He gazed upon the necropolis. "Why here, Illum? Why this awful place?"

Remy shrugged. "For the moment, bird, I've not a clue." He narrowed his eyes and pointed at a spire wreathed in illum, jutting upward from the center of the city. "But instinct says some semblance of an answer lies within."

At that, both Varésh and Remy disappeared.

Theailys took a deep breath to steel his nerves, then started on his way.

"Do you get the feeling, Ronomar, we ought not be here?" Raelza asked for the umpteenth time. They were well aware this was a dream, an illum dream to be exact, one they had traversed many times before. They stood before the ruins of a great city, white with years of snow, preserved by endless frost. "What I mean to say is, do you think Mistress Khal will be angry?"

"Considering we're an ocean away and we snuck out of the Hall one night before assessments began, probably," Ronomar said. "Probably more so when she learns we commandeered her surname in order to fund this little excursion."

"Free travel out of Ariath for Master Illumurgists," Raelza said, grinning. "Who could blame us?"

They looked the frosted, gate-less archway up and down, shivering. The chill of this place lent itself to a city lost to time. Ouran'an —the dead city of a dead race, the first race. One didn't happen upon such a majestic mausoleum by chance. Finding Ouran'an had taken years of research, of sifting fact from fib. Years of honing their abilities as Illumurgists, though apprentices they were. One did not wander into history on a whim, and one certainly did not go unarmed, especially to a place like this.

The twins conjured illum blades, motes of light coalescing at the hilts. They crossed the old threshold into Ouran'an, though not before they gave a final glance to the path and landscape they'd traversed. Snow and rock for as far as they could see. Had there ever been grass or trees?

Raelza coughed. "The air is thick."

"Like a tomb in summer, but worse." Ronomar stepped a few paces past their sibling, wrinkling their nose. "The promenade, the angular architecture and the spires—it reminds me a bit of home, though decidedly less lively."

"So many buildings. Where do you think the journal is?" Raelza asked. It was a good question. "Research suggests it lies in one of three or four locations, but who can say? It's just as well we decided it was optional, eh?"

"Yes. But think of what secrets those pages hold," Ronomar said softly. The Reshapers and their fall... Ghosts returned to life in ancient ink. An optional desire, a side quest to an undertaking of immense scholastic import and personal pride.

"The better question," Raelza said, "is where the Prime Vault sits. Do you think it's under guard?"

Ronomar shivered in their cloak. "In a city like this, Raelza? In a city long dead and near erased from history? Undoubtedly. Whether by glyphs, or ghosts, or something more, only time will tell."

Ronomar scanned ahead, vision obscured by light snow and sunlight bouncing off the ice. They could tell, though, a number of once great spires and towers had been reduced to half their true heights. As they and Raelza pushed ahead they saw that one stood out amongst the rest—taller, bearing tarnished, half-shattered stained-glass windows.

"Impressive," Ronomar said. "Even after so many years. Could that be their refuge? Might that be the Reshaperate Spire?"

Raelza stopped and pulled a map from their cloak. The twins had spent years reconstructing the city layout through what information they had gathered; it was as accurate as anything anyone could hope to find.

"I would say so." They stowed the map away and started forward, snow and ice crunching underneath their boots.

What must Ouran'an have looked like in its prime! Golden streets and silver spires floated through their minds. Fantasies, they knew; no one was quite sure what color scheme had graced the home of the Reshapers, but it was certainly fun to ruminate.

The further down the promenade the twins went the more rubble-cluttered Ouran'an became. Stone and glass remained encased in ice, one with the natural landscape that had, over centuries, begun to stake its claim on the corpse of Ouran'an. It was so obstructive that they found themselves walking half a mile east in order to bypass the great stone mounds. They ducked through the remnants of what could have been a house and came to the start of a path that ran toward the Reshaperate Spire.

"Did you see that?" Raelza asked. They brought the tip of their blade level with their shoulders. "It looked like—"

THEAILYS PAUSED, glancing back. He'd heard voices...hadn't he? He looked at the bodies, wondering if perhaps a soul or two might still remain. He recalled the church in Tal, shivering at the momentary recollection of the slaughtered town, of the screaming souls he'd heard.

Breathe, he thought. In this place, this necropolis...it was best to have one's head on straight. As straight as was possible, at least. He inhaled the cold, dead air, held his breath, then exhaled slowly, continuing toward the spire in the center of the city.

"A SPIRIT," Ronomar said, catching sight of the wispy figure as it ducked behind a wall of dark hoarfrost. They looked at Raelza—this was a new development in the dream.

The twins stepped in unison, each footfall measured and precise so as not to make too much noise. The spirit peeked back from around the corner and waited, watching with misty blue eyes. It wanted them to see it, to follow, or so they assumed.

"An echo wraith?" Raelza posited. Such spirits were rare, but it felt right to assume that Ouran'an might host a few given the profoundness of the power that the Reshapers had wielded.

"Maybe," Ronomar said. They weren't entirely convinced. "Could be necromancy."

"This doesn't feel like necromancy," Raelza said. "It feels..." They held their free hand out. "Sad."

If this spirit was not some poor reanimated soul, or an echo wraith, what was it?

The twins rounded the corner, the spirit several paces in the lead as they passed through a valley of splintered towers and tree trunks. Something crunched beneath Raelza's boot—it was not snow.

"Perdition," Raelza gasped, looking down. "A skull." They knelt as Ronomar continued on. The fragments were black as pitch, something Raelza had never seen before. They shuddered and rose to follow after Ronomar, who had stopped and was eying more black skulls, dark bones.

"What do you think did this?" Ronomar asked. "Do you think it still resides in Ouran'an?"

A sharp, ethereal hiss drew their attention before Raelza could respond. The spirit glanced back at them again before fading to mist at the door-less threshold of the Spire's eastern entrance.

The twins exchanged tense glances and approached the old tower of Reshaper rule, the frigid darkness as foreboding as it was enticing.

THEAILYS STOOD in the antechamber of the spire. He'd grown increasingly sure someone or something was following him. Was it the gentle silhouette he sought? Instinct said otherwise. He'd not seen the silhouette since entering the city ruin.

"So long ago we danced here, you and I," a voice said from across the room.

Theailys trembled at the voice, a distant memory from a dream. "Ana?"

From the shadows of the frozen sepulcher she came, as beautiful as the day he'd reaped her soul. Theailys crossed the cracked floor, ignoring the gossamer threads of mirkúr as they hissed and begged he reap her once again.

"Come," she whispered, extending her hand.

Theailys reached for her.

"Come," she repeated, dissolving to mist as Theailys touched her hand.

He stood there, mouth agape. So close. He'd been *so close!* He tensed his jaw, pushing back the anxiety. He would find her—he had to. He glanced about the room, searching, pondering. His eyes fell upon the hallway to the left, the least obstructed of them all. That way, instinct said.

So, he went.

THE ANTECHAMBER WAS ENORMOUS, with a domed roof several hundred feet above. Stalactites hung from the bannisters and over-hangs of the ascending floors, and stalagmites rose from the floor like cold, dark columns.

"It reminds me of a ballroom," Raelza said as they twirled away from their twin.

"Not any ballroom I would want to dance in," Ronomar said, gesturing with their blade. "Look. More of those awful bones." They shuddered to think these belonged to the Reshapers, that they and Raelza had more or less desecrated a mass grave.

Not that it was very sanctified to start. The deeper into Ouran'an they'd come the less majestic the city's mystique grew. In fact, Ronomar partly felt they had wandered into a dark future, that Ouran'an was home—Helveden—in ruin. They closed their eyes and took a breath.

"Where now?" Raelza asked. "Our tour guide seems to have wandered off."

Ronomar opened their eyes and glanced at the rime-encrusted floor. The hint of an inlay caught their eye. Was it a bird's beak?

"Beneath the Raven's wings," they uttered, a passage from their research coming to mind. "Beneath the Raven's wings—"

"Is where the mirkúr keeps," Raelza finished. It was a poem, or so the twins had been told; a line from a poem used as Reshaper

code. There was a decent chance that in this instance it referred to the Ouran'an catacombs.

"I've learned to trust the tingling in my gut," Raelza continued. "What do you think? Into the primordial abyss, or shall we wait and hope the spirit returns?"

"Below," Ronomar said. It made sense for a vault to be underground. But it also made sense for danger to lurk beneath the earth as well.

Still, they had come this far. There was no turning back, not with history waiting to be found and held. Not when they had ventured further into this dream than ever before. The question now was where to go, how to access the catacombs. Ronomar scanned the antechamber, illuminated by an illum wisp they had conjured. There were several collapsed archways, but the one farthest to their left looked to be just wide enough to crawl or duck beneath. It was anything but sure, but it was a start.

"Snow," Raelza said. They held their free hand out, the prismatic flakes collecting in their palm, falling from a hole high above. It melted as it touched their flesh. "It would be pretty if this place weren't in ruins, ruled by death."

No one seemed to have a clue as to why or how the Reshapers had vanished. History harbored hardly anything about the first race to start. Judging by the black bones, though, the twins figured the Reshapers' end must have been moderately violent at the very least.

Crawling underneath the collapsed archway brought them into a circular room half the antechamber's size, the stonework chipped with age and stained with something black as fresh ink. Ronomar brushed a hesitant finger across the stain and frowned. It was solid but appeared to have at one point been liquid, maybe membrane-like.

"Blood?" Raelza asked.

"I don't know," Ronomar said. Their wisp's radius increased at their will, giving light to more of the stains strewn across the walls, floor, and ceiling. There had been conflict here, they sensed, violence. They couldn't say for certain why they knew—they just did.

"North or further west?" Raelza asked.

Ronomar shifted their wisp toward the western corridor. It was spotless by comparison. "North, with the stains."

They walked on. Raelza jotted notes and hurried sketches into a small leather book, having dismissed their blade for a minute of scholarship. They tucked the book away and took up their radiant arm as the path veered west, then north, then east.

The switchback network of rime-encrusted corridors spilled into another small, circular room in which there stood three doors of a peculiar make. Beneath the frost they looked to have once been white or silver. On their facades were etchings and inlays of glyphs, some of which were also engraved.

"Just like home," Ronomar said. There were plenty of doors locked and warded using similar systems of privacy. Had Reshaper methods somehow made their way to Ariath?

The twins approached the middle door and cleared the ice away with their blades, revealing the intricate face. They had never seen glyph work like this in their lives, and yet they felt a familiar air about the door. Shrugging, they reached forward, calling on their illum, and traced the engravings until they were ablaze with white illumination. A faint clicking ticked behind the stone and the door parted down the center seam, each half receding into the frame.

"No stains here," Raelza noted as they both stepped forward. "They stopped just outside." Behind them, the door scraped shut. "Oh, hell."

"I don't think we're locked in," Ronomar said, gesturing to the twin engravings on this side of the door.

"I certainly hope not," Raelza huffed. "Hmm. A study? Two desks, bookcases, and— What do you think this is?" They plucked a glass square from one of the desks and held it level with their eyes. It was filled with some sort of dark matter that folded into itself before expanding to encompass the entirety of its prison. It seemed to react to Raelza's presence, for as they set it on the desk the dark matter froze.

"Fascinating," Ronomar said, crouching by the desk. They put their fingertip to the glass and the dark matter finished its recession, this time with a burst of light that left it snow-white instead of black.

They watched it for a minute or two, transfixed, and noticed that the light had dimmed ever so slightly.

"Keepers," Raelza laughed. "It's a time piece, an hourglass of sorts! How ingenious." They clapped their hands lightly. "What else do you suppose is in here?"

"I would say it's a safe bet there's a descending stairway," Ronomar said, gesturing to a half-concealed passageway, at the entrance of which a spirit had appeared. It flickered beckoningly, its yellow eyes a stark contrast to the study's murk and rime. This was not the spirit they had seen initially.

"What are you?" Ronomar tried.

The spirit's head cocked. Did it understand? Could it not speak? It gestured to a mouthless face before fading into mist.

Ronomar stepped toward the stairway.

"Down we go."

THEAILYS PRESSED down into the tower's bowels, following the occasional dot of light. He could feel her presence growing stronger the further he descended; Ana's face was a vivid image in his mind. It led him to a spiral stairway, at the bottom of which was a hallway bereft of death. It was smooth and led to a room of pedestals and orbs. Theailys ignored this, instead focusing on the ghostly figure at the far end of the room. Behind her stood an open door. Beyond it, darkness.

"Close, now," she said. *"Come. You're so very close."*

So, they went.

THE STAIRWAY DESCENDED in a spiral that seemed to stretch forever, which was reasonable, Ronomar decided, if in fact it led them to the catacombs. A people as clandestine as the Reshapers would take no chance at having their secrets uncovered.

That brought to light another question: how had the twins gotten this far into Ouran'an, dead city or not, without some sort of innate resistance? As Ronomar lingered on the thought they began to feel a bit sick and uneasy—they had been allowed to delve this deep. But why, and at who or what's will?

The stairway leveled out into a corridor of smooth stone untouched by the frost and rot above. The spirit flickered intermittently as they went, eventually leading them to a chamber of pedestals and crystal orbs, some empty, some bright, and others black as pitch. The spirit gestured frantically at one of the dark orbs.

"What should we do?" Raelza asked.

Ronomar frowned and pressed their finger to the orb, the black-

ness shifting, hissing at their touch, at their illum, they realized, fingertip aglow. They hadn't called upon it, so what was happening?

As the square of glass in the study had, the orb exploded in a blaze of illumination. "O Celestials… At last!" a wispy voice came. The spirit looked at the twins, a pale smile drawn across even paler lips. "Thank you. Thank you!"

The twins took a step back. "You can talk," Ronomar said, blade extended. "Were you restricted before?"

The spirit nodded. "My heart essence was corrupted. Celestine and Feran locked me away in this orb to preserve me until they could return to cleanse my blight." It seemed to shiver. "So long I was in there…but I understand. A nasty business, that plague. Is everyone well? Has it passed?"

The twins looked at each other. "Have you looked outside?" Raelza asked.

"Of course," the spirit said. "Beautiful streets, white as snow. Empty, but beautiful."

Again, the twins exchanged awkward glances. "They aren't white," Ronomar said slowly. *Keepers, but this dream was getting odd.* "I mean they are, but with actual snow. What does Ouran'an look like to you?"

The spirit hugged itself, stammering. "Such a question. Something is wrong. Tell me, what year is it?"

Ronomar swallowed. "Mid Year, eleven fifty-five."

The spirit moaned. "I've been in here for… Perdition. It's been centuries. The city…?"

"Sits in ruin," Raelza said softly. "None live. We've seen many bones."

The spirit bowed its head. "Celestine and Feran Dov'an, I pray your spirits rest well."

"Were they your friends?" Ronomar asked.

"Friends and progenitors. I am called Nether. I was their familiar. Celestials, did they hate that term," Nether chuckled. "Derogatory, they said. They preferred to call me their research partner. They were brilliant, they were.

"It's strange. I suppose the plague must have twisted my perception of reality," Nether continued. "I thought you two were Celestine and Feran for a moment." Nether raised his face, as if inhaling. "You bear a similar scent. They were twins too, you know. Maybe it's a twin thing. What are you doing in Ouran'an?"

"Research of our own," Raelza said. They sensed no ill will in Nether. "We've come looking for the Prime Vault so that we might learn more about the Reshapers and their lost history." Then, with a raised eyebrow and a chuckle: "We fancy ourselves scholars."

"The Prime Vault," Nether mused. "The fact we're having this conversation says more than words ever could. It takes something special to bypass the door to their study. Noble intent. Scholastic yearning. I find myself genuinely impressed, if not indebted."

"Could you take us to the vault?" Ronomar asked hopefully.

"Yes," Nether said, "but you will not get far. There is a remnant of the plague that haunts Ouran'an. I can feel it as plainly as I see you now."

"What about the journal?" Raelza whispered to Ronomar.

Nether eyed the twins. "Journal?"

"The journal of Remulus Dov'an," Ronomar said.

"Ah, Remulus," Nether sighed. "I fear he is gone too. What a kind man. If Celestine and Feran were the most intelligent of the Reshapers, Remulus was most certainly the kindest. He had a

certain fascination with the mortals. It irked much of the Reshaperate, but then again, they always were a bit wound up.

"Alas, I know not where his journal might be," Nether said,
"but I can take you to the Vault if you so desire. Follow me and be
on your guard."

———

THE HORRIBLE SENSE of familiarity and longing grew the
further in Theailys went. The network of hallways, the
labyrinthine feel to it all as he descended deeper yet…had he
done this all before?

He came to an anteroom. There were nine doors total: four
on either side of him, and one larger at the far end. Each door
bore a symbol. The largest was engraved with a raven, its
wings outstretched. Theailys approached. Ana was nowhere
to be seen.

"Do you really think it wise, opening that door?" Varésh
asked, materializing to Theailys' right.

"Do you think it *un*wise, bird?" Remy countered, manifesting to Theailys' left.

"That door is sealed for a reason," Varésh said.

"Yes, and the point of revisiting this dream is to apparently find out why," Remy said, glaring at the winged man.
"Honestly, for someone so concerned with our wellbeing,
Varésh Lúm-talé, you seem incredibly wary of whatever lurks
beyond that door. Skeletons in your closet, perhaps?"

The room fluctuated as the city had earlier, and for a
moment Theailys saw the anteroom caked in gore, two
figures fighting for their very lives, wielding illum blades.

They looked horribly familiar. He reached for them, but the fluctuation ended, and the room returned to its current, barren state, save one tiny difference.

"Ana." Theailys eyed her standing just a foot before the door.

She glanced at them, holding Remy's gaze for an extended period of time. She smiled softly at him, as if they were old friends, then turned her attention to Varésh, glaring. The winged man dissolved, leaving Theailys and Remy to question Ana.

"Whatever it is I'm meant to find is behind that door, isn't it?" Theailys asked.

"*Yes.*" She furrowed her brow, looking from Theailys to Remy and back. "*But...you'll not like it.*"

"The truth is never easy, is it?" Remy said. He held his hand out to Theailys, nodding.

Theailys took the silhouette's hand, the two becoming one. The room fluctuated again, each instance of the chamber overlapping one another in triptych: barren; gore-filled; occupied by several inverse silhouettes. Theailys approached the door, walking through each third of the triptych. Instinctively he placed his palm on the door, letting his illum flood the engraving until the door dilated inward with a groan.

"*The truth,*" Ana whispered, gesturing to the darkness beyond.

Theailys ventured inside.

Ana screamed, and everything was bathed in light.

THE PEDESTAL CHAMBER bore a second door, beyond which sat another labyrinth of hallways and corridors leading Keepers knew where. The entirety of the network bore a musty, earthen scent, having not been used for centuries.

They kept to a course that went something like left, right, right, left, left, right—so many times until the twins thought Nether might have forgotten where he was going, as everything seemed the same. They passed many doors, these too locked and sealed, before they halted at a heavily warded egress.

"Beyond this," Nether said, quivering, "sits the Prime Vault anteroom." He flickered, his pastel figure mottled with faint gray spots. "I can go no further, I'm afraid. The remnant would corrupt me should I pass beyond this ward. I would not be of much use either. We familiars are lacking in that respect."

The twins summoned their blades. "We'll come fetch you when it's destroyed," Raelza said with a nod. They looked to Ronomar. "Ready?"

"As always." The twins placed their free hands on the door, imbuing the glyphwork with illumination until they heard a click.

Nether withdrew from the egress. "Best of luck!"

Ronomar pushed the door ajar and they stepped into the gore-filled antechamber. There were nine doors total, the first eight of which stood parallel to one another. The last, the Prime Vault, was further on. Each bore a labyrinth of grooves, which extended outward from a unique symbol carved in the center of the door. The crests of the eight Reshaperate families, the twins assumed.

"It smells awful," Ronomar said, wrinkling their nose as they approached the door at the far end of the room. "Like death."

The door was all but concealed behind a thick layer of whatever this membrane-like substance was. Raelza wiped a hand across the door, revealing the engraving of a raven. "This must be it."

"Auntie Cela, Uncle Feran," came a small, disembodied voice. "Have you come to play? It's been so long since we've played…"

A small figure, black as pitch, with bright white eyes, materialized in the stains, rising up to meet the twins. It smelled like sunbathed rot. "Why won't you play with me anymore?"

"Oh…" Ronomar extended their blade. "It's…a child, Raelza."

"Was a child," Raelza said. "The poor thing."

"Please hold my hand," it gurgled. "I'm so scared here in the dark."

The twins stepped back. They could feel the anteroom shifting around them, bent by the dark will of this dream-thing. Had this ever been a child, or was it some malevolence keen to play horrific games?

"Please," it begged. "We can be a family again. Stay here with me, always and forever."

It lurched at the twins. Tendrils of gore shot toward them from all directions. Whatever this was did not want them to reach the end of the dream. Ronomar swung their blade in a circular arc, deflecting the incoming assault with a momentary illum shield. Raelza followed their example and the twins fought to subdue the entity, whatever it was.

The mirkúr giggled, echoing in their minds. "Auntie, uncle, we can play here in the shade, always and forever."

Ronomar and Raelza cracked their blades together and an orb of light exploded. The mirkúr recoiled into itself, shrieking, hissing. The tendrils melted back into the stains, crackling with smoke, leaving only the frail, muck-covered corpse of a small child.

"Keepers," Raelza uttered. "It really was a child."

"Do you realize what this is?" Ronomar asked. "The shifting, the mastery of the mirkúr—Raelza, it's one of the lokyns! This means our enemy originated all the way in the Deep Rock."

"A reach, but it makes sense," Raelza said. "Maybe not precisely lokyn, but most certainly its predecessor, which makes me wonder how it got all the way to Ariath to start." They paused. "It's strange to think our armies might be fighting something that the Reshapers could not quell."

"Which makes opening the Prime Vault even more important," Ronomar said.

They turned to the corpse. "The child needs a proper burial."

"In a dream?" Raelza arched an eyebrow.

Ronomar shot them a scathing look, then led them toward the Prime Vault door. The twins hacked at the membrane until it came free, burning and recoiling at their light.

The door was smooth stone; the engraved raven's wings were stretched wide. There was no seam. How were they to open it? Ronomar looked about for something that resembled a lock while Raelza examined the door for any irregularities they might be able to exploit.

"Puzzle."

The twins started at the voice and raised their blades to the corpse rising from the floor. No—not a corpse, they saw, as the membrane darkness fell away. A little girl with azure skin and snow hair, clothed in rags. The twins were confused, though they sensed no illness as she neared.

"Puzzle," the girl said again.

Ronomar knelt before the child. "Are you all right, little one? What's your name?" They pulled their cloak from their shoulders and draped it over the girl.

"Puzzle. Auntie and uncle made a puzzle on the door." The child eyed the twins with a tilted head. "You're like them. You can solve it. You can get inside."

Puzzle. Ronomar turned to the blank door, lips drawn to a straight line. They reached instinctively for Raelza's hand and the two stared long and hard.

"'Phantom to unworthy eyes,'" Ronomar uttered, as if they had known the words all their life. Glyphwork manifested like invisible ink beneath the raven's wings and they sensed that Raelza could see it too.

"Pretty symbols," said the girl—Puzzle, Ronomar decided to name her. "Lines of illum."

The twins pressed their hands to the door, flooding the glyphs with increased illumination. A seam split down the center and the door withdrew into its frame with a loud grinding sound.

Then—a flash of blinding luminescence.

THEAILYS GASPED as the meadow came rushing back. He was sprawled in the grass, looking up at the dusky orange and purple sky, sweat trickling down his face. *Did...did you see?* he asked of Remy.

"No," Remy answered. *"Just light. Blinding, scalding light."*

Theailys exhaled raggedly. All of that, chasing Anayela through the ruins, and nothing, save further questions. What was that place? Why had it felt so terribly familiar? Who were the two figures he had seen for just a blink? What was in that vault? He sat up, tearing at the grass.

"Your agitation is understandable," Remy said. He sounded

vexed as well. They were one and the same, after all. *"But perhaps this is our mind's way of telling us we aren't ready for whatever lies within. That we've repressed that part of the dream because it's too dreadful to relive."*

Or, Theailys thought, *it's telling us we* need *to see what's in that vault.*

He stood, starting back to camp.

"Do you intend to dream your dream again?" Remy asked. *"Tonight?"*

Yes, Theailys said. Where fear of the unknown once had ruled, now dwelled curiosity and determination. The tingling in Theailys' gut implored he see the truth in madness, the clarity beyond that blinding light. His dreams—this one and those that'd come before—were more than dreams, and he intended to learn their truths.

12

HAUNTED

Theailys inhaled and heaved a contented sigh as they crossed the threshold into Avar. As it had before, the town smelled of fresh apple pie and rain. There was something soothing about the amalgamation, perhaps that it made Theailys think of childhood. He'd always loved the smell of rain and his mother had made the best pies in the world.

"Perdition, but it's good to be beneath a roof again," Cailean sighed as they stepped into the inn. He fingered a small cut on the underside of his jaw and let out a low growl of discomfort. "Blasted itchy bastard."

"You could be missin' your jaw entirely," Leyandra reminded him, "and then how would you be able to complain so often?"

"I'm sure he'd still find a way," Theailys jabbed. Cailean had somehow gone face-first off his shaghound the previous night. He'd been surprisingly, yet unsurprisingly drunk. "He's got a talent for such things."

They wandered to the bar, and Cailean's glare faded as the barkeep strolled into view. He was a young man, perhaps no older than his thirtieth year, with dark hair pulled back behind his ears, a stubbled jaw, and green eyes.

"You lot look awfully weary," the barkeep remarked. "Take a detour through Perdition, did you? Have a rest there and I'll fetch some ale. I daresay you could all use a drink or three."

"Way ahead of you, sweetheart," Cailean said, raising his flask in a grateful, inebriated salute.

Theailys rolled his eyes. "You're a walking, one-man tavern." He turned up his nose. "And you smell like a full-tavern washroom."

Cailean waved him off with a snort. "And I suppose you think you smell like springtime grass and flowers, eh? You drink a lot yourself in case you forgot, and if I recall correctly, which I think I do, weren't you the one who pissed yourself in the Naldun Woods over an owl's hoot?"

"Didn't sound like a fucking owl," Theailys muttered.

"Truth be told you all could use a bath," the barkeep said, setting three mugs of ale on the bar. "You've got a scent about you—summer sewage soaking in the sun, I'd say. Drink up, then wash up, and I'll see that your clothes get a good rinse as well." He snapped his fingers at a barmaid and two barmen, then wandered off, barking orders.

Cailean slipped his flask away and hoisted up the mug. "Cheers! May your nightmares vanish like the men Leyandra courts."

WHEN THEAILYS CLOSED HIS EYES, he saw leering silhouettes. When he was awake every shadow seemed to move, and every breeze seemed a whisper begging he fall back into his dream and see what lay behind that door beneath the city. He'd dreamt a few more times to no avail, each time ejected by a blinding flash of light. He took a sip of rum from his flask and sighed, the alcohol smooth and warm against his throat.

"You look haunted, love," Leyandra said. "You have since we arrived, and even through the drink." She dropped onto the porch stair beside him, wrapped in a cloak, hair pushed back out of her face. "You want to try talkin' about it again?"

Theailys rubbed his thumb and index finger together, conjuring a wisp that set the inn's porch aglow. "I think it's driving me a bit mad," he said, chewing at his lower lip as the end of the dream flashed across his mind. "The chamber door, the woman, Ana… I don't think this is just some dream. I haven't since Remy walked me through it that night." He'd come clean to Cailean and Leyandra about the new voice and the new dream. "It feels like a…vision, or a memory."

"You think the drink'll help you puzzle it out?" Leyandra said, chuckling softly. Her smile faded and she moved a bit closer to Theailys. "It may do Cailean good, but I think it's important you look at this dream with a clear head."

Theailys nodded, watching people wander through the night, the street lamps casting shadows here and there. They grinned eyeless grins and Theailys blinked them away. "You said the other night you'd been pretty adept at illumancy before the lokyns stole your light. Am I going crazy or do you think there might be something to these dreams?"

"Hard to tell without havin' seen or felt what you did for myself," Leyandra said. "I'd wager you're probably right, though—that your dream is something more. An omen, perhaps."

"But of what?" Theailys murmured, more to himself than Leyandra.

"Only time will tell," Leyandra said, nudging his hand. "Mind if I have a toss?"

Theailys handed her the flask. Goose pimples surfaced as he lingered on her words and the bitter taste of ale and dinner teased his tongue. "I'm going to destroy the Heart," he whispered through a rictus. "Maybe that'll put a stop to all this madness in my head."

Leyandra touched his arm and gave it a squeeze. "We'll all be rootin' for you," she murmured. Then with a chuckle: "When you do, you come find me for a drink. I daresay you'll have earned one."

She took another sip from the flask and leaned against Theailys, the pair looking out at Avar, the inn tavern at their backs and bursting at the seams with drunken mirth.

ANA SCREAMED *and everything was bathed in light.*

But Theailys did not wake. The brilliance dispersed and he found himself before an open door, beyond which lay a darkness colder and more smothering than anything he'd ever felt. He set foot into the blackness without a moment's thought, immediately overcome by an aura of profound sorrow and guilt. A pain unlike anything he'd known before, yet at the same time felt he had.

"*Endurfaithe,*" *hissed something from the back of the chamber. More words came, but they were gurgled. Theailys hastened his steps, eyes searching for the source of the disembodied voice.*

"*Endurfaithe,*" *it came again, and a chill washed over Theailys as he realized the word was* his. *A pained screech erupted from his mouth as he dropped to the ground. His head was spinning. It felt as though his body had turned to smoke.*

Then Varésh was standing before him, one wing aglow with illum.

Garbled, ethereal words escaped Theailys. Varésh shook his head. "I am sorry. I do not understand."

Theailys cried out indiscernibly, then in a rush of smoke retreated to the back of the chamber. It was here, he knew, and he needed Varésh to see, to take the journal for his own. The winged man followed suit and knelt before Theailys, looking deep into his eyes. Theailys mewed weakly and extended a wispy thread of a hand toward his old journal.

Please...he thought at Varésh. Please! The journal was everything.

Varésh plucked it from the ground.

"*Please!" Theailys wailed, and in a burst of mirkúr ceased to be.*

THEAILYS JOLTED, tumbling out of bed, body slick with sweat. A scream caught in his throat and instead came out as a hoarse gasp. He picked himself up off the floor and sat at the edge of the mattress, face resting in his hands, body trembling as the feeling of incorporeality gradually faded from his mind.

What the hell was that?

He gnashed his teeth as the dream persisted in his thoughts, as the emotion of its nightmare end endured. The pain, the sorrow, the guilt...but why? What had he—what had whatever he'd become done to evoke such profound anguish?

Theailys squeezed his eyes tightly shut.

"Breathe," came Remy's voice, soft and soothing from the center of Theailys' mind. *"You are safe. You are in the waking world."* Despite his placid tone, Theailys could tell Remy too was shaken by whatever that had been. *"We are...whole."*

Sometimes dreams are more than dreams, Theailys thought at Remy. *If so, then what did any of that mean?* The question festered like an open wound, and for a moment he imagined Faro's distant cackling in his mind.

Be silent, Theailys commanded, though his thoughts were shaky, insecure at best. *Just leave me be. I'm done with you, you were banished. Obey!*

The star-eyed silhouette manifested in his mind, its chasm-mouth stretched into an endless grin. *"You cannot run from who you are, Theailys An,"* the ghost of Faro seemed to say. *"You are shadow, shade, and silhouette—humanity's fear of the dark. Embrace reality lest you falter like the light."*

Theailys opened his eyes and the room rushed into focus. Faro's disembodied voice faded into silence, his final, taunting whisper tickling Theailys' ears.

"Will you be able to find sleep this night?" inquired Remy.

Theailys laughed.

And laughed.

And laughed.

IT WAS A DARK DAWN.

Theailys sat atop his shaghound at the edge of Avar, just beyond the gate. Cailean sat mounted to his left; they were waiting on Leyandra. Theailys tugged his hood up so it rested just above his eyes. He heaved a sigh, listening to the distant thunder rumbling overhead.

"You look like you hardly slept," Cailean said, turning to face Theailys. "Keepers, you look worse than I've felt after a night of nursing bottles. You're haunted, aren't you?"

"Leyandra said the same thing last night," Theailys said. "Is that the proper term?"

"'S the *easier* term," Cailean said. "People flinch at the mention of trauma. Don't like to think they've been afflicted." He brought his mount beside Theailys and clapped him on the shoulder. "I can't claim to understand what's going on inside your head, to understand the things you see behind the darkness of closed eyes, but I damn well feel your pain, you know I do."

Theailys swallowed. He wasn't sure he was ready to tell either of them about the dream he'd had last night, about the chamber door opening and the progression of events. "I just want to know what they mean. I can feel it, this new dream driving me insane. How do you keep yourself from dreaming such horribly profound things?"

"The drink," Cailean said. "Sometimes, and you knew that already. Honestly, talking helps me sort through shit. 'S not the answer you're looking for, I can tell, but it's the hard truth. Ain't any illum that's going to erase nightmares from your mind."

"Being out there, fighting on the front lines," Theailys whispered. "Facing down the lokyns, facing down night-mares incarnate for days and months and years...how does anyone stomach that?"

"'S what we're trained to do," Cailean said. "Training as a Faithbringer or a Warden...'s not all fun and games. Often times it makes you wish the lokyns were laughing in your face. We braved darkness of a different kind in order to combat and vanquish Te Mirkvahíl. I can't explain it any better than that.

"But hey." Cailean squeezed Theailys' shoulder and held his grip. "When you complete The Keepers' Wrath and take it to the Heart, you can be damn sure I'll be there with you. That's a promise."

Theailys smiled despite his gloom. "Thank you."

"Sorry for the hold up," Leyandra apologized, riding up behind them.

"Let's get a move on," said Cailean. He squeezed his mount into action and led them west, their trots becoming gallops, the cobblestone highway rattling beneath their haste.

THE GUARD WAS FAR TIGHTER at the southern peripheral gate than it had been when Theailys had departed Helveden roughly three weeks ago. Theailys noticed a great many more Illumurgists, Wardens, and Faithbringers peppered in between the usual longsword and heater shield-bearing gate watch.

They were met halfway toward the gate by a platoon of mounted soldiers, who drew rein to block their way. The captain was a Faithbringer of some import, judging by the length, width, and black coloring of the scabbard at his waist.

"Identification if you would be so kind," he requested, extending a gauntleted hand, his words measured but firm. The other guardsmen around him looked equally tense.

Theailys nodded, rolling up his sleeve to reveal the glyph announcing him as an Illumurgist; Leyandra did the same. Cailean showed a similar symbol on his arm marking him a Warden.

"Your cooperation is appreciated," the Faithbringer said. "With the way things have been the last several days we can ill afford to take any chances with who we let in and out of the city."

Cailean raised an eyebrow. "Care to explain?"

"Dissident insurgency," the Faithbringer said, and Theailys knew the man was full of shit. It was doubtful they would learn much more than that.

"Right."

Theailys gave a half-hearted salute and squeezed his shaghound into motion. He felt little, if any relief as he rode through the farmlands, Cailean and Leyandra at his heels, the pair muttering to one another about the Faithbringer's bull-shit response. A simple man would have seen the distant spires of Helveden as a welcome sign, an indication of normality falling into place. To Theailys they were the teeth of something monstrous, and the path he rode its maw.

"What're you going to do?" Cailean asked, pulling up beside Theailys.

"After we return the hounds?" Theailys thumbed his nose. "Not sure, really." There were several options, and nearly all of them were shit. "Maybe I'll drink myself to sleep. Not like I slept a lot the last few days. Not well, at least. What about you?"

"Pay my respects to Searyn," Cailean replied, expression softening. "You know, provided they gave her a proper burial, the hiltstroking fucks. Khoren better pray I don't get drunk enough to seek him out in prison."

Theailys allowed himself a smirk. Khoren had never been the most physically intimidating man. Even with a lame arm and hand Cailean could probably break the general in half.

But it's probably better if he doesn't. Theailys wished death on Khoren, but not before the general stood trial for his crimes. Not before Theailys got to look him in his traitorous eyes.

"What do you think that shit at the gate was all about?" Theailys asked.

"Dunno," Cailean said. "Nothing good, I'll tell you that. Someone must have pissed off Khoren if the Faithbringers are crying insurgency. Probably sweeping the city hoping to find the poor bastards."

"May the Keepers bring them luck, then," said Theailys. After a moment: "I expect we'll be back on the road within a week. Once I've forged The Keepers' Wrath."

Cailean nodded. "No sleep 'til death or victory. Not a proper one at least. I'll make damn sure I'm out there with you when the Heart's destroyed, and we can have a piss and a drink atop the ruins of that shithole once we've brought it down."

They rode in a silence a while longer, thunder rumbling intermittently.

"I'm going to leave when this is done," Theailys said eventually. Mar. Anayela. Searyn. He could feel his anguish of their deaths trying desperately to root him here in Ariath, as if suffering was what the world meant for him to do until his final breath.

"I understand," Cailean said. "All this death..." His expression darkened, and he furrowed his brow. "Any thoughts on where?"

"No," Theailys said. "Just...somewhere." Someplace he could breathe and forget this nightmare of a life he'd lived thus far. Somewhere dreams were only dreams, devoid of talking birds and corpses rising from a pile of ash.

Anywhere but here.

13

ATROCITIES

"I saw somethin' last night," Fenrin said.

He and Serece had withdrawn from Helveden in the dark of night. General Khoren was dead by demon hands unknown. His mutilated corpse had turned up in the farmlands yesterday. In retaliation, a sect of Khoren's followers had rounded up any dissident they could find—men, women, *and* children—and cut them down in cold blood. If you weren't an Ariathan human, you were as good as dead. If you were of demon blood, you were absolutely fucked. Suffice it to say neither Serece nor Fenrin had been keen on the prospect of running afoul of the murderous lot.

Serece peeked out the window of the ruined home they'd taken refuge in. Dawn shone faint behind a sea of black and gray. "What was it?"

"A ruin. Banerowos," Fenrin said.

The Dead City. A Place Where the Sun is Silent. Serece shivered at the name, at the distant memory of its touch. She wished this recollection dead and gone, yet somehow it persisted to torment her on occasion. "What do you think it means, you seeing that? How much did you see? *What*, exactly, did you see?"

"Black spires wreathed in illum," Fenrin said. "Mirkúr emanatin' from the streets to permeate the world without." Serece looked back at him, his silver eyes aglow. "The end time, maybe."

Serece withdrew to Fenrin's side. "Anything else? Any*one* else?"

Fenrin shook his head. "Wasn't anyone there to begin with."

Serece leaned against the wall and sighed. Truthfully, she hadn't a clue as to what to do now. Helveden was swarming with opposition, seen and unseen, severely limiting the ease with which she and Fenrin could gather information. Paranoia had kept them laying low, sneaking whispers from the streets and stealing thus-far-fruitless moments in the city archives when they could. Keepers, but she wished her aunt was here. Fiel would know what to do.

"You think Banerowos is the key?" Fenrin sounded more uncertain than usual.

"To what?" Serece asked, grinding her teeth at the name.

"To learnin' what the endgame is," Fenrin said. "Maybe we need to go there."

Again, Serece shivered. "I hope not."

Fenrin perked up. "Why not? You been there before?"

"Once." Serece swallowed. "I don't know what the city used to be or what it housed but there's a curse about its ruin now. One of rot and resurrection of the blackest kind."

"I see," Fenrin mused. "What d'you know of this...curse?"

"It brings the dead to life," Serece said. "But... Look, let's talk about something else, all right?"

Fenrin eyed her, relenting with a firm but gentle hand upon her knee. "All right."

Serece grasped the crystal vial hanging from her neck, allowing the chill of the snow within to momentarily occupy her thoughts. It permeated her dry, plagued flesh, soothing her from the inside out. Her urge to scratch dissipated quickly and a low sigh escaped her lips.

"Do you have children?" Serece asked. She caught Fenrin's melancholy smile in the corner of her eye.

"*Did*." His words were soft, reminiscent. "Haven't talked about them for a while, now. Memories are painful enough, you know?"

The question sounded, *felt* almost accusatory. As if Serece couldn't comprehend the agony of such things! Memories of children, babes bundled in their blankets... A malevolent chill emanated outward from the center of her chest. She turned to Fenrin, looking deep into his forlorn eyes, her ugly blue-eyed likeness staring back. She hated him for having dreamt of Banerowos and she loathed herself for having ever sought deliverance from its poisoned depths.

She collapsed into Fenrin's arms, sobbing into his chest as the brief but vivid memories of her daughter bloomed.

"There, now," Fenrin murmured, holding her. She tried to speak but could only manage gulping breaths between each sob. It'd been so long since the last time she had wept over that night. "Let it come, let it out. Far worse to keep it in, that pain. *Far* worse…"

"…Why did she have to die?" Serece finally whispered. "She… Keepers, she was my *child*…" Eyes like the sun, soft sunset-purple skin, a tuft of black hair atop her tiny head. Vhora, the phantaxian word for spring. "My own little season."

She remained in Fenrin's arms a while longer. They were silent as the clouds withdrew to let the sunlight peek into the ruin, as a gust bestowed upon Serece's sense of smell a scent like earth, stone, and snow. Her ears twitched at muffled words, and she stood from Fenrin's hold to peek outside, overwhelmed with desperate joy and puzzlement.

There, within the shadow of the trees and growing nearer, was a giant white wolf, atop which sat a pair of grinning twins, both of whom were waving vigorously at Serece.

Serece rushed from the ruin, stopping just short of the newcomers as the twins dismounted and her aunt transformed. Serece leapt into Fiel's arms and hugged her tight, for a moment afraid if she let her go, her aunt might disappear for good. Fiel returned the embrace, stroking Serece's hair.

"Keepers," Serece whispered, "it's good to see you."

"Mmm. Likewise," Fiel murmured. "I sense we all have much to talk about."

Serece shuddered at the notion, at the myriad black thoughts that had been running through her mind. She pulled away and allowed herself a moment to scrutinize the twins. Strange things, they were, with their unnaturally round eyes…and their perpetual grins. Keepers, why were they still grinning?

They approached her with outstretched hands. "Ronomar and Raelza Tír. A pleasure."

Serece arched an eyebrow. Did they expect her to what... shake hands? She glanced at Fiel, who too had a grin spread wide across her face. Serece frowned at her aunt's amusement. Then, sighing, briefly grasped their hands. "Serece. And...a pleasure. I suppose."

"Quite the brooder," Ronomar whispered to Raelza.

"Reminds me a bit of Theailys An," Raelza said. Serece tensed her jaw. Raelza perked up at that. "Oh! Do you know him? Ronomar, I think she knows Theailys!"

"We've met." She shot a glare her aunt's way.

"Perhaps it's best we take this inside," Fiel said. "Before we draw attention to ourselves." She cast her gaze toward the derelict house Serece and Fenrin had taken refuge in and smirked. Fenrin was watching from the window.

"All right." Serece started for the house, the twins humming lightly in her wake. It was going to be a *long* day.

It seemed absurd to Serece, the phantaxians reaching an accord with the Ariathans. Military aid in exchange for the remains of Vare Tal-úlm. Even more outlandish was the fact her aunt and father had swayed the council to their side, a feat without which the former would not have been possible. Imagine—the council siding with her "mad" father and pariah of an aunt! Instead of her queen mother! How Serece would have loved to have been a fly on the wall for that.

She eyed the twins. They were odd, uncannily upbeat,

their round eyes bright. "So...you're the Hands of the Seraph." They nodded with a nonchalance suggesting this was common knowledge, though Serece felt confident in thinking hardly anyone really knew. "And you think this letter from the queen is a forgery." Another nod accompanied by grins. Serece cocked an eyebrow. "Well if that's the case why do you both look so happy?"

"Since we returned from the front some months ago," Raelza said, "we've suspected *something* lurking in our midst. The letter from the queen, dear General Khoren's face...well, it certainly narrows down the possibilities, wouldn't you say? Te Mirkvahíl or otherwise, I can confidently say the object of our worry sits atop the Ariathan hierarchy."

Serece furrowed her brow. "How can you be so sure?"

"Think about it," Ronomar said. "Te Mirkvahíl and the lokyns are deception made manifest. You and Fenrin both felt something off about Mistress Khal when you encountered her in the prison. Fenrin said her eye color was different than usual, an impossible change for the Celestial race.

"What of the recently 'deceased'"—Ronomar made a gesture in the air—"General An? I read the report detailing the circumstances of her arrest, the charges levied against her. Raelza and I served beneath her on the front. Where might her ability to wield mirkúr have come from if not already innate?"

"An intriguing question," Fiel opined.

"A dark question," Fenrin said. "It certainly suggests... you know."

"What do you propose?" Serece asked. "We can't just sit idly by, even with the city in such chaos."

"Agreed, of course," Raelza said, looking at Ronomar, who nodded. "What say we infiltrate Helveden and see if we can't figure out the font of all this madness, hmm? The Bastion is a place of interest as it's the seat of power in Helveden, but the Hall might also be worth looking into if Mistress Khal is not herself."

"What would we be looking for?" Serece asked.

"Oddities, I suppose. Things out of sorts," Ronomar said. "Raelza and I will investigate the Hall. We apprenticed there for the better part of fifteen years, after all, and Mistress Khal…well, we've a certain fondness for her."

"I think we'll know what we're lookin' for when we see it," Fenrin said. "Like the twins said: deception made manifest."

"True," Serece said. "But what if it's like Khal said the other night in the prison? What if what we find, we only find because Te Mirkvahíl meant for us to?"

"Then that is the way it is," Fiel said. "Either way, whatever we find might help us discern this entity's endgame, which to this point remains a mystery." She frowned pensively. "Such slaughter and madness—why?"

"The joy of death?" Serece said, though she knew that was not the case. The demons did find amusement in slaughter, but she could feel in her gut whatever was going on in the city was meticulous, that everything happening was being carefully orchestrated. But what was the endgame? The Faithbringer Khar Am had preached that his followers, his disciples discern truth from madness, and in this moment Serece wanted nothing more. Even if the Ariathans and the phantaxians were doomed to some horrible end, she at least wanted to understand why.

"Even monsters have souls," Rejya once had said.

So, if this was Te Mirkvahíl they were dealing with, what did the demon's wretched soul desire most? What did it hope to gain from all of this?

"Shall we depart?" said Raelza, standing from the dusty floor.

Serece clutched her vial of snow tightly. "Yes. The longer we wait the more inclined I'll feel to say no."

They stood and withdrew from the house, starting through the shadow of the trees. Serece knew they were going to find something in the Bastion, that the twins would find something in the Hall. It was the uncertainty of what, exactly, those somethings would be that made her hair stand on end.

"A place permeated with sorrow. You come here often, Remulus," Behtréal said, staring at the hooded figure seated at the base of the oak tree. "Why do you continue to torment yourself so? What do you hope to achieve?"

Remulus made no movement. "I do not come here hoping to achieve a single thing. If you understood, brother, if you understood the concept and power of love, then you would understand the nature of my frequent visits to this tree." His shoulders rose slightly, then fell with his exhale. He stood to face Behtréal.

"I find sorrow in my hours here, but there is also the joy of memory. Are you able to comprehend joy, Behtréal, or is that, too, as

foreign and forbidden as affection?" Remulus stalked past Behtréal, his snarling breath a cloud of frosty mist. He paused, turning back. "What is it you hope to achieve by coming here?"

"I hope only to absolve your pain," Behtréal said. "Twenty years, Remulus. Twenty years and still you seek this tree. Still you wander Harthe, Athéro at your side, preaching perseverance in the wake of loss, to mortals no less—and for what? What good has it done you? What good has it done our people?"

"Our people?" Remulus sighed heavily. "Your egotism wounds me. We are gods, Behtréal. We create and we destroy. We reshape the old world in favor of the new. Our people populate the whole of Harthe, but you and the Reshaperate are still too obsessed with what goes on behind the walls of Ouran'an to give a care."

"Too obsessed with..." Behtréal stammered. "Celestials curse you, Remulus! Too obsessed? Too obsessed? Ouran'an is being gradually ravaged by this...this plague. The very same that stole Annabelle from you!"

"And you would have me do what, exactly?" Remulus asked. "Forsake them? Leave them all to rot while sitting idly by behind the walls of Ouran'an? They have nothing to ward against this infection. To us this plague is but a winter cold, Behtréal. We'll survive just as before. The mortals, though?" Remulus shook his head and started off.

Behtréal closed his eyes and tensed his jaw. Obsessed? Obsessed? He exhaled slowly, the air escaping through his teeth like a hiss. I will make you see. I will make you see the damage wrought by your infatuation with that woman you claimed to love.

Behtréal opened his eyes. His blades manifested in his hands, fluctuating light and shadow. To eradicate a plague, you had to stop *it at the source, and once that source was little more than ash you had to cut away the tainted flesh until the purity of old returned.*

Behtréal started toward the oak tree.

THE MEMORY TRICKLED from Behtréal's mind. "I was such an angry man," he murmured to the darkness of his sleeping chamber. He did not yet feel like letting the sun kiss his stolen flesh.

"*You are still an angry man,*" Te Mirkvahíl said. "*And a weak man at that.*"

And you are a still a monster, Behtréal thought. *You are mistaken as always though: I am not weak. Reflection of one's past self is not a sign of imperfection—quite the opposite, in fact.*

"*What of guilt?*" Te Mirkvahíl asked. "*What of the guilt your memory evokes?*"

It makes me realize I was wrong to fell the oak tree, Behtréal thought. *That anger breeds recklessness. I still harbor distaste for Remulus having thrown our people to the wayside, but part of me understands now what I did not then, what my fury and feelings of abandonment concealed.*

"*Pray tell, Te Luminíl, what might that be?*" sneered Te Mirkvahíl.

In that moment he was right to believe the Reshapers' immortality would win the day, Behtréal thought. *But more than that, the path he chose was done so in the name of love, out of respect for the memory of a woman he adored.* Behtréal swallowed the lump that'd formed in his throat. *As is my own.*

Te Mirkvahíl chuckled. "*Are you so sure? You claim love and the memory of your people as your motivation for this undertaking, but perhaps you do so in order to ease the guilt of knowing you took far more lives than did the plague."*

Behtréal tensed his jaw. *I am aware—*

"I speak not of mortals," hissed Te Mirkvahíl, *"or is the memory so horrific that you forced it from your thoughts? Recall the old Reshaper wars, Te Luminíl, and the many throats you slit, the many* children *that you felled—and all before I ever came to be."*

You lie, Behtréal thought.

"Think that if you wish, if it helps you go about your task," Te Mirkvahíl said. *"But know in the depths of what you call a soul that I am right."*

Te Mirkvahíl dissipated from Behtréal's thoughts, leaving him to ponder, ruminate in the darkness of the room. He remembered nothing of the Reshaper wars, of spilling blood and slaughtering children. Had he blocked this memory or was it merely the monster in his mind attempting once again to wrest control? He wasn't sure, and it frightened him, almost as much as the notion of failure did.

"The sooner I succeed," he whispered, rising from the bed, "the sooner I absolve myself of such a monstrous thing."

───────────────

It'd been unsurprisingly easy to infiltrate the Bastion grounds, easier than re-entering Helveden. Cloaks and hoods were commonplace during the rain, and Serece was sure whatever entity had taken up residence in Helveden had afforded them an easy entry. That and the fact they were amidst a throng of citizens Serece supposed were here to walk the Bastion gardens. They were something of an attraction, or so she'd heard.

She pulled her hood a little further past her eyes. Beneath her cloak she clutched a vial of snow, her second of the day; it was getting harder to keep the rot at bay. She could feel it underneath her skin, spreading like a fire fanned by wind, expedited by the foulness of her phantom quarry. It made her long for the Phantaxis Mountains and she hated that.

"So. How *did* you and father sway the council?" she murmured to her aunt.

"Rather easily," Fiel said. "It seemed the majority had grown, shall we say…disillusioned with your mother's rule. 'In times of war, let bad blood fall fallow when a common enemy arises,' or something along those lines. The lokyn raids in the Phantaxis Mountains seemed to have been the final straw."

"You're surely joking," Serece said, arching an eyebrow. "What a bunch of cowards, holding their tongues so long; letting my father make a fool of himself to our people." She balled her hand into a fist, quickly swallowing the urge to strike the hedges to her left lest she draw attention.

"They argued in your favor," Fiel continued, and Serece nearly choked. "About the Avatar and Shades."

Serece narrowed her eyes. In the last days' chaos, she had nearly forgotten about that night, about how she'd murdered Taür, how she'd slaughtered Rejya all those years ago. "Kind of them, but they're fools to have done so."

"The stress of war induces rage," Fiel said.

"And we are taught to temper Yssa in order to keep it

from enraging," Serece argued. "Regardless of what the council believes, the fact remains I killed my sisters. I lack mental balance, Aunt Fiel." Which meant they all were lucky Yssa was dead because Keepers knew Serece was a knot of anguish, fury, and paranoia. "I don't deserve their faith."

"You think that now," said Fenrin, just a foot or two behind Serece. "It's the guilt, the blood stains on your soul. But it'll pass, and when it does, you'll see you deserve their forgiveness, that you deserve to forgive yourself."

"Did you see that in an illum dream?" Serece spat. "You can soothe me all you want, the council can say my invocation of the Avatar and Shades was forced, that I was under duress, but it doesn't change the fact I did what I did. My sisters are dead by my blades, and I'll never, ever absolve myself of that."

She crossed her arms to her chest, following Fiel as they continued winding through the periphery of the Bastion grounds. *Wish I hadn't asked,* she thought. Only weeks ago, she had sought her mother's forgiveness, had wished to be looked upon with sympathetic eyes. And now? Now she despised it. She didn't deserve exoneration for such atrocities. She spat on the ground. *Fuckers probably did it in order to curry favor with father.* If the council had truly put their faith in Undrensil then what better way to appease him than to amnesty his daughter?

"Best we split up," Fiel spoke from ahead, and she melted into the crowd.

Serece turned to Fenrin, but he too had disappeared. She frowned and made her way west. *Right. It's not like Te Mirk-vahíl doesn't know we're already here.* She shivered at the notion.

Eyes everywhere, the uncertainty of whether or not the people around her were puppets dancing on strings. Why the hell was she still alive? Why was anyone still alive?

Serece ducked down a garden path lined with tall hedges and bright blue flowers. At least it smelled nice—for the moment. She felt in her gut whatever she found, whatever Te Mirkvahíl allowed her to see was going to smell and look foul enough to make her retch.

But only time would tell, what little of that they had left. Whatever game Te Mirkvahíl was playing was nearly at its end. The chaos about Helveden, for all its subtleties, was palpable enough to make the air feel thick.

Serece stopped and sat on a stone bench, feeling disoriented. She closed her eyes and massaged her temples, inhaling slowly, focusing on the amalgamation of flowers and rain. Listening to the raindrops on the stones and leaves, sounds of the wild, of the mountain world she'd grown in long before the plague ripped freedom from her people. It'd been a long time since she'd heard them, somehow. She hadn't realized until now.

If I could bottle a sound... She exhaled shakily, feeling the tension in her body wane.

"Are you all right?" came a soft but strong voice, snapping Serece from her trance.

Serece blinked. Before her stood a woman with hair like dark fire, mid-year face peppered with the occasional scar. She'd seen war, no doubt about that.

Serece tilted her head. "Fine, thank you. Uh..." The woman looked terribly familiar, and after a moment Serece realized why. "You're a friend of Theailys An, aren't you?"

"I am," the woman said. "Name's Leyandra."

"I remember you from the mountains," Serece said. "You had that mouthy, one-eyed man with you as well. Tell me…" She paused, considering what she'd said and the fact she could have very well just implicated herself. This woman had been one of Theailys' companions, but who was to say she was who she claimed to be, that she didn't already belong to Te Mirkvahíl?

"Tell you…what?" Leyandra asked.

"Is Theailys well?" Serece said finally.

"He is," Leyandra said, eying Serece. "Are you sure *you're* well? You seem skittish."

"The paranoia of war," Serece said. "You can feel it, right? The tension in the air."

Leyandra stepped toward her, so they were little more than a foot apart. "Yeah, I can feel it," she murmured. "Guards at the outer gate claimed it was a dissident insurgency. They're full of shit."

"They're in a desperate frenzy," Serece said. "Demonry. Something killed General Khoren yesterday and the Faithbringers are pinning it on the dissident. Hell, on anyone not human."

She stood, motioning for Leyandra to follow. It was too obvious, the pair of them huddling there in the rain. They had to at least appear as if they were simply enjoying a flowery stroll, bundled in cloaks.

Words spilled effortlessly from Serece's mouth the longer they walked, questions and answers. She had learned a hell of a lot more than she had anticipated—and she hadn't retched or felt the urge to. Still, everything Leyandra had relayed was troubling, most of all Theailys' dreams. Odd things, they were. Outlandish. Nightmarish. Surreal. And possibly something more.

"It's all comin' to a head, isn't it?" Leyandra asked as they withdrew from the gardens some time later, heading south and away from the Bastion.

"Feels that way," Serece said. "Whatever *it* is."

"A balancin' act, perhaps," Leyandra said. "An attempt to set the world in order."

"What the hell does that mean?"

"Nothin'." Leyandra sighed. "Somethin' a friend told me. Entropy and Law: two sides of the same coin. One inevitably brings about the other. Keepers know I've seen enough in my years to put stock in such a notion."

"It's a bit abstract," Serece said, trying to make sense of it, trying to apply it the current state of her world. "In order to have peace, there must first be madness?"

"Somethin' like that."

They parted ways at the Bastion gates, offering nothing more than nods. Serece was sure that Leyandra would tell Theailys about their encounter, about their exchange of information. Just as well she did.

What now? She snuck a backward glance at the Bastion, rising up like a jagged tooth in the fog and rain, and trembled. She hoped Fiel and Fenrin were faring well, but she dared not try to imagine what they had found, if they had stumbled upon anything at all.

Serece walked on, melding with the throng, weary and lost in thought.

THE ILLUM NETWORK was an interesting thing. Puzzling, really. In all his eons Behtréal had yet to truly comprehend exactly how it worked. He understood the illum of various individuals overlapped, that it was possible for Illumancers to occasionally catch a glimpse of someone else's thoughts and memories. What he didn't understand was why. It was horribly invasive, even if it was accidental.

"*Though you have little reason to complain,*" Te Mirkvahíl hissed, "*seeing as how this little...imperfection has given you the means to manipulate your martyrs like the little puppets that they are.*"

The monster had a point. Despite its invasiveness it was undeniably beneficial to Behtréal's cause. The things he'd learned of the drenarian, Fenrin, and the phantaxian, Serece, were useful to say the least. Sad, too, enough to earn his sympathy.

"*Fear not, Te Luminíl. Soon they will cease to be,*" Te Mirkvahíl said.

I know, Behtréal thought. *Thus, they will never come to feel pain.*

He pushed Te Mirkvahíl away and looked at the twins standing before him. They had come to see Mistress Khal. Behtréal grinned and took them both in a large embrace. "Ronomar. Raelza. It's been some time."

"Indeed, it has," said Raelza, pulling back and smiling. Celestials, but they had unnaturally white teeth. "I'm glad to see you are well."

"Likewise," Behtréal said, releasing them both. He

motioned they take a seat beside his office window; he had always liked the sea view it'd afforded him. "So, what brings you here?" It was an honest question in two parts. Behtréal was genuinely glad to see the twins, but he was also curious about their motivations, especially since he couldn't detect a hint of illum about their characters. They'd always been tricky, even as children.

"Nostalgia," Ronomar said. "War has a way of making one long for simpler times."

There was truth to what they said, but Behtréal was quite certain the twins weren't here simply because they were homesick. They knew something, or at the very least were suspicious of something.

"It *has* been some time since Ariath knew peace," Behtréal agreed, allowing himself a melancholy smile. He was not entirely proud of the things he'd done, of the war he'd waged. His undertaking had ruined innocent lives and for that he felt immense shame.

But pain is nothing to those who never come to be, he reminded himself for what felt like the millionth time. He wasn't sure how much he actually believed that anymore, if at all, and it made him sick.

"How have things been here?" Raelza asked. "The Faith-bringers seem riled."

"Aren't they always?" Behtréal said.

"I suppose," Raelza said. "But this is different. It's fanatic zeal. Furious, even."

They know, Behtréal thought, and he was unsurprised by the notion. Ronomar and Raelza had always been different, more attuned to the abnormalities of the world. It was part of what made them so endearing. Their fierce curiosity was admirable.

"Does it pain you," hissed Te Mirkvahíl, *"knowing that you'll have to spill their blood?"* Behtréal's left eye twitched and the monstrous voice cackled. *"I can hardly wait to taste their illum."*

Behtréal pushed against the voice. *Sleep. This is—*

"No time to interfere?" Te Mirkvahíl mocked. *"Someone needs to keep your mind on track, Te Luminíl, lest your infatuation for these parasites dooms this undertaking to its end. And then how would you feel, knowing you let Aveline and little Jor remain ghosts of memory so this sentient plague could persevere?"*

"Are you all right?" Ronomar placed a hand on Behtréal's arm. "Mistress Khal?"

Behtréal blinked, Te Mirkvahíl's cackling fading to silence in his mind. "Yes. Just—it's been a long few days."

"Care for a walk?" Raelza asked, standing from their chair. "I find working long hours indoors a bit monotonous." They offered their hand to Behtréal. "Would you not agree?"

Behtréal took it and the twins led him from the office. "Where did you have in mind?"

"Anywhere, really," Raelza said. "Anywhere at all."

A VAGUE RESPONSE *to a question with a very specific answer,* Behtréal thought. "Anywhere at all," had really meant a few miles east of Helveden to a patch of forest so incredibly dense it was impossible for sound to echo. A few threads of gray light peeked through the trees, though they did little to illuminate the woods.

Behtréal arched an eyebrow at Raelza. "Anywhere at all, hmm?"

Raelza conjured an illum wisp, its pale light bestowing a soothing aura upon the trees. "Do you not remember this place?"

"I don't," Behtréal said. He took a few steps, looking aimlessly about. "Should I?"

"It's where you found us nearly forty years ago," Ronomar said. "Two crying babes, abandoned to the darkness of this silent place. Left to die by hands unknown. Do you truly not recall?"

"I…"

"*You could snuff them out,*" Te Mirkvahíl urged, manifesting at Behtréal's side as a towering white-eyed silhouette. It snaked around him, flicking tongue just inches from his face. "*You could take their illum, reap it for your own. You're hungry, I can tell.*"

I require noth —

"*Oh, Te Luminíl… It amuses me how often you forget, how often you desire that the truth be fiction,*" sneered Te Mirkvahíl. "*What I require, so too do you, for we are one and the same. It would do you well to remember this, to accept this. You want to see them again, do you not? Aveline, Jor, the rest of the Reshapers? Our success shall bring about their restoration.*"

"Mistress Khal." Again, Ronomar drew Behtréal back, their voice helping to quell Te Mirkvahíl. "Do you remember?"

"No," Behtréal murmured, leaning against the tree nearest him and rubbing the spot between his eyes. Why were things so foggy all of a sudden? No, not all of a sudden. They'd been murky, questionable the entire day, ever since he'd risen from bed. Now he felt…weak.

He looked up at the twins. They were before him now, above him; when had he fallen to the ground? Were these tears? He made to wipe his eyes, only to find he couldn't move, that everything around him was fading to black.

"Wh-what…"

"Truth from madness," Ronomar murmured, reaching for Behtréal's face.

THEY SAY *the light is darkest just before the dawn. I hold that statement to be true. This war has lasted far too long. I pray to Vara'szen for strength enough to subjugate Te Mirkvahíl's will but still its progeny come. For every thousand troops we arm Te Mirkvahíl sends two thousand more. I fear our forces will be tragically outnumbered by month's end. Keepers help us, we already are…*

Every day we march to try and gain a foothold on the outskirts of the Heart, and every day our forces are repelled. I have asked the Church for aid. I have pleaded for more Illumurgists. Those we have, have begun to feel the tolls of war. They spread their energies too far. Some have all but lost their light. Others…others have burned out. With their illum stretched thin by overuse, we cannot hold our own in battle. What hope does the Ariathan army have when its numbers fall so quickly to the lokyn swarms? We have seen too many of our own claimed, souls reaped from freshly dead flesh. Something has to give.

Ronomar looked up from the journal, quill held lightly in their trembling hand. *Wartime fear,* they thought, looking for somewhere they might catch a glimpse of the countenance they wore.

"General?" a voice called from outside the tent.

"Come," Ronomar called, and the voice sounded horribly familiar.

Third General Szen entered and approached, giving the formal salute.

Ronomar returned the gesture, their faint reflection in his war-scarred breastplate confirming that this memory belonged to one Searyn An. Their friend. "Well?"

"Vahnyll and his scouts have returned," Szen said. His face was hawkish, his graying hair pulled back and braided in several areas starting near his temples. He acknowledged her with yellow eyes. "They have found a breach in the Heart's defenses."

Then this is it, Searyn thought, adrenaline coursing through her like a spring stream.

"How close?"

"Half a day," Szen said. Anticipation swirled in his eyes.

Searyn stroked her ear pensively. She narrowed her eyes, lips forming a straight line. She had served her country since her youth. Keepers knew she'd love to see this monstrosity of a war end before her thirtieth year. She missed home. She missed Theailys. It'd been a couple years since they had seen each other.

"Speak with Nharmais and Lugus," Searyn said. "Broach the idea of infiltrating. If they seem favorable…"

Szen gave a silent salute and withdrew.

Searyn sighed and paced her tent, catching the occasional glimpse of her sword. That beautiful, brutal dragon's tooth of a blade. She felt complete when wielding it, yet at the same time longed to put it down. She'd spent more than half her life training to and being used by the Empire as a weapon. She'd spilled blood, innocent and not, and she was tired of it all.

"Khar Am, give me strength," she whispered, returning to her makeshift desk.

She tore a blank piece of parchment from her journal. If the other generals favored this breach the scouts had found, it meant they'd all be marching into chaos and their possible ends. It would be foolish, Searyn decided, to descend with total arrogance. Nothing of this war had given her the privilege of being so. She took up her quill, dipped it in the ink, and started writing.

It took Searyn little time to finish the letter to Theailys. She sighed, narrowing her eyes. Her lids felt heavy, *everything* felt heavy. Her partial intent for the letter had been some semblance of catharsis, but it had instead served only to magnify her fears and reservations. Not that she had needed to—Theailys understood her well enough to know.

Searyn folded the letter and sealed it shut, deciding to hand it to the courier before the day was done. She stood and started from her tent. She pulled the flap back and ducked out into the world, greeted by the darkness that the skies had known nearly as long as Searyn was old.

THEY'D MADE camp at the outskirts of the breach earlier in the day. Now, sleep was nonexistent to Searyn. Never had they been this deep inside the woods. Leaves were scarce upon the trees, which gave her clear sight toward the sky. It was dark as always but there was something *more* to it. Something sick and eerie, something sentient. She was not the only one to notice.

"These woods are foul," said Nharmais, joining Searyn at her tent. "Listen."

"Silence," Searyn noted several minutes later.

"Not a cricket's chirp to lull the night," said Nharmais, narrowing her red eyes. "Something is off. I can feel it in the air and in my bones. A wood this vast should not be ruled by silence so profound."

Searyn nodded. It was more than just the sky that tugged her nerves, it was the atmosphere itself. She observed her soldiers as they circled on patrol.

"No sound," she uttered breathlessly. "Their footfalls make no sound."

"I agreed to this because the plan was sound, the information firm. But…" Nharmais paused, chewing on her lip. "It all feels wrong."

"Then may Khar Am and the Keepers give us strength," Searyn said, clapping Nharmais on the shoulder. She had never before seen the Fourth General tremble so apparently.

"I will pray they do," Nharmais said, standing. "In a few short hours we march toward fate, whatever it may be."

Searyn bid the general goodnight. She watched her soldiers walk about, gradually shifting her attention to the woods again, to the silence, and the foulness of the sky.

Te Mirkvahíl surely watches us, Searyn thought. *It knows of what we try…and yet we must.* She felt warmth coursing through her, surging like the tide. She glared into the night, westward past the twisted branches in the direction of the Heart. *We are on your doorstep, monster, and we will see your end. The light is darkest just before the dawn, and when we finally meet, it will be my blade that sets the fire in your eyes and wipes you from this world.*

THE LACK of sound had made its mark upon Searyn's soldiers as the night endured. Their courage would not sway, though, and they marched ahead, growing closer to the breach with every step. She marched at point with Lugus at the rear and Szen and Nharmais at her sides.

We near fate. We near the end of war and the start of peace, she told herself, her jaw clenched tightly as she gripped the hilt of her sword. *Whatever menace lurks below will fall.*

"There," said Nharmais.

Before them stood the entrance to the breach, a cavernous maw of stone deprived of light. Searyn glanced at the sky, shuddering. Had the darkness *grinned* at her? She set her gaze upon the breach and drew her blade, the others doing as she did. She ventured toward the entrance, blade extended forward. Should anything approach them she would spear its life away.

They descended silently into darkness. Searyn saw no reason for a speech. The outcomes were clear, and she knew her soldiers would follow her until the end. She had earned the titles of First General and First Faithbringer and that was something none of them would question. Her resolve was theirs, as was her courage. She had their respect and they hers.

Passageway illuminated by wisps, they delved deeper, walking straight for Keepers knew how long. The walls and floor were simple gray stone, nothing special, but eventually they began to change. Where the walls and ceiling met a slick membrane had developed, seeping toward the floor and reeking horribly of…well, just horribly. Had this tunnel been a disposal of sorts at one time?

Wouldn't make much sense, Searyn thought of the possibility. *Not for the lokyns, at least.* The demons weren't keen on keeping hostages. You either escaped captivity or you died.

They emerged inside a wide, high-ceilinged chamber. It was comprised of the same rough stone as the passageway and smelled equally as nauseating. The source—*sources,* rather—of the smell hung from the ceiling.

"Keepers have mercy on their souls," whispered Nharmais. Her eyes looked past the dangling suits of flesh, resting on a naked figure in the center of the room. "You there…"

"Vahnyll?" Searyn started toward him. Nharmais followed as the others fanned the room. "Vahnyll, are you all right?" He had not left basecamp, and so far as Searyn knew, the scout was supposed to have taken a day's rest before heading south. She reached out toward the trembling man. "Vahnyll…?"

His arm shot forward, grabbing hers. Searyn gripped her sword tighter. Vahnyll tittered, looking frantically around the room, then leaned in toward her ear.

"We are *fashion,*" he uttered. Oh, how his breath *reeked*! "We are suits and dresses, flesh veneers for masquerades."

His tittering melted quickly into tears. He held his arms up, revealing swirling black glyphs. *"Please!* I do not want—"

Searyn shuddered as the man went still. She glanced at Nharmais, who had her crystalline longsword at Vahnyll's neck, then withdrew, greaves clanking with each step. Searyn gripped her blade with both hands and brought it level with her eyes, extending parallel to her feet. Szen and Lugus neared. The four generals circled Vahnyll slowly, the man's eyes frozen wide and fixed upon the ceiling.

"I do not want to be a mask," he sobbed, causing everyone to start. The glyph marks on his arms began to glow. Vahnyll fell to the floor, flopping like a fish, shrieking. "I DO NOT WANT TO BE A MASK! END ME! END ME NOW BEFORE—"

"Keepers have mercy on his soul," Lugus said.

Vahnyll wailed, flesh sundering down the center of his body, starting at his forehead. A mass of...something slithered from his body and ascended quickly, taking Vahnyll's flapping corpse and hanging it amongst the others.

Then, they came.

The blackness whirled around the room and slapped itself inside the meat suits. Figures slopped to the floor and launched themselves at Searyn and the others. She cut them down with no remorse—they weren't people anymore.

She moved in tandem with Nharmais, the pair striking down lokyn after lokyn. Truth from madness—that was one of Khar Am's ancient teachings, and apparently one some of her soldiers were having trouble with.

Searyn broke from Nharmais and rushed an Illumurgist

cowering on his knees, wailing, begging for his wife to forgive him.

"I was away from you... My fault you are dead..." he sobbed as a blonde-haired girl in rags approached.

"You said you loved me!" she wailed, descending on the Illumurgist. "You said that we would be together, always and forever! HOW COULD YOU LET ME DIE?"

Searyn severed head from neck and kicked the body away, watching as the blackness—the lokyn's true form—rose into the air. She gripped the Illumurgist by the shoulder and pulled him to his feet.

"It's not her!" she yelled. "Truth from madness! Come on!"

Searyn parried several of the creatures as they came then knocked them forward. She drew illum from the crystals hanging from her neck, raised her sword high, and plunged it toward the floor. Crystal punched easily through the old stone and a wave of brilliant energy radiated outward, disorienting the lokyns within its immediate vicinity. Nharmais and Szen followed her example, bathing the chamber in a light so hot and blinding Searyn felt her hair might catch fire. Instead the lokyns shrieked, and when all settled, they were gone.

Searyn dropped to her knees, hands still on the hilt. She felt winded, drained.

Wailing filled the air. Soldiers ripped their ghost-white helmets off and tossed them to the floor.

"You killed them all," said Lugus, advancing on her, anguish in his eyes. "You killed your *own*."

Searyn frowned. "What are you talking about?"

She stood, hilt clutched tightly as she looked upon the faces of nearly three quarters of her force. Black glyphs on their foreheads and cheeks. They drew closer. A hand raked across her greave. Searyn whipped around, watching Nharmais crawl toward her.

"No. No!" Searyn readied her blade. *Fashion,* rang Vahnyll's terrified voice. Was that all they were? Was that all they ever *had* been?

One by one the remaining Faithbringers, Wardens, and Illumurgists removed their helms and advanced, glyphs shining brightly on their sweaty skin. They circled her, wailing, lashing out.

"You killed her! Monster! You struck my daughter down as if she were a piece of wood!" cried Szen, sweeping toward her.

Searyn ducked the attack and swung at Szen, blade glancing off his right flank. He turned and lunged again, speed catching her off guard. How long his body would hold up she did not know. Probably not much more. The glyphs on his face were beginning to glow. She parried another strike and dodged another blow. All around her glyphs began to burn. Laughter trickled through the room, watery and wicked. It tickled her ears, trying to distract Searyn.

Truth from madness, she recited, fighting for her life. *Truth from madness.*

The lokyns withdrew from their hosts. They bent, twisted, and splintered plate, leaving Searyn's soldiers dead and gutted on the floor. She withheld the urge to retch and instead readied herself to strike, horror and fury welling up inside her. She gripped the hilt of her blade so tightly she thought her knuckles would go numb, watching the darkness swirl overhead. Instead of multiple entities, though, she was met with a singular figure whose presence was so pervasive it made her legs wobble.

Te Mirkvahíl.

She brought her blade behind her shoulder and swung, only to stop halfway as the figure's features came to light: dark skin, purple eyes, bald scalp, clean shaven. A blade hung sheathed at his side. Searyn's own clanked to the floor.

"No…" She whispered. "It can't be."

"Truth from madness," said Te Mirkvahíl. "Five hundred years of peace because he made it so, imprisoned me beneath his flesh. Khar Am was strong, he was resilient, and over-powering and devouring his soul took time, as did fashioning another force. But it is done. My people shall be remade, and I will watch their resurrection through your eyes."

Searyn shook away the dread. She drew upon the last of her illum and lunged for her sword. Te Mirkvahíl was quicker and kicked her away. She hit the wall with a crunch.

"That might take a couple months to heal. No matter." He knelt before her, holding Searyn's gaze as he drew a knife and placed its tip just over her heart. "I really *am* sorry about this next part. Bonding with new flesh tends to leave a few scars."

Searyn shrieked. Her illum burned away as the blade pierced her plate and plunged straight into her heart. Her life flashed before her eyes. Home. Friends. Theailys. She watched Khar Am's pilfered corpse melt away, turning into mist. She felt cold, numb, violated. Dead. Searyn slumped to the floor and everything went dark.

BEHTRÉAL GASPED as he came to. The world around him was dim and muffled. He pushed himself to sit up from the ground and look about. To his left lay Ronomar, eyes glazed over, trembling as Raelza tried to shake them from whatever trance they were in. They had been deep inside Behtréal's mind, they had seen Searyn die that night, and perhaps even more.

Mirkúr coalesced around Behtréal's hand. Te Mirkvahíl hissed in his mind, urged him on. He approached the twins, chest tight, throat near constriction, and grabbed Raelza by the face, saturating them with dark energy until their desperate retaliation ceased.

Ronomar made no effort.

"Go," Behtréal whispered to them, and they rose from the ground and started toward Helveden. He leaned against a tree, sighing raggedly. What he'd done to the twins just now...Celestials, but he'd have felt less shame for having killed them. Instead...

"They are yours, Te Luminíl, puppets for the greater good," Te Mirkvahíl said, and Behtréal started after them, serenaded by the monstrous cackling all the while.

AUNT FIEL and Fenrin had found nothing out of the ordinary in the Bastion. Nothing at all. But it was that absolute normalcy that'd made them privy to the influence within the city's seat of power. Whispers, Fiel had said, and a thickness in the air, one palpable enough to cut with a knife. Serece was sure it'd been a warning. "I see and know all," it seemed to say, and that realization made her feel horribly, jarringly small.

Serece walked through Helveden, bundled in her cloak, face concealed by her hood as the rain fell. It hadn't stopped all day, though it was considerably lighter now. She could even see a sliver of moonlight through the dark clouds.

Her mind drifted back to the conversation she'd had with Leyandra, specifically the part about Entropy, Law, and balance. Was that really what was going on, the reason for Te Mirkvahíl's longevity—to bring Law back from the brink, to give the world a nudge toward restoring balance? The more she thought about it the more ludicrous it sounded. Te Mirkvahíl had its purpose, all right, but she was quite sure it was not showing the world the error of its ways, however helpful that might have been.

Or maybe, a voice in her head whispered, *Te Mirkvahíl is Law and you people are the chaos, the Entropy.* Somehow that notion made a lick of sense, enough to numb and terrify Serece. The phantaxians were victims of Ariathan brutality and prejudice, but she knew her people sure as hell weren't innocent of their own atrocities. She was proof enough of this, illustrated by the deaths of Rejya and Taür.

She drew a ragged breath then exhaled. She narrowed her eyes, curiosity rising as a familiar figure staggered out of what appeared to be a church. She hastened her steps, following at a distance, close enough that she could hear the poor soul muttering to himself.

"Dear, sweet Theailys An. We meet again," Serece

murmured. Truthfully, she was glad to see him alive, though she could hardly call him well. She hurried after him, following just a foot behind. "You look typically agitated."

He jumped, and Serece afforded herself a much needed chuckle.

Theailys wheeled around. "*Serece?* What in Perdition are you doing here?"

"Sight-seeing," she said, and Theailys raised his eyebrow. "Not the fun kind, I promise. The kind that makes your skin crawl and begs you question your sanity as a shadow falls across your world. I've been here two weeks and you would not believe the shit I've seen, Theailys An. Or maybe you would. You've lived here your entire life, after all."

They walked aimlessly in step. "I've seen my own fair share of shit these last couple weeks," Theailys said, and he told Serece everything that'd transpired on his journey after having departed the Phantaxis Mountains.

"And even after all that you still plan to forge that weapon, don't you?" Serece asked. Theailys' silence told her all she needed to know, and it made her want to punch him in the face for being so stupid.

"I need to," he argued. "It's our only chance at ending this war, at destroying whatever's lurking in the city."

"It could also *destroy everything*," Serece hissed from the depths of her hood.

"You don't think I know that?" Theailys snipped as he started from her.

"I know you know that," Serece replied, "and that's what's so frightening! You know, yet still you're going through with it. What happens if you're wrong? What then?"

269

"Then I've killed us all," Theailys snarled. "Is that what you want to hear?"

"What I *want* is for you to think—just for a fucking *minute*." Serece took a deep breath. Temper Yssa and all that bullshit. "If you forge The Keepers' Wrath and history repeats then there's a damn good chance Te Mirkvahíl or whatever's lurking uses it to…to…" Keepers, but it sounded stupid as a thought, and Serece could only imagine how it would sound aloud. "Alter time."

Theailys snorted, then guffawed. "*Alter time.* Have you gone insane? It's impossible. How would one go about such an undertaking? And how the hell would The Keepers' Wrath help? It's a power focus—*a weapon*! And how do you make the leap to Te Mirkvahíl wanting to alter time? What possible reason would a monster like that have for doing such an impossible thing?"

Serece bit back her frustration and the urge to smack Theailys An as hard as she could. He wasn't looking at the bigger picture. He didn't know what she knew. "Fenrin and the twins think this entity might be an old Reshaper." Theailys cocked an eyebrow at the word, giving Serece the confidence to continue. She explained what little she knew about the Reshapers, about Yssa's temple and Te Vétur Thae. About the city Ronomar and Raelza had seen in dreams.

Theailys was trembling by the time she finished, by the time he fumbled for a response. "The city…Ouran'an was it?" Serece nodded. "I've seen it in my dreams as well. I've been inside…" He trailed off, eyes widening. "I saw the twins in my dream, like…I don't know how to explain it except it was as if we were in the same place at different points in time."

"A bright light at the end?" Serece asked.

"Yes," Theailys said. "Except I've also seen the dream's end, and I've no idea what it means. Your aunt is adept at illumancy. Do you think she might be able to help me understand what it is I'm seeing?"

"Ask her yourself," Serece said. "Come on."

They started on their way from Helveden, making for the ruined house in the woods. Hopefully Aunt Fiel and Fenrin could discern the truth within this dream. Serece couldn't say why, but she knew it was important.

Behtréal observed Fiel and Fenrin through stolen eyes. To his right stood Ronomar, arms crossed to their chest. Behtréal's own arms were crossed—the twins' mannerisms were as identical as their flesh for the most part.

This feels wrong. It was his own thought, not Raelza's. The Illumurgist's cognizance was locked away in the abyss of their mind, granting Behtréal dominion over what was more or less a vessel. Raelza would regain control over their body once Behtréal allowed it so, but even still...

"*These things you put yourself through...*" Te Mirkvahíl mused. "*I would venture to guess you're a bit of a masochist.*"

Pain in the name of love, or something like that, Behtréal snipped.

Te Mirkvahíl chuckled, then went silent.

"Fenrin. Aunt Fiel." Into the ruined home walked Serece, Theailys An in tow. "I've brought a guest with dreams in need of scrying or clarification or whatever you want to call it." She looked at Behtréal and Ronomar. "Apparently you've had similar."

"Have we?" Ronomar chirped. Even under Behtréal's influence their curiosity shone through as endearingly as ever. "Ruined cities, screaming shadows, and the like?"

Serece nodded. "Before we get to that, did you learn anything of Mistress Khal?"

Theailys frowned. "Something wrong?"

"There was a thought," Behtréal said, "she might not have been entirely herself. Eye color being wrong and all that." He looked from Fenrin back to Theailys. "Ronomar and I can confirm, however, that dear Mistress Khal is...well, she's a bit ill, hence the amber eyes."

"What have I missed?" Theailys asked, and they took a moment to fill him in. Behtréal took an extra moment to assure everyone that Khal's "illness" was the product of some Celestial rule she had violated, though she had neglected to mention more than that. Those were, in her own words, "reserved for privileged ears."

"You sure about that? She's just...*ill*?" Fenrin asked. He was not easily swayed.

"Not entirely," Behtréal said, shrugging. "But what else could it be? What we know of the Celestial race suggests that they are far more complicated than our own, and Ronomar and I saw nothing, felt nothing that would suggest Khal had been compromised by Te Mirkvahíl or otherwise."

"Dunno," Fenrin murmured. Somehow *that* had silenced him, and for that Behtréal was thankful. His plan was close to coming to fruition, and he could ill afford to have things fall apart now.

Behtréal clapped his hands together and grinned at Theailys. "So. Dreams, Theailys An." He approached the young
Illumurgist and sniffed his face. Theailys recoiled with a
glare. "Oh, come now—it's mere curiosity!"

"Express it differently," Theailys said, glaring at Behtréal,
then at a chuckling Ronomar. "With words, perhaps.
Questions."

"All right." Ronomar approached, arms crossed, staring
into Theailys' eyes. "We can scry your dreams for meaning, if
you'd like. In one of two ways, maybe three, though the latter
is a bit...brutal."

Behtréal looked at Ronomar and shook his head. "No
need to knife Theailys An, Rono. Illumancy and lacrimancy
are perfectly suitable means to entering The In Between."

Theailys stared at them incredulously. "You were thinking
of *stabbing me*?"

"Of course not," Behtréal said. "Well, that is to say, I don't
think Ronomar was planning on actually following through
with their suggestion."

"Why suggest it all?" Theailys snapped.

"Aunt Fiel did the same to me, for what it's worth," Serece
muttered.

"Most of you are crazy," Theailys said, sighing.
"*Anyway...*"

"Do find a semi-comfortable place to sit, Theailys An,"
Behtréal said. He took a deep whiff—the air smelled only of
rain, stone, and dirt. Theailys An, however, smelled of something new, and that troubled Behtréal. Gone was the shadow
that'd hung over him all these years, replaced with something, *someone* else.

"*Be sensible,*" Te Mirkvahíl warned.

Of course, Behtréal thought. Illumancy was a more efficient way of interpreting dreams, of scrying them, but it also made the Illumancer vulnerable to counter-scrying. Lacrimancy on the other hand…

"Hold still," Behtréal said, making a fist. "This is going to hurt a bit."

Then he decked Theailys clean across the cheek.

"WHAT THE FUCK IS WRONG WITH YOU?" Theailys snarled, picking himself up off the floor, and Behtréal smiled at the tears trickling down his cheeks.

"Quite a lot, I'm sure," Behtréal said, reaching forward to catch the tears on the tip of his finger. "This is the least invasive method, if you cared to know." He licked them from his finger and immediately felt their memories stirring as his illum probed the tears. He took a seat on the floor and closed his eyes. "Oh. Well this looks familiar."

BEHTRÉAL BLINKED the ruined home into focus as the dream ended. He felt disturbed. Ronomar and Raelza's dream had shown an impossibly accurate rendition of Ouran'an, as had Theailys An's, but it was what had transpired in the vault that really put a chill in his blood. If he was piecing this puzzle together properly…

Then that means Theailys An is my brother. Remulus. Behtréal looked at him, a maelstrom of confusion, loathing, and disgust churning in his gut. *But that's impossible.*

"*Because you watched him die that night in the Reshaperate Spire,*" Te Mirkvahíl confirmed.

Behtréal remembered that well, or at least he did now that Te Mirkvahíl had reminded him. He blinked slowly and took a deep breath. He could ill afford to let unfounded notions rile him into recklessness. Remulus had been well and dead after his skirmish in the Reshaperate Spire—hadn't he?

"Are you all right?" Serece asked, drawing Behtréal back. "Raelza?"

"S-sorry," he stammered. "Just…collecting my thoughts. An interesting dream, that." Dear Varésh Lúm-talé had been there too, luminous wings and all. "Similar to our own, yet different too. It was as if…" He paused, tilting his head. "As if Theailys was experiencing this city at different points in time. How strange."

"So, what do you think it means?" Theailys asked. "The city. The vault. The…me as a silhouette. The journal." He was shaking, beginning to crack. That was…good.

Behtréal shook his head, frowning. "I don't know," he lied. "You're sure you've never been to Ouran'an, not even unknowingly?"

"Positive," Theailys said. "I don't even know where the thing stood." He rubbed his temples. "Keepers, this has to mean something, though. I can feel it does. I feel it's something more, that it's not *just a dream*."

"A memory, perhaps?" Behtréal asked.

"Maybe." Theailys narrowed his eyes and sighed. "Either that or I've learned to look into the past, whoever's past it is."

"Some rest might do you well," Behtréal said, though he

knew he'd see Theailys again before the night was done. "Some rest might do us *all* well."

"Right." Theailys stood. "I've got a weapon to forge come dawn."

He bid them all goodnight then started from the house, muttering indiscernibly to himself.

Behtréal stood next, he and Ronomar following suit. When they were far enough away from the others, he withdrew from Raelza, spirit tumbling through the void until the bright lights of Eisley Khal's office pulled him out.

"Always a strange sensation," he murmured. "Traveling through The In Between."

He smoothed his cloak, stood from his chair, and started from the room. Theailys An would soon be here.

BEHTRÉAL SAT beside Theailys in the Hall courtyard; they'd been talking for a while. He felt sick, something more profound than shame for what he'd done to Ronomar and Raelza. His stomach gurgled at the thought of his shadow puppets hiding in plain sight, at the notion they were now gears in his machine.

Focus on the moment at hand, he urged himself. It felt very much like the night before Theailys had left. The air was crisp, the moon bright, the two of them reminiscing on what a shit day, what a shit *month* it had been. Behtréal was not fond of such profanities, but they were an important part of Eisley Khal's personality, at least where Theailys was concerned.

He inhaled from his pipe then passed it off to Theailys,

letting the smoke escape his lips in threads. *Closer, now,* he thought. *To success.* He tensed his jaw at a twinge in his chest, just above his heart, and allowed himself to frown.

"Searyn's really gone," Theailys said, and the weight of that reality, of that sad acknowledgement hit Behtréal like a maul. Using his mirkúr he attuned himself to Theailys' thoughts, listening to the internal strife as Theailys worked to push the black pictures from his mind, his nightmare manifestations of what Searyn's end might have been like, of what it might have felt like for her. He instead tried to focus on her as she'd been before she'd left for war, before the both of them had sold their souls to abetting in their nation's death.

Do you see what we have done? Behtréal thought.

"*Every great cause has martyrs,*" Te Mirkvahíl replied. "*And who better than the man who at one point might have been your brother, hmm? After what you saw in those dreams, what they suggest, how can you harbor remorse for such a man as this? How can you harbor remorse for a man whose predecessors abetted in the slaughter of your friends in Zorahl half a millennium ago?*"

Behtréal sighed. Those were both good questions. He thought a moment. *Because Remulus died eons ago. Theailys An is someone else. Faro Fatego was someone else.* Another thought occurred. *I created Theailys An. Who's to say that dream wasn't of my making as well? A happy accident that served to further bend him to my will?*

Te Mirkvahíl chuckled. "*Think that if you wish, Te Luminíl.*"

"I need this all to be over," Theailys whispered, looking up. Behtréal met his gaze with a forlorn expression of his own. "I need you to tell me it will all be over soon."

Behtréal squeezed his arm, nodding. "It will be. I promise.

The Keepers' Wrath will see to that. We all of us will see to that, and once it's over we'll be able to start anew and properly mourn the dead. We'll be able to put this madness in the past where it belongs."

He leaned back on his elbows, a wistful yet contemplative smile drawn across his lips. *Play the part,* he thought. "Temporal alteration—" A chuckle escaped, and Behtréal gave himself a moment to let the amusement pass. "Imagine the possibilities."

"It's pure conjecture," Theailys said, though Behtréal could sense he'd put a bit of stock in what he'd learned. "A fool's fantasy to think we could ever change things in such a profound way."

Behtréal arched an eyebrow. "Is it? With everything going on, with everything that's happened, do you really believe it's such a reach to think we might be able to rectify our wrongs, to reset the world and do things right?"

"I *think,*" Theailys said, "you've let my nonsense make berth in the space between your ears. It's better to focus on the task at hand lest we distract ourselves from the monsters lurking in our midst."

Behtréal's jaw tensed momentarily. "Perhaps you're right." He took up the pipe and drew another breath, smoke leaking from the corners of his mouth. "Searyn would probably have said the same thing."

Theailys allowed himself a smirk at that. "Of course she would. We're twins."

Were *twins,* a voice inside Behtréal hissed. It was not Te Mirkvahíl. It just *was,* and Behtréal's thoughts drifted momentarily to what Ronomar had seen inside his mind.

"I'm going to leave when this has passed," Theailys said. He stood, offering his hand, and pulled Behtréal to his feet. They walked toward the entrance of the Hall, eventually bidding each other goodnight and going their separate ways.

"You should rest," Te Mirkvahíl said as Behtréal wandered through the labyrinthine streets of Helveden. *"You've spent yourself this day, and the endgame is nearly upon us."*

I shall rest once all is said and done, Behtréal thought.

Te Mirkvahíl grumbled. *"What now, then?"*

Behtréal said nothing as he made for the inn at the end of the street. He knew he was foolish to be doing this—he'd been foolish for a lot of what he'd done—but Celestials damn it all, it was too hard to resist. *Just this once,* he told himself as he ducked into the shadow of the inn. *Just this once.*

BEHTRÉAL HAD SEEN this woman twice before, the first time ten or fifteen years ago at war, and the second earlier in the day, a companion to Theailys An. Leyandra, she was called, but in his desperate fantasy she was Aveline, for they looked so terribly alike. Had he not been married to the past…

"You are a fool," Te Mirkvahíl chided. *"Just as you were a fool to have commiserated with Theailys An in the courtyard. Did you expect yourself to have sewn shut the wounds on your heart in such a short amount of time?"*

Behtréal ignored the voice and instead kept his focus on Leyandra's sleeping form, little more than a silhouette. He reached out with a trembling hand to caress her cheek, taking care to do so lightly enough that she wouldn't wake. She was beautiful, and her battle scars served only to enhance her elegance. They were a window of sorts, a peephole to her memories and soul.

Such pain, Behtréal thought, tapping into the modicum of illum that remained beneath her flesh. *Pain for which I am responsible.* He had been there the night his lokyn brood had reaped her light. Not all, but enough that she could no longer channel it. "I am sorry," he murmured for that and so much more, withdrawing his hand.

"*The irony of your infatuation with this mortal woman is pathetic, almost as comical as the guilt Theailys An stirs within you and as the shame you feel for having marked the twins,*" Te Mirkvahíl sneered. "*If you care so dearly for these things you once were strong enough to realize were a plague, then perhaps you ought to slit your throat and let them be.*"

Behtréal said nothing.

"*You won't though, will you?*" Te Mirkvahíl said. "*Because I'm right, and I know how much you hate when I'm right.*"

Have you no empathy? Behtréal thought. *Truly?*

"*Have you no spine?*" Te Mirkvahíl countered. "*The end is drawing near, Te Luminíl—no time for second thoughts. You either forge ahead with staunch determination, emboldened by the thought of holding your beloved wife and son again, or you fold and cede ambition to uncertainty and guilt.*"

Aveline. Jor. Behtréal squeezed his eyes shut, trying to call upon a memory of his wife and son, anything at all. Something strong enough that he might feel their phantom presence pressed against his chest. Celestials, how long had it been, how many years since he had held them in his arms?

"Time has little meaning to forever people," he

murmured. Something Aveline had said to him once. If she could see him now, she would understand how horribly wrong she'd been. Time was everything to Behtréal, it ruled him, had molded and transformed him into what he was today. And that was…what, exactly?

He withdrew from Leyandra's room, formless, traveling in the shadows cast by light. This led him out and away from the inn, south to the burial mounds from which he'd resurrected ghosts from years and centuries past. He took up the shape of a wispy silhouette and wandered on his way.

14

VULTURES

There was sunshine, and the meadow was ablaze with gentle light. The air was sweet with the scent of myriad perfumes, yet pungent with the tang of iron. Cailean held Bar's body close. It was still warm despite the blood crying around the dagger impaled in Bar's chest. *You fool, Cailean thought, choking back tears. You fucking beautiful fool.*

In his heart of hearts Cailean knew Bar's death had been for the best. The fallen angel had said so himself in his way. "From Entropy, Law. From both, balance." Peace. Cailean wondered what that might feel like. He'd jumped from one war to the next, though searching for what, he was still unsure. It certainly wasn't this. This was just chaos of a different kind, the chaos brought by Law, and Keepers did it hurt something fierce.

Cailean laid Bar down in the grass and sobbed as uncertainty claimed his world for its own.

To Cailean, restlessness was as familiar as his flesh was scarred. He slept little these days. Most of the time it was a nap induced by drink, and even then, he found himself roused from sleep by the profoundness of his dreams, as had been the case tonight.

He stood on the small balcony his room at the inn afforded him, looking out into the black night. The air smelled of coming rain, of horse shit, smoke, and piss. Nothing new. He took a sip from his flask, letting the whiskey saturate his tongue for a couple seconds before he took the liquid fire down his throat to let it settle in his gut. The sensation elicited a sigh, letting Cailean know he'd picked a good thinking whiskey. He'd been awfully pensive these last few days in Helveden, a strange, unsettling amalgamation of confusion, curiosity, and déjà vu.

Smells like that night, he thought, Bar's face rising from the depths of memory. *You sure flipped that coin mighty fucking hard, you beautiful prick.* Instinctively he rubbed his hand along his chest, lingering on the inch-long scar above his heart, the place where nearly sixteen years ago Bar's blade had parted flesh and bone. It itched like hell, and the very thought of Bar, of what'd transpired in Harbanan all those years ago, sent agony flaring outward from his heart. Cailean clenched his teeth to keep the tears at bay.

"Once marked, always marked."

Cailean started at the ethereal voice. He wheeled around to the darkness of his room, and from a twist of light emerged an inverse silhouette with eyes like setting suns. Cailean clutched his flask with a trembling hand. *"...Bar?"*

Obscurity melted from the silhouette and pooled around

its feet. Bar was lithe, fair of skin and fair of hair, garbed in a snow-white suit with polished shoes. He looked exactly as he had that terrible night in the Drahl Muuz cathedral.

"*Cailean.*" His voice was soft, grating, like flies on a summer breeze, and it was all Cailean could do to keep himself from lunging at the man.

"How? Bar... I killed you," Cailean said. "*You* made me kill you."

"*You can't slaughter memory, my sweet,*" said Bar. "*You can cast away my mortal flesh, and you can send my spirit to Perdition or the Second Life, but you can never rid your memories of me. Once you let the devil in your bed there is no letting go.*"

"Once marked, always marked," Cailean murmured. "Why now?"

Bar cocked his head. "*I'm afraid you'll have to answer that yourself, my sweet.*"

"Or"—Cailean slugged the whiskey in his flask—"*you* could answer that."

"*Truly, I cannot,*" Bar said. "*Not the way this works. I am little more than memory, and the meaning of a memory, the reason for a memory rousing from its sleep, takes time to understand.*"

Cailean tossed the empty flask into the room. "You telling me I need to quit the drink? Is that it?"

"*On the contrary. You were always more perceptive when you drank,*" Bar said.

Cailean arched an eyebrow. "Haven't had *that* kind of whiskey in a while. Fuck all, but I barely remember how to make the drink of the Galrun Muir. Even if I did...not like I have the means."

Bar smiled. It was soft and inviting and it served to magnify his monstrousness. Beautiful creatures, beautiful things were often times the deadliest. Cailean allowed himself to shudder. He knew Bar would take it as a compliment of sorts.

"Things are coming to a head," he told the fallen angel. "I can feel it in my gut."

"*You never liked the feelings in your gut,*" said Bar. "*Nor I, mine.*"

"It's like you said—the coin has flipped," said Cailean. "Or, it's on the verge of flipping." He furrowed his brow. "I just don't know what comes next, and that terrifies me to no end."

"*What do you* think *comes next?*" said Bar. It was more a challenge than a question. "*If you learned anything from the night I broke your heart or the morning that you took my life, pray tell, my sweet—what comes next?*"

Cailean leaned against the balustrade. "Chaos. Doesn't matter which way the coin has flipped. Chaos follows Law, chaos follows Entropy. That's just the way of things." He turned to face the night, gazing far into the blackness. "Why'd you do it, Bar?"

"*Do what?*"

"All of it." Cailean kept his back to the fallen angel. "Harbanan. Killing me in the cathedral. Resurrecting me. Forcing me to kill you in the meadow. What was the truth in your madness? You said it was about restoring order, balance, but it has to be more than that."

Cailean turned to Bar, but the fallen angel was gone, and that was answer enough. *Suppose I always knew,* he thought, and the scar on his chest screamed as he allowed the truth to finally sink in.

Sometime later a knock on the door drew Cailean's gaze. "Come in."

The door opened and in stepped Leyandra. "Surprised you're awake."

"Could say the same of you," Cailean said. "Dreams?"

She nodded. "Nightmares, really. Not going to sleep anytime soon. Walk?"

"Sure," Cailean said, and he took a moment to quickly dress himself. "Where to?"

"Anywhere," Leyandra said, and they withdrew from the room and the inn, into the night.

FOR THE FIRST time in her life, Serece found herself wishing she could wield illum. Aunt Fiel could, so why not her? Why not the rest of phantaxians? She rested her arms on the balustrade of the tower's highest point, gazing out into the blackness of the night as the question stewed. What she would give to walk The In Between, to relive dreams and memories of yesteryears, to hold her daughter tightly in her arms as she and Rejya laughed at something their father had said.

Suppose I could knife myself, she thought, remembering how Fiel had drawn her to The In Between. *Or not. Stupid idea.* She was low enough on vials of snow to the point that trying something so bold would probably lead to her death—and wouldn't that be a terrible way to go? She curled her lip at the notion of dying in Helveden, at the increasing possibility that she might. Her ears twitched and she tensed her jaw.

"Your anger is justified."

Serece started at the voice, nearly tumbling over the balustrade. She turned to its source—Rejya stood before the balcony door, arms crossed to her chest.

"Rejya?" Serece blinked several times, but her sister remained. "H-How? I—" She reached for Rejya, grasping air as her hand passed through her sister's arm. She swallowed, choking back tears. "Did I drink something weird? Keepers, I'm not dead, am I?"

Rejya shook her head and approached the balustrade, each graceful step leaving gossamer threads of luminescence in its wake. *"Memory is a fascinating thing. The ways in which our minds react to the world without are more extraordinary yet."*

"Is that what you are?" Serece asked, turning to Rejya. "A memory?"

"A fragment," Rejya replied. *"An echo."*

"But…how am I seeing you?" Serece asked. "How are we even having this conversation? Why?"

"I can't answer that," Rejya said. *"You're going to have to dig deep to understand."*

Keepers, but there were a great number of possibilities. Guilt, fear, and shame seemed the strongest candidates though. "I'm scared, Rejya." Serece's ears twitched rapidly, and she reached to steady them with her hands. "The uncertainty of everything in this wretched place…"

"You're right to be," Rejya said. *"Only a fool would claim otherwise."*

"The absence of evidence, Searyn An's death, and the

dreams…" Serece wrapped her arms around herself, shuddering. "They make me feel colder than I already am." She gazed out into the night, eyes unblinking.

"But something else makes you absolutely frigid," Rejya guessed.

"The possibility, however ludicrous it seems, of Te Mirkvahíl altering time," Serece murmured. "Rewriting history and erasing everything and everyone."

"And would that really be so terrible?" Rejya asked. *"All of this misery and madness gone as though they'd never been. A second chance at a better life, to keep this plague from ever coming to be."* She approached Serece, stopping so their noses nearly touched. *"To hold your daughter once again, to watch her grow before your eyes."*

Serece chewed her trembling lower lip, allowing the tears to fall. All of that…it was horribly tempting. A chance to start anew. Maybe then her mother wouldn't look at her with shame. And maybe then… "We could be together, you and I."

Rejya nodded. *"I would like that very much."*

Keepers, the notion of a better life was so horrifically seductive. Serece gripped the balustrade, her nails scratching the stone as Rejya whispered sweet tales of possibility in her ear.

Would it be so wrong to seek it out? Just the fact she had asked herself turned Serece's flaking flesh to goose pimples. She was balancing on the precipice of no return, on the edge of desperation. *To simply ask? What could it hurt that hasn't been already?*

Serece took a breath, then exhaled raggedly.

"You know where and how," said Rejya, as if having read

Serece's thoughts. She was a memory after all, a projection of Serece's mind. *"You need only ask. Like you said—what could it hurt that hasn't been already?"*

Serece nodded, starting for the balcony door.

The Bastion called to her.

THE STREETS WERE empty save the occasional late-night wanderer or guard. Every step felt heavy, every breath a struggle, as though the city sought to keep her from this thing with every ounce of strength it still possessed, which at this point wasn't much. The nearer Serece grew to the Bastion, the more palpable the blackness over Helveden grew, until she found herself brushing strands of shadow from the air. Dark curiosity and adrenaline kept her on the path, and eventually the city's last stand against her desperation died.

Serece stood at the Bastion gates, yawned open so she might pass. She was not surprised. The Bastion itself rose into the night, its pinnacle devoured by the clouds and its interior illumination turning its many windows into watchful eyes. She swallowed, set her jaw, and started in with measured steps, failing horribly to keep herself from trembling as she went.

She stopped in the center of the courtyard, in the center of a crescent moon-shaped inlay. Instinct bid she go no further until whatever lurked in wait invited her inside.

A minute passed.

Then another.

And another, until Serece could not say how much time

had elapsed. It could have been five minutes, it could have been an hour. She supposed it didn't really matter. Whatever came next would have been the same regardless of how much time had passed.

Her ears twitched. Footsteps approached from behind. She turned her head ever so slightly, enough to catch a pair of silver eyes.

"Serece." Fenrin stopped beside her, though his gaze was fixed upon the Bastion.

Serece said nothing, and Fenrin offered nothing more. She wondered if the same idea had crossed his mind and knew she wouldn't blame him if it had. Everything he'd lost, everything he'd seen... The notion of a second chance was captivating, especially when all attempts to save their current world seemed to have been in vain. Serece knew loss, and this was a war they had lost even if no one cared to admit so yet.

The Bastion doors swung open and a silhouette emerged. Its presence forced Serece and Fenrin to their knees and Serece was certain this was *It*—Te Mirkvahíl. The silhouette approached at a measured pace, each footfall rousing whispers in Serece's ears, voices from an age long dead and gone. Their words were foreign, but that mattered not, for they brought to life myriad pictures in Serece's mind. A city like the one Theailys and the twins had seen in dreams. A raven, and an oak tree in a meadow underneath a triptych sky.

"I know it hurts," Te Mirkvahíl said, and its voice was nothing like Serece had thought it'd be. It was not monstrous nor cold, not hungry nor something from the abyss. It was soft, *soothing*. "More than anyone, I know. The loss, the remembrance, the agony of it all."

Serece hadn't realized she was crying again. Te Mirkvahíl knelt, reaching to wipe away her tears. She allowed this, and the demon's touch eased her trembling and allowed her heart and mind to relax. No fear. Just…solace.

"I have done horrible things, and I will do more before this night is done," Te Mirkvahíl said. "Know this brings me pain. Know this brings me guilt. I am not proud of what I have done and plan to do…but it is necessary. I just want you to know that."

"W-What comes next?" Serece stammered. She felt small before this thing, this entity, however old it was.

"Pain," Te Mirkvahíl said.

Fenrin sputtered. Serece turned her head, stifling a cry. Mirkúr blades protruded from his chest and blood dripped down the corners of his mouth. Fenrin's head lolled to the left, the brilliance fading from his eyes, the color from his flesh as Te Mirkvahíl took his illum for its own. The blades dispersed and Fenrin dropped to the ground, blood pooling, threads of mirkúr rising from his wounds.

"He thought his coming here would alter things. He was wrong." Te Mirkvahíl sighed. "Such sorrow. Such agony. Perhaps it is better he will never come to be. Life, regardless of the path, eventually leads to pain."

Never come to be? You fool, Fenrin. Serece longed to cry, to mourn his loss, but she dared not do so. *Though what would it matter if I did? Surely death is better than this life, a life soon to be rewritten.*

"Come," Te Mirkvahíl said, pulling Serece to her feet.

"Where?" she asked, trailing the slender silhouette.

"To see Theailys An."

BEHTRÉAL STOOD *atop the highest tower of Ouran'an, watching dawn creep through the clouds. The plague had taken lives, but in the end his people had persevered. Two years later and it all still seemed a wonderful dream from which he hoped he never woke.*

"How do you feel?" a gentle voice inquired from behind.

Behtréal turned to find her standing there, his Aveline. Her gray eyes shone like gems, her waist-length mane like dark flames. "More alive than I have in quite some time."

She approached, raising a hand to caress his cheek. "You gave up your illum. You spent it all to eradicate the plague, to save our son, to save them all. Even now I find myself unable to say—"

Behtréal pulled her close and pressed his lips to hers. They melted into one another and, in this moment, there was nothing else but them. "You need not say a thing," he said, pulling back to look at Aveline, to commit her face to memory. "I would do it every time. I would risk it all, I would give it all to keep you safe, to keep our child safe—to keep them all safe."

Aveline smiled and brushed a strand of hair behind her ear. "I know."

They stood there a while longer, letting the sun warm their skin. It felt good, refreshingly cathartic after the years of coldness the plague had brought. Aveline sighed against his chest.

Her breath was cold as ice.

Behtréal pulled back from Aveline as she fell to ruin at his feet. Below, the city erupted into screams. He should have wailed to see her dead, naught but ashes scattering in the breeze that had come, but the only thing Behtréal thought of now was Jor. He leapt the balustrade, melting into smoke as he hurtled toward the streets. He regained physicality once outside of the Reshaperate Spire grounds and broke for home.

Failure met Behtréal at every turn, falling from windows, stumbling from alleyways and doors. Eyes ringed black with the infected mirkúr that he thought he'd quelled, reaching desperately for this man they years ago had called their savior. Turning to ash as he passed them by in a panicked sprint.

The trees were black and gnarled as Behtréal leapt the small fence surrounding his home. The grass was dead and dusted with a snow he'd not been privy to 'til now. The front door swung ajar and little Jor staggered out into the yard, wailing, reaching for his father. Behtréal ran, heart caught in his throat. He reached to scoop Jor into his arms.

But there was only ash.

BEHTRÉAL WALKED THROUGH HELVEDEN, Serece trailing several steps behind. Her fear was palpable and rightly so. The threat of something monstrous stealing everything you knew? It was something with which he could intimately empathize. And the fact her people had been able to endure their mirkúr plague where his had not? Well, that was of interest as well.

"*Stay the path,*" Te Mirkvahíl hissed. "*We're so very close, Te Luminíl.*"

I am quite aware, Behtréal thought.

"*Yet once more these lesser things tug at your heart,*" Te Mirk-vahíl said. "*So weak.*"

You love to call me so, Behtréal thought. *But you would hold your tongue if you truly understood. Empathy is not weakness, nor is reflection, as I have tried explaining to you many times before. To empathize with others is to know their minds and hearts.*

"*What good is that?*" Te Mirkvahíl asked. "*Why seek to understand such fragility?*"

I would have thought the answer obvious to you, a thing so heavily reliant upon manipulation, Behtréal thought. *If you need tangible proof, look no further than the Faithbringers, Wardens, and Illumurgists of this realm. War manipulates men and women into unified machines of violent capability. It peels away all logic and instead appeals to the most primal of emotions. If you want something more concrete...* Behtréal trailed off. *Look to Theailys An, look to the suffering we've subjected him to.*

Besides, Behtréal continued. *Her people spat in the face of the mirkúr plague where mine could not. There is something to be said for that.*

Te Mirkvahíl was silent. Behtréal had made his point.

He turned his thoughts to Serece. Would she linger here to die or follow him into the Temporal Sea? The agony of remembrance was an awful price to pay, one he wasn't sure he could impart on someone else, least of all against their will. *My dear daughter of the mountain,* he thought. *Whatever will you do?*

Behtréal stopped and turned to Serece. "What do you wish?" She swallowed. Her lips parted but she failed to speak. He reached for her trembling hand. It was warm despite her kind being incapable of comprehending heat. "Please. Tell me."

"To not hurt," she whispered, and fresh tears welled in her eyes. "To fix things."

Behtréal nodded slowly. "I too long for the same. I have done such monstrous things. I have slaughtered through the centuries. I have twisted families against each other. I have hurt the ones I loved. But I intend to rectify it all, and you may help me if you wish, for my time is the seed from which this sorrow bloomed."

Serece said nothing.

"Consider as we walk," Behtréal said, towing her gently. "As chaos claims the night."

He called to the lokyns with his mind, called to them through the incorporeal mirkúr network through which they were bound to his will. *Awaken from your sleep. Cast away your veils of flesh and reap this city of its soul. Vengeance for the sake of... Behtréal sighed. Just reclamation. He had lived amongst these people—most were noble. It wasn't fair for sons and daughters to pay for the sins of their fathers and mothers, but that was life— unfair.* His heart ached for having issued the command, but he could not afford a heavily armed response, not again. This time would be different. This time he would succeed.

CAILEAN WASN'T sure how long he and Leyandra had been walking. They hadn't spoken much either. *So much for talk,* he thought, though he wasn't really complaining. The walk did him good, helped to clear his mind. The air still smelled like shit here in the farmlands, but at least it was *clean* shit.

"So. Nightmares," he said, hoping it would prompt Leyandra into conversation.

"Nightmares," she echoed. She had a faraway look in her eyes.

Cailean raised an eyebrow. "…About?"

She took a deep breath. "The night I lost my illum. Have I ever told you?"

"In passing," Cailean said. He squeezed her arm. "Say what you need."

"Having your illum reaped from your flesh…" She spat in the grass. "It was so cold I thought they had lit me on fire. And I've had to relive that moment every night for the past three days. Always burning in my sleep as those creatures force their way beneath my skin and steal a piece of me, knowing I can never get it back. D'you know what that feels like, losing something irreplaceable?"

Cailean furrowed his brow. "You know I do," he murmured, taking Leyandra's hand. "Often times I think of Bar, of Harbanan, of that stupid mistake that left me looking like the ugly fuck I am."

"But have you ever had a piece of you *removed*?" Leyandra asked. "Do you understand that violation, Cailean?"

Cailean was silent a moment, then he nodded. "Bar, he…" Fuck all, but this was hard to admit. He'd not told a soul in all the years since. "That night in the cathedral—he killed me, Ley. Drove that dagger through my heart and left me there to die. He stole my life…and then he gave it back, and how do you think that feels? Comprehending what's beyond, only to have your murderous husband bring you back to knife him in the heart." He took a deep breath, resisting the urge to retch.

They walked in silence for a time. Cailean thought he smelled smoke in the air, but the odor went as quickly as it'd come. He felt nauseous from their brief conversation, for having learned Leyandra's pain and spouting his. What was it he'd wished all those weeks ago? *Amnesia and a second dead eye,* he recalled. *Maybe a blow to the head or a blade through the heart. Whatever it takes to forget.*

"Except that isn't what you want." For the second time that night, Bar emerged from a twist of light. *"For all your woe, you know you want to keep your memories, the history that's made you who you are."*

Cailean said nothing lest Leyandra think him crazier than he already was.

"I can hear your thoughts," said Bar. *"I'm memory, after all, and memory"*—he tapped Cailean's skull—*"resides within."*

Fuck you, then, Cailean thought. *You must be stupid to think I want this rattling around inside my head. All the bullshit, all the sorrow...why in Perdition would anyone want to hold on to that?*

"Like I said, my sweet. History," said Bar. *"Introspection as a means to personal growth."*

And I suppose you know all about personal growth, do you? That's rich coming from the man who slaughtered half a city then left his husband dead in a fucking cathedral. Cailean spat in Bar's direction. It passed through Bar and hit the grass. *Why would I want to remember any of that? Why would I want to remember you?*

"You'll have to find the answer to that yourself," Bar said. *"I can't speak for the dead."*

Wish you wouldn't speak at all, Cailean growled.

Bar shrugged, dissolving into the night.

Cailean reached into his jacket and cursed. He'd forgotten his flask. He took another whiff of late-night air, wrinkling his nose. "Does it smell like smoke to you?"

"Smells like shit," Leyandra said. Humoring Cailean, though, she raised her nose. "Faint, but yes, it smells like smoke." She turned about, settling north toward the city proper. "Cailean…"

But he'd already turned, swayed by the cacophony of distant screams. The city was aglow with bursts of illum, swirls of mirkúr braiding, twisting in a violent dance as fire licked the walls. Shrieks of varying pitch sent shivers up his spine. Without a second thought he sprinted north, Leyandra at his heels. Fuck all, but if they were going to die, they were going die with blades in hand and lokyn ash on blade.

Cailean knew they were fucked the moment they entered the city proper, and it wasn't because of the myriad lokyns ripping flesh from bone. Leyandra had dropped to her knees and was retching something black that reeked of death.

"F-F…uck," she gurgled, looking up at Cailean. Her eyes were stark white save a small black dot of a symbol where her pupils once had been. Her face had begun to crack; black veins webbed outward from her eyes. "…ailean —rrruuuuuun…"

She could tell him to run, but she couldn't tell him how or where. He scooped her up into his arms and started back the way they'd come, into the farmlands now ablaze and half concealed by acrid smoke. Cailean coughed every several steps, and Leyandra wailed. *Keepers, what the fuck am I doing?* And where could he go? What could he do?

He started as a lokyn shambled from the smoke, wearing the flesh of a little girl. Another followed, this one a little boy, and another, a woman, presumably their mother. Cailean had seen a lot in his years, but this was one of the worst in recent memory. He shifted course and headed east before the demons could make him.

Screams ruled the night as Cailean ran. It was hard to tell where exactly he was going, but he didn't care. Eventually the smoke began to thin. In the distance he could make out the burning ruin of a manor house, swarmed with lokyns slipping into suits of flesh. Beyond that, a small copse. He shifted course a second time, praying to the Keepers that he'd not been seen. Considering how thunderfooted Cailean was, and Leyandra's gurgling, it was a fucking miracle they'd made it this far.

He jogged into the copse, keeping on until his legs gave out beneath him and he tripped. Leyandra flew from his arms and landed with a thud. She rolled a couple of times before coming to rest on her back, wispy threads of mirkúr leaking from the cracks on her face. Her deep red hair had burnt to black and Cailean knew—he *fucking knew*.

She reached for him, face contorted in a rictus of whatever it was that people felt when they knew they were at the end of their line. When their friend knew they were at the end of their line. Cailean crawled to Leyandra, fresh tears welling in his eyes. He forced himself to his knees and pull her into his arms, clutching her to his chest.

How? How the fuck—

Bar watched from beside a black stone entombed in the grass a few feet from where they were. His expression was solemn. Tears dripped from his eyes too, telling Cailean all he needed to know.

"P...whee...se. Caaahleeuh..." Leyandra garbled, with one hand clawing at her face. "I...on'd...wha..nt..." She tugged weakly at his jacket with the other, as if she had known the dagger would be there.

"Ley—" She tugged harder, and what could he do but oblige? He nodded, a lump in his throat. "Fuck," he whispered. "*Fuck.*"

Time felt slow as he finally drew the blade, slow and horribly surreal. There was moonlight peeking through the leaves, and the farmlands were ablaze with ravenous light. He wasn't sure how long he'd sat there holding Ley. The air was sick with the odor of burning flesh, pungent with the tang of blood.

Cailean cradled her against him, dagger hovering over top her heart. "Look at me," he whispered to her. "Look in my eyes, love. Look here, all right? Just look..."

He didn't watch the dagger punch through flesh and bone, didn't watch the life leave her eyes, but he felt it in her body going limp. Felt it in her body growing colder as the minutes passed.

Eventually he did look. He cupped her cheek. It possessed a modicum of warmth despite the blood crying around the dagger impaled in her chest. The very dagger with which he'd been forced to slay Bar. "You fool," he hissed of himself, choking back tears. "You ignorant fucking fool."

Once marked, always marked.

He closed his eyes and wept as entropy claimed the city for its own.

15

SORROW

Serece could see the Hall rising up in the distance, as of yet untouched by pandemonium and fear. She looked at this thing she trailed, watching it take the shape of a woman she knew to be dead—Anayela An. She felt sick at the implication this ghost of yesteryears evoked. For a creature that claimed itself ashamed of what it'd done and planned to do, Te Mirkvahíl seemed quite intent on making Theailys' end a festival of wretchedness and everlasting pain.

"You mean to kill him," she said. She knew the answer in her heart, but she needed to hear the demon say it, whether for peace of mind or something else, Serece was unsure. "Theailys An. You mean to make his death a horrible thing. Why?"

"I do," Te Mirkvahíl replied. "But there is more to this than death."

And wasn't that a vague response? Serece wasn't sure what to make of it. As far as she could tell there was *only*

302

death and the possible subconscious joy that torturing people brought. After all, the lokyns took horrendous pleasure in the pain of those they killed.

"Such as?" She hadn't meant to ask, but curiosity was a beast uncaged. The closer they drew to the Hall, the more she longed to know. Not necessarily about temporal alteration, but rather what made a creature like Te Mirkvahíl the way it was. What made this murderous, melancholy demon tick?

Te Mirkvahíl glanced back and—were those *tears* in the demon's eyes? It turned its head before Serece could properly analyze what she'd seen. What sorrow could this monster feel that was profound enough to elicit *tears*? She racked her mind, partially hypnotized by the demon's swaying hips, initially awkward, eventually graceful, as though this walk was something familiar and practiced.

Oh Perdition. The realization sent a shiver through Serece. Had Anayela ever been real, or had it always been Te Mirkvahíl? If the latter were true, poor Theailys An had been a puppet since the start.

Serece scratched at an itch beneath her cloak, then shifted focus to the night. Her trembling had subsided some ways back; she was running on adrenaline, now. Adrenaline, curiosity, and fear. If she were to abet Te Mirkvahíl in altering time, in forging something better than this miserable reality that'd come to be, she needed more than simple truths. She needed to understand the reasons why, lest she follow out of fear and reckless despondency.

"Did you..." Keepers, but it was such a peculiar question to ask of this...this *entity* in whose presence she felt little more than a speck of dust. "What I mean to say—"

"Is did I care for him?" Te Mirkvahíl asked. "As I said, there is more to this than death"—the demon's shoulders slumped, and the slump elicited a sigh—"and I have hurt the ones I loved."

Serece furrowed her brow. Not in confusion—and she *was* confused—but in commiseration. "I know what that feels like." And before she knew it, she was telling Te Mirkvahíl of her sisters and child, though the demon had apparently gleaned this earlier in the night. Or time. It was hard to know considering how ubiquitous the creature was.

"Will you tell me something of yourself?" Serece inquired.

"Perhaps," Te Mirkvahíl said. "What do you wish to know?"

"Did you have a name?" Serece asked. "*Do* you have a name?"

"I did and I do," Te Mirkvahíl said. "Behtréal Dov'an."

The twins had sought a journal with that surname in their dream. "And who is Remulus?"

Te Mirkvahíl was silent a moment. "My brother. But he is dead."

Serece had struck a nerve, as the demon offered nothing else in the way of conversation, let alone a passing glance. *So many stones unturned,* she thought. This thing was more complex than she had ever dreamt.

"*And what will you do, Serece?*" asked Rejya, manifesting at her side. "*You harbor fear, yet with every passing second curiosity seeks to reign supreme. Destruction gives you pause, but the mystery of Te Mirkvahíl puts haste in every step.*"

She *was* walking a bit faster.

"*Renew your people. Learn the genesis, the history of Te Mirk-*

vahíl," Rejya urged. "*How long have you yearned to be free from your shackles, to see the world beyond the rock and snow to which your flesh and soul are bound?*"

So terribly, achingly long. Serece had never ventured very far.

"All right," she said, drawing a look from Te Mirkvahíl. "I'll help."

The demon offered a tiny nod, and they continued on their way.

THE CITY WAS SILENT, *and this was music to Te Mirkvahíl. It was a melody of ignorance, one that roused in him a surfeit of delight. Contrary to his actions to this point, Te Mirkvahíl enjoyed the act of slaughter. He adored it. He always had and always would. Unfortunately, the severity of his enterprise required he refrain from spilling blood, and what a shame that was.*

A terrible thing indeed.

He continued up the tree-lined campus promenade, its entirety wreathed in the wonderful uncertainty of night. In the distance stood the Hall, its windows bright with the light of its studious occupants. He ached to put them down, to end them, but he knew should they look his way the coward in his flesh and mind would keep his urge to reap at bay.

"*You look well tonight,*" *a passing acolyte said. His face was slick with sweat, pupils at rest with the accomplishment of a hard day's work.* "*Keepers be with you.*"

Te Mirkvahíl smiled and bowed his head. He wore the skin of Anasharon Anor, Faro Fatego's dead wife. "*May They light your way." The voice inside him clucked its approval as* Te Mirkvahíl *continued on his way. It was perhaps the sorriest thing he'd heard in years, and he frowned.*

"What's another soul preserved, another body spared?" *Te Luminíl inquired.* "When we rewrite history, none of this, none of them, will have ever come to be. Why care about such trivial things?"

Because, *Te Mirkvahíl thought.* Destroying them brings me joy.

THE CITY SHRIEKED and it was music to Behtréal's ears. It was a melody of anguish, one that roused in him a surfeit of despair. Contrary to his actions to this point, Behtréal did not enjoy the act of killing. He despised it. He always had and always would. Unfortunately, the severity of his enterprise required spilling blood, and what a shame that was.

A terrible thing indeed.

He continued up the tree-lined campus promenade, its entirety wreathed in the mystery of night. Serece trailed silently behind him. In the distance stood the Hall, its windows dark with the fear of its studious occupants. He need not put them down, but he knew should they try to block his way the monster in his flesh and mind would take their illum and their souls.

"You don't look so well," a passing acolyte remarked. His face was slick with sweat, pupils dilated like a spooked cat. "Are you all right?"

Behtréal smiled. The voice inside him hissed contentedly

as a thread of mirkúr speared the acolyte through the chest. "Better now," he said, extending his hand to reap the fallen soul. Its objecting scream was perhaps the sorriest thing Behtréal had heard in years, and he frowned.

"*What's another body in the grave?*" Te Mirkvahíl inquired. "*When we rewrite history, none of this, none of* them, *will have ever come to be. Why care about such trivial things?*"

Because, Behtréal thought. *Destroying them brings me pain.*

"I'LL HELP."

Serece thought on the words she had uttered little less than half an hour ago. She thought of the acolyte lying dead on the promenade, reaped of his light. She thought of the chaos sundering a night that'd once been calm and wondered —did she really *want* to help? To abet in torment of a magnitude such as this? Death on such a scale? She chewed her lower lip, drawing blood.

"*No such thing as a bloodless reclamation,*" Rejya said, and Serece started at the voice. "*There is always a price for such things, Serece. You should know this by now. After all, you gained a father and all it cost you was your mother's love.*"

She never loved me, Serece bit back. *She would much rather have seen me dead. She said so herself, or do you not recall that evening in the temple?* Her ears twitched at the memory, at the shame. *Maybe—* What? Maybe she could change that, change how her mother felt if she committed to breaking this world in favor of building another? Serece had had some crazy thoughts in her life, but Keepers this one may have taken the cake as the Ariathans liked to say.

She chewed her lower lip as she went, ears twitching at every other thought that popped into her head, fingers aching to wrap themselves around the hilts of her blades.

Now there's *a stupid idea.* Turning on Te Mirkvahíl. Keepers, what a situation she'd gotten herself into now. A lose-lose if ever there'd been one. Attack the demon, lose her life. Aid the demon and affirm her monstrous tendencies. Her selfishness.

Her heart pounded against her chest with every step. She was thinking of her father, now. What would he do? Would he have ever considered siding with Te Mirkvahíl? Shit, what about Phantaxis? Te Mirkvahíl had killed him, but what had they spoken of that night in the mountains? Had Serece's blood father tried negotiating with this thing?

She sighed to herself. *Maybe I'm asking the wrong questions of myself.* Phantaxis was little more than blood, and Undrensil, for his love and tenderness, was always last to the blade; he abhorred violence. So... *What would mother do?*

Serece knew the answer before she'd finished asking the question, and that was enough.

THE HALL INTERIOR WAS WARM. *The pale light of illum wisps reflected off the polished floor, and the mirth of achievement soaked the air. Te Mirkvahíl walked with measured steps, a smile drawn tight across his borrowed lips. The merriment of apprentice exploit brought him joy, the joy of knowing that their light would soon be his, the coward voice inside his head be damned.*

"Only him," *Te Luminíl said.* "Only Fatego."

What's another body in the grave? *Anasharon inquired.* You said it yourself: when we rewrite history, none of this, none of *them,* will have ever come to be. Why care about such trivial things?

Because, *Te Luminíl said.* Destroying them brings me pain.

Te Mirkvahíl chuckled inwardly. Pain is the blood of life. Pain lets you know you're alive. It would do you well to remember that. Think where you might be without it. One incapable of feeling such an awful thing would not be here, a moment away from possessing the means to alter time. Guard your pain as you would your heart.

Te Luminíl held his tongue, and Te Mirkvahíl continued through the Hall. He could smell Faro Fatego and he ached for his attentive gaze, hungered for the agony his eyes would weep when he beheld the beautiful, shambling corpse of Anasharon Anor for the first time since her death.

THE HALL INTERIOR WAS COLD. The pale light of moonbeams reflected off the polished floor, and the silence of fear infested the air. Behtréal walked with measured steps, Anayela's resurrected lips drawn to thin line. The whispers of apprentice terror brought him sorrow, the regret of knowing that their light would soon be his, the murderous voice inside his head be damned.

"*All of them,*" Te Mirkvahíl hissed.

What's another soul preserved, another body spared? Behtréal asked. *You said it yourself: when we rewrite history, none of this, none of them, will have ever come to be. Why care about such trivial things?*

Because, Te Mirkvahíl said. *Destroying them brings me joy.*

Behtréal hissed inwardly. *Then you know little of joy. Joy is the warmth in your heart that lets you know you're alive. Joy is holding your son. Joy is kissing your wife. Joy is knowing you're a moment away from possessing the means to alter time. Guard this feeling with the same ferocity with which you ache to kill.*

Te Mirkvahíl held its tongue, and Behtréal continued through the Hall. He could smell Theailys An and feared for his attentive gaze, trembled at the agony his eyes would weep when he beheld Anayela's beautiful, shambling corpse for the first time since her death.

SERECE DREW HER DAGGERS. The best she could do was slow the demon down and hope Theailys An was keen to their presence in time to flee. It was folly to think she was going to make it out alive and she accepted that. *So, let this be my expiation.*

She charged Te Mirkvahíl, but the demon side-stepped easily, sword manifesting, emerald eyes glistening hungrily. Serece snarled, taking a defensive stance.

"I wished otherwise," Te Mirkvahíl said, nearing at a walk, mirkúr blade gripped tightly in one hand. "But I knew you would turn. They always do in the end. Tell me, what swayed you, Serece?"

"Does it matter?" she asked, retreating as Te Mirkvahíl advanced.

"To me, yes," the demon said.

There was sincerity in those words. Serece gripped her daggers tight. "Because," she said, "I have sins to pay for. I don't want to be the monster I think I am. Willingly killing a man in cold blood…" She shook her head. "No."

"I admire that," Te Mirkvahíl said.

The demon lunged, closing the distance between them with unnatural ease. Serece deflected the blow, but the force behind the attack sent her staggering backwards into the wall. Her head ricocheted off the stones and a sharp pain spread through her skull.

"You are quicker than most," Te Mirkvahíl said. "But still not as quick as you'd like. I expect it's the plague, the internal decay. The atrophy my presence incites."

Like smoke, the demon stood before Serece and dragged its blade across her gut. Blood spewed from the wound. She shrieked as she fell to the floor. Never had she felt such agony. The sundered flesh and entrails, the mirkúr slithering beneath her flesh, hastening her decay. She smelled horrible; the wound already reeked of rot.

Te Mirkvahíl dismissed its blade and knelt before Serece. The demon cupped her cheeks with hands like ice, boring into her with the emerald eyes of a woman lost to dirt and worms. "The end will be here soon. I am sorry that it came to this. Truly. I had thought perhaps our mutual abhorrence of the Ariathan Empire would have been enough, but I was wrong."

Serece parted her lips to speak, but she could only manage

a pained gasp. *Mutual...abhorrence?* She clutched at the wound as if doing so would make it right, would subdue the entrails threatening to leak between her flesh.

"*You are a fool,*" Rejya said. She stood several feet behind Te Mirkvahíl, leaning against the opposite wall, arms crossed to her chest. "*You always were. You were offered a chance at reclamation and, predictably, you let your blades lead you astray. Once again, your selfishness prevails. You are a monster. You are the worst of our mother.*"

Tears trailed down Serece's cheeks. Maybe Rejya was right. Maybe she had been selfish to refuse Te Mirkvahíl and the chance to rewrite time. And maybe she'd let her daggers point the way because violence was the thing Serece knew best, because it was what her mother knew best. An old and trusted friend, the most bitter of drinks. Little pleasure and a lot of pain.

Te Mirkvahíl leaned in and kissed her forehead. "Farewell, my dear daughter of the mountain. Should we meet again I doubt you'll have any memory of this night, if you ever come to be at *all.*"

The demon stood and started on its way, gossamer threads of shadow trailing in its wake. Serece sat there against the wall, the blood loss and the stench of her dying body pushing her closer toward unconsciousness, not that there was anything she could do. She'd no vials of snow on her person, and even if she had, there was little she could do with such a trivial amount.

Her head lolled to the side and her vision shifted in and out. Rejya's lips were moving but the words were soundless. Instead, Serece thought of her companions. Of Fenrin, lying dead in the Bastion courtyard. Of Theailys An, surely soon to be dead. What of Ronomar and Raelza, of Aunt Fiel?

Serece retched. The blood and bile smacked her shoulder and dripped down her arm, pooling on the floor with the occasional sad plop. *What a shit end.* She thought of Theailys, the man who'd no doubt forged the weapon of their end. And here she was, the woman who had nearly sided with Te Mirkvahíl. She wept at the stupidity of it all. *At least we screwed this up together, right?* Keepers, how the hell could she have ever come so close to following Te Mirkvahíl, to abetting in the slaughter and annihilation of an entire world? The tears came heavier at that thought. So many dead, massacred, and for what? What had the demon meant by "mutual abhorrence?"

She was sobbing now, pain erupting from her gut as every violent breath unknit her flesh a little more. "You could have…a-at l-l-least let…me underst…and." Even monsters have souls, Rejya once had said, and in this moment, it resounded horribly with Serece. What loss, what tragedy had driven such a creature as Te Mirkvahíl to all this trickery and death, to deciding time and history should be rewritten to its whim?

Does it really matter? hissed a voice from deep inside her mind. *We'll soon be dead. Why linger on a question for which you'll never know the answer?*

It had a point, she conceded. *Maybe you're right. Maybe this is what I get for slaughtering Rejya and Taür. For trying to resurrect my little Vhora. For allowing myself to be swayed by a monster.* She squeezed her eyelids shut at the memories, sucking in a ragged breath. *Maybe I really was meant for this, to suffer and fail.* That was all her life had been these last years. Perdition, that was all her life had *ever* been. A bastard child whose mother looked on her with shame, whose deity father had doomed her to a life of misery amongst the snow and rocks. This was a fitting end, then, to a child unbidden by her blood.

Serece placed her hand to her heart and prayed to Vol'anan. "Mother of Souls," she whispered, "ferry my soul to the fair skies above. Love me in the Second Life as fiercely as my mother loathed me in the First."

———

BEHTRÉAL LAMENTED her end as he went. He hadn't wanted that. Such pain and misery—he'd been sincere in wishing she would join in him in the Temporal Sea. In wishing they might keep her people, the phantaxians, from the plague. But this was how it had to be, and he accepted that.

He turned attention to Theailys An, to The Keepers' Wrath, dragging the tip of his blade along the floor as he went. It served as a warning, and he hoped the Hall's occupants discerned it as such. He didn't want to spill unnecessary blood, not anymore. The majority of the Illumurgists here were acolytes and apprentices, and why should they have to suffer for the sins of their mothers and fathers? If they wanted to escape the destruction of this place, he would allow it. His war was against those who had brought the war to him those many years ago. The Faithbringer generals, the Master Illumurgists, and the Lord Wardens who had razed Zorahl. The crown itself.

"The endgame is all but here," Te Mirkvahíl hissed gleefully.

They had all but brought the city to its knees, and the queen would soon be dead if Ronomar and Raelza hadn't finished her already. Once Helveden was destroyed, there would be no stopping Behtréal.

Funny. He allowed himself a melancholy smile. *I thought the same thing last time and look how well that turned out. Foiled by Khar Am.* Behtréal had been far more careful this time, more calculating in his methods, and it showed.

He continued on his way before stepping out onto the grass of the garden. The garden wrapped around the rear of the Hall, and at its center was an oak tree for which Behtréal had a particular fondness.

Theailys held The Keepers' Wrath in the palm of his hand. Years of theory and three straight days of forging had finally seen the creation of this weapon to fruition. He should have felt the weight lessen, should have felt the tightness in his chest subside even the smallest bit, yet he did not. Instead, as Theailys held this power focus, no bigger than an apple, he felt a combination of uncertainty and dread, laced with a trace amount of desperate hope, as if all the opposition to this weapon's genesis had finally made its home in the center of his mind.

Theailys placed the orb on the pedestal beside his desk. His hands were trembling horribly, and he clasped them together in an effort to calm himself, the little good it did. The trembling made its way up his arms, to his shoulders and torso, and he found himself shaking, shivering almost, as the weight of his reality pressed itself upon him like a serpent strangling its prey.

Breathe, he urged of himself, though he struggled even at that. Each breath was ragged and apprehensive, the opposite of what his mother had taught him as a boy. He closed his eyes, hoping the darkness might see fit to ease his troubled mind, but it only served to chill his blood.

"Shift your focus elsewhere," Remy said. *"To a memory that brings you joy. To a thought that fills your heart with hope. Think of a distant land bereft of war and death. Think of the ocean breeze against your face as you set sail for this new and wondrous place."*

Theailys *had* said that he would leave the country once the war was done, and it was ludicrous to think he might go back on that. What was left for him here? Why remain in the city in a country where his life had been an anxious wreck at best?

I've always wanted to visit Liosene, he thought. *Good whiskey from what I hear.*

Remy scoffed. *"Liosene is a cesspool of rape and slaughter."*

Theailys shrugged. *Still sounds better than Ariath. Than Helveden.*

"Quite a low bar," Remy said. *"But I suppose I understand."*

Theailys twiddled his thumbs, gazing at the open door at the far end of his office chamber. *What do you think of temporal alteration, Remy? At first it seemed a ludicrous notion, but...I don't know. Serece seemed hellbent on the possibility, on the idea that Te Mirkvahíl might rewrite history. Let's pretend all this is true: what reason would Te Mirkvahíl have for wanting to accomplish this?*

"If I were to venture a guess," said Remy, *"I would say the ruined city Ouran'an is at the center of it all. Both you and the*

twins have seen this city in your dreams, walked its dead halls, even, and the consensus seems to be that Te Mirkvahíl is an old Reshaper. So..."

You think Te Mirkvahíl is trying to save its city? Theailys asked.

"Perhaps. I can think of little else," said Remy. *"If...if you were Te Mirkvahíl and your city had been destroyed, would you not do everything in your power to see it restored? Would you not try altering time if you possessed the means?"*

Theailys frowned. *You're asking that I empathize with Te Mirkvahíl in an entirely hypothetical situation. You do realize this, right?*

"I do, and I did for the simple fact that empathy allows for a better understanding of the enemy," Remy said. *"Ariath has fought this entity for years, centuries, even, yet has anyone ever thought to inquire as to why Te Mirkvahíl saw fit to start this war, or if Te Mirkvahíl was even the one to start it?"*

Those were dangerously bold questions, the latter of which had never even occurred to Theailys. He had always been taught, always assumed that Ariath had simply retaliated toward hostile intent. But what if the truth was more complex? He felt cold at the notion that the war might not be as straightforward as he'd always thought. From that came a queasiness in his gut, one that grew more violent as he gazed upon The Keepers' Wrath.

A faint whisper rippled outward from the center of Theailys' mind, growing louder the longer he looked at the orb. Somehow, sitting here, transfixed on the fruit of his theory and craftsmanship, felt...familiar. He reached for The Keepers' Wrath, but stopped a couple inches short, hand quivering as the whisper's volume rose. At first, he thought it was Faro, struggling to flip the coin, to wrest control from Remy and supplant him as the dominant voice. But the whisper grew to a distressed murmur, and Theailys realized Remy was the source.

"I have lived this once," said Remy. *"This scene, this calm before the storm."* He wailed with such affliction that Theailys thought his skull was going to crack. *"The Keepers' Wrath must be destroyed."*

Theailys steadied himself, head still pounding. *What are you talking about? Remy, what—*

He grabbed the orb, lurching from his seat against his will, and started toward the oaken door at the far end of the chamber, leading out to a patio at the rear of the Hall. Theailys pushed, trying to wrest control of his body back, but Remy, in all his fear and desperation, was undeterred. In fact, his control of Theailys seemed only to grow as they opened the door and stumbled out onto the grass.

WHAT IS GOING ON?

Remy held his tongue, but fractured recollections flashed across Theailys' mind. An office chamber—*his* office chamber—flooded by Illumurgists with threads of shadow leaking from their eyes. In the center of the chamber stood a man, strikingly, terribly reminiscent of Theailys in the face save purple eyes instead of gray. In one hand he held a mirkúr blade, in the other The Keepers' Wrath. It was identical to the very sphere he carried with him now.

Reality melted as Theailys ran, as he became the figure in the scene.

"They have come to claim it in his name," said Remy. *"Faro, you must run."*

Theailys—*Faro*—lunged at the lokyn nearest him (he was undoubtedly sure that was what these creatures were) and swung the mirkúr blade clean across the demon's gut. Blood, smoke, and a sick black liquid leaked between the flesh and robes, and the creature shrieked as Faro reaped its spirit for his own, drawing the dark essence into the orb. He finished the other three off in a similar fashion. They'd obviously been lesser demons, and those stood little chance against a Master Illumurgist such as he was.

Faro turned, starting for the door at the chamber's rear, but stopped abruptly at the call of his name. He turned, a cold sweat dripping down his face and neck, down his spine as a slender silhouette took shape some hundred feet away in the dimness of the hall. It walked with measured steps, with swaying hips, a pair of blue eyes shining brightly in the gloom.

"My dearest Faro."

The chill beneath his flesh intensified. Faro knew the master of the voice and knew her well. To hear her whisper such a name was agonizing. Only one had ever called to him like that, and she was four years dead.

"Anasharon."

He approached this thing, this reflection of his wife with guarded steps, The Keepers' Wrath and mirkúr blade still tightly in his grip. She seemed to float, to walk the air like faeries do. Her tresses fluttered in the breeze her steps conjured.

"Come now, Faro," said this thing, his wife. *"Come now, let*

me feel your touch." A sob escaped her phantom lips and she reached a quivering arm his way. *"So cold. So cold where I have been. Won't you..."* The darkness melted from her frame and pooled around her feet. She stood before him, motionless in winter-white with silky hair and eyes of blue. Her skin was fair, her thin lips pink, as though she'd not been touched by death. She was just as he recalled and looked exactly as she had the night that they'd been wed.

"Won't you hold me as you did so long ago? Faro?"

He jumped. Her voice had shifted, now filled with life, so unlike the haunting call he'd heard. He dismissed his blade and stepped toward Anasharon, yearning for the sweet familiarity of her voice. He reached his hand to her face. It was cold as death, if not more so.

"How could you let this happen?" she inquired tearfully. Darkness wreathed around them and the Hall dissolved, a forest rising up from memory to take its place.

"Anasharon?"

She spun away, dancing sadly through the skeleton trees, her dark tresses bouncing as she went. Her eyes shone bright amongst the gloom, never straying from his face. They bore into Faro, slicing open wounds he'd done his best to suture shut. A throbbing pain shot through his chest, one he hadn't felt in years, not since he'd reaped her soul, then held her as she'd died. In the burial mounds he'd placed her corpse and carved her name into a stone. He'd sat beside that grave for hours every day, wish her back. Yet she stood before him now, dancing about the trees. But there was something different in her eyes, something cheerless, odd, and hollow. Something dead.

"Anasharon!"

Like smoke she was before him, seething. "YOU DID THIS TO ME, FARO! YOU STOLE MY SOUL AND KEPT IT FOR YOUR OWN!"

Faro watched her twirl away, mouth agape, eyes about to burst.

"You let me wilt away so long ago," she whispered. "You let your memories of me fade. Are you ashamed of me, my Faro? Have you no desire to keep me in your thoughts? Was my soul the only thing you hungered for?"

Faro fell to his knees. "How could you think such awful things, Anasharon?" he croaked, on the verge of tears. "What you say, it isn't true! Of all the things my mind has fractured, never could I let it break my thoughts of you. You are always constant in my dreams. Never once have I forgotten you." He bowed his head. "Never once I have ignored the shame I feel, knowing that you're dead because of me."

Anasharon said nothing. Her blue eyes turned a somber gray, then she slipped away. Faro leapt to his feet and chased her through the trees. He would not lose her a second time.

She led him to a clearing where the night sky shone. It was a twisted, ugly mass of charcoal, lightless and bereft of life. Behind her stood the remnants of a church, a crumbling thing with toppled spires stretching toward the clouds and stained-glass windows where the eyes of the long-dead looked out at nothing but the darkness of the grove. The trees around the church were bare and dry, the ground beneath it cracked. Fog hung in the air, and mist crept through the trees. There was a sense of hopelessness about this place, and Faro knew that he had found it. He had found the place—

"In which I died," Anasharon said, as though she'd read his mind.

Faro turned his gaze to her. A cold breeze slipped between the trees and snaked around the woman. Departed was the gilded portrait memory had bestowed, washed away beneath the ashy night, replaced instead by the truth that was her hollow, rotting corpse. Faro wiped away the tears, his emotions threatening to rend him from the inside out. Sorrow, grief, and desperation consumed him. She'd been so real, so very real.

Faro stood before her, letting memories pass through on repeat before they fizzled into nothing, leaving him alone once more. Anasharon drifted toward him, placed a ghoulish hand upon his cheek, and wiped away his sorrow as he mourned. She took up her lively form once more, whispering softly in his ear.

"Stay with me, always and forever."

And for a moment, yet again, Faro fell prey to her lifeless mouth, aching horribly to say, "Of course, my Anasharon, of course I'll stay." But he kept his tongue, watching as his seconds-long delusion vanished in a breeze, replaced again with death. He glared into its eyeless holes and snarled, "You…you are not my Anasharon. You are a foulness from the trees and if you linger but a second more your death shall come again." The corpse, the thing, did not relent, and Faro pushed its clammy hands away. "Just leave me be."

Anasharon whimpered sadly as he shoved her to the side and stalked his way to the church. He placed a hand upon the heavy, oaken barrier and pushed. He could see, could smell the gore-filled reality of the Hall within and longed for its ugly, terrible comfort, to be away from whatever thing had come to him. The doors creaked open and he slipped into the forlorn, antique temple, Anasharon vanishing from sight, her voice an echo out of time.

"Always and forever…"

Faro gasped as the Hall materialized around him. His chest stung, and blood spilled from his mouth. Anasharon stood before him, a grin spread wide across her face, the hilt of a mirkúr blade clutched tightly in her hand. She relented, and Faro dropped to his knees, reality undulating as he dragged himself across the floor.

"I wish I could say I was sorry," Anasharon said, trailing at a walk. "Rather, the coward inside me does. I would like to say thank you for the tremendous amount of work. Without you, Faro Fatego, my undertaking might not have come to fruition."

Faro dragged himself through the chamber and collapsed by the pedestal, The Keepers' Wrath rolling from his hand. Tears dripped from the corners of his eyes, blood from the corners of his mouth. *Keepers, what have I done?*

Anasharon extended a hand and tugged on his soul.

Keepers…

He could see his corpse on the floor as he floated toward the demon.

what

Faro could see, feel amidst a swirl of smoke the demon taking up his corpse and wearing him like a suit. Could hear the monster's incorporeal laugh and the shrieks of myriad stolen souls.

have I…

More Illumurgists flooded the chamber, blades in hand. Faro knew they were doomed.

done?

The memory dissolved, and Theailys screamed as the waking world came into focus with the ferocity of a fire eating grass. He stumbled, tripping over his feet and falling to ground before a giant tree. An oak tree.

Remy was screaming too, trying desperately to force Theailys to his feet, but the shock of the memory kept him planted where he was, trembling madly.

I WAS HIM. I WAS HIM. FARO FATEGO.

"GET UP! GET UP, THE DEMON COMES!" Remy shrieked.

He could hear the screaming now, to the distant west but loud enough to know the storm had come. That it wouldn't stop until it'd claimed its prize. He clutched The Keepers' Wrath to his chest and cursed himself for having ever been so foolish.

"Please," Remy whimpered. *"You have to get up. You have to run from here. You have to destroy The Keepers' Wrath lest it annihilate us all."*

So many questions. So much pain. Tears leaking from his eyes, Theailys forced himself to stand and stagger past the tree. Beyond it, though, was something he had not foreseen—his darling wife, as beautiful as she'd been the night she'd died. Urine ran down Theailys' legs at the sight before him, as he stood there, stuck in place.

"No..." he croaked, lower lip trembling, a lump in his throat. "No, I...*I killed you.*" Anayela approached, boring into him with that beautiful emerald stare, the skirt of her gown fluttering with every step she took. "This isn't real."

Like smoke she was before him. So quickly he'd not seen her disappear nor reappear. She just was. She reached up to caress his cheek, and he could see there were tears in her eyes too. He faltered at her touch and dropped to his knees, but Anayela went down with him, tipping his chin up with her thumb so she could look into his eyes.

"I really *am* sorry," she whispered. "Our love—I want to you know it was real." She leaned in to capture his lips, and she tasted like honey, like she always had.

Remy was still screaming, but the sound had faded to a dull buzz. *Everything* had faded to a dull buzz, and the world was nearly black as pitch. There was rain, too, and the cold was nice. It'd numbed him long enough to mask the pain of sundered flesh and the heat of blood.

Anayela pulled away, taking care to remove the blade from his chest with a gentle hand. When had she summoned it? "It will all be over soon."

It must have been the blood loss and the torment. He imagined Anayela taking up the orb. Felt a tugging on his soul as sorrow spilled from Anayela's eyes.

Keepers…

Theailys could see his corpse on the ground, just as Faro Fatego had so long ago.

what

He could hear the monster's gulps and sobs, the shrieks of myriad stolen souls.

have I…

His spirit floated toward the silver moon that would end the world.

done?

BEHTRÉAL LAID Theailys gently beneath the tree and closed his eyes. He had brought this man two lifetime's worth of pain. Closing his eyes to the darkness of this world was the very least he could do.

"Someday, somehow, in another time perhaps, this will all make sense," he whispered, looking over Theailys' still and battered form. Behtréal placed his hand on Theailys' chest, over the spot where he had run the poor man through, and with his mind he tugged, calling Theailys' illum, calling his soul. Taking it with him away from this ugly place—*that* was the very least he could do.

"I told you pain would rule this night," he whispered, half to himself, half to the memory of Serece in a firm but gentle tone. It was a shame she had turned, but then again life was full of shame, was it not? "What is done, is done. Soon the real work begins." As if these last centuries had been little more than leisure. He stood and started from the tree.

"*Where now?*" Te Mirkvahíl inquired. There was such monstrous glee in that voice.

To a Place Where the Sun is Silent, Behtréal said, and in a rush of shadow he fled, leaving Helveden to its violent end.

16

PREMONITION

The Sixth Month, Illum Year 1144

L eyandra had always been skeptical of illum dreams. Her mother and aunt both swore by the damned things and her father claimed to have foreseen Leyandra's birth in one. To Ley they were fantasies, little more than gilded pictures formed by the darkness of sleep or the intoxication of alcohol and smoke. To say her opinion of divination was a popular one was to say the sun refused to set.

What she was *not* skeptical of was instinct, the feeling in her gut that told her what she'd dreamt this past night with her illum's aid was real—there was a way to escape this hell she called home, a way to save Bringer and end the Radichian War that'd been waging for seventeen years. All she had to do was shove her knife down a five-year old's throat and hope the value of his death was enough to grant her entry into the Temporal Sea.

Ain't that a bitch.

Leyandra wrapped herself in her fur blanket and withdrew from the relative warmth of her shaghound tent. The triptych sky had shifted. The azure blue of day was dominant now with the sun concealed behind a mass of eastward rain clouds gray as ash. The air was cold and ripe with smoke that reeked of burning flesh.

Leyandra cocked a brow and spat. "You've made your point," she snarled at nature, at the world and everything she'd dreamt. "It's a damn fine day to kill a kid." And there was little time to waste.

She wandered past the fire at the center of her camp; no one said a word. These days energy was better spent on fight and fuck. She entered the armory tent, eyes scanning hastily for her prize—a crystalline dagger like a dragon's claw, nastily curved and as long as her forearm. *So much for a knife.* She snorted, snatched the gleaming beauty from its rest, then withdrew from the tent. The weapon drew a couple of eyes but again nary a word was uttered nor spat.

THE WALK to Helveden was roughly a mile long. Leyandra didn't mind, it gave her time to think about her dream and the brutality of its message. *Bleed a child and dystopia dies.* Such had been the case through histories old and new. Violence was the fashion of forever and she found her body tingling madly at the notion of a world and time reprieved of such a thing.

Best hope your conscience takes the morning off, she thought. *Or else this killing thing is going to be severely hampered by morality and tears.* Theirs, not hers. The last time Ley had cried was seven years ago because her favorite knife had dulled.

THE STREETS WERE slick with blood, empty save the several sorry souls who'd taken to mopping the crimson from the cobbles. Towers speared the sky, tall despite their crumbling ruin, and the smell of burning flesh clung yet to the morning air like a thirsty babe to a tit. To an outsider, to someone visiting Ariath, the city would have looked as though it'd just been massacred by some mirkúr-frenzied fucks. The reality was that Te Mirkvahíl had not attacked for months. Helveden's ruin was its own, perpetrated by the illum wielders who'd been driven mad by radich, the wild temporal energy for which the war was named and the means by which Leyandra hoped to swim the Temporal Sea.

Along with a child's death. Make sure to a carve a crimson grin, that way everyone knows the final moment was the happiest of their short and shitty life! Leyandra spat again as she wound through alleyways and headed east. *I hope my stupid dream was right.* If she knifed this kid and the Sea decided "Fuck you, try again!" she knew her inner voice would cease to hold its tongue.

"You're an idiot," it would snarl.

"You're a moron," it would hiss.

"Theailys An was just a child!" it would shout. Ley knew she'd rather fuck herself with a rusted pole than subject herself to *that*.

VARÉSH LÚM-TALÉ SAT in a chair with a glass of Liosenean whiskey in his hand. By his count he had gone through a bottle and a half of the stuff; he planned to consume at least a half dozen more. He had seen what violence the day would bring and thus endeavored to be as blackout drunk as possible before the Blood Time came. His eyes sought darkness, ears silence, and morality the void regarding his adopted son, Theailys An.

Even in this thread you're a shitty parent, Vare thought. He remembered well the other timelines of this world, especially the one from which this current iteration had diverged. The planet Harthe was of his own making after all, formed and molded by his energy, radich. Possibility, in the Celestial tongue. Vare had learned all of this only yesterday after being struck repeatedly by lightning. This really *was* a violent instance, if he said so himself.

If only I'd been spared the painful truth. A legacy of failure. A legacy of lies. He sighed, watching little Theailys toss a ball across the room, then raised his glass to irony, to the fact his newfound knowledge had replaced his ability to swim through time. To do anything, really. For all intents and purposes, Varésh Lúm-talé was a mortal man with fabulous long-term memory and a drinking problem.

The doorknob rattled, then turned, and through the open door came death and hope on legs like Vare had never seen—not in this life, at least. "Leyandra," he said, and cursed himself for the smoothness of his speech. He downed his drink and poured another. "Come to—" He slid his index finger across his throat, nodding toward the child ignorant of impending doom.

"Did you have my dream as well?" she asked. Her eyes were soft, and her calm demeanor made Vare shake.

"I suppose that's one way of putting it." He took a sip then offered her the glass.

Leyandra waved it off. She brushed a strand of gnarled scarlet hair behind her ear, eyes falling to the child ignorant of her presence at the far side of the room. "Will it work?"

Vare tilted his head. "*It*, meaning…?"

She looked him in the eyes and Vare felt cold.

"Yes," he said. "The price of temporal alteration—of attempting it, at least—remains the same. The life essence of whomever you desire to save." What a shit brand of magic this was.

Leyandra leaned against the wall, eyes narrowed in the way one does when things make little sense, yet at the same time, all the sense in the world. She reached into her cloak and from its darkness drew a blade so beautifully brutal in its make. Vare grasped for the whiskey bottle and chugged as silent words escaped Leyandra's moving lips.

Chugged harder as the room was bathed in the pale blue

light of radich swimming, twisting, braiding toward the weapon in Leyandra's hand.

Harder yet as Leyandra knelt behind his son and dragged the dagger clean across his throat.

Would he remember any of this in the world to come?

THE END OF BOOK ONE

GLOSSARY

1. **Black Year**—The last four months of the year.
2. **Channeling**—The act of imbuing a person or object with illum.
3. **Dawn Year**—The first four months of the year.
4. **Dissident**—A lokyn sect no longer bound to the madness of Te Mirkvahíl. They dwell predominantly in the Ariathan capital of Helveden.
5. **Dren**—A phantaxian epithet; also means father.
6. **Illum**—A secondary stamina or energy; the light of the Keepers, bestowed upon the Illuminated at birth. Presently wielded by Illumurgists, formerly wielded by the Reshapers.
7. **Illumancer**—One adept at using illum to interpret dreams and premonitions.
8. **Illumancy**—Divination through the use of illum.

9. **Illuminated**—Individuals born with illum. Primarily dissident or human.
10. **Illumurgist**—One who wields illum.
11. **Illumurgy**—The manipulation of illum for a variety of purposes.
12. **Lokyn**—Demonic tricksters, malicious in nature. They take pleasure in the suffering of their prey.
13. **Mid Year**—The middle four months of the year.
14. **Mirkúr**—A secondary stamina or energy; the inverse of illum, the power of demons. Presently wielded by Te Mirkvahíl and Theailys An, formerly wielded by the Reshapers.
15. **Perdition**—The realm in which the souls of the damned dwell.
16. **Phantaxians**—A plagued, mountain-dwelling people wrought by the Season God, Phantaxis.
17. **Rapture**—The realm in which the honored dead reside. Also called the Second Life.
18. **Reshapers**—The first race. The dead race. A powerful people capable of wielding both illum and mirkúr.
19. **Te Luminíl**—The Light, or My Light. Translations vary.
20. **Te Mirkvahíl**—The Darkness, or My Darkness. Translations vary.
21. **Tem**—A phantaxian epithet; also means mother.
22. **Yssa**—Bestial rage and frenzy made manifest; wild energy wielded by the phantaxians.

ACKNOWLEDGMENTS

To quote Dante Alighieri's, *The Inferno*, "I found myself within a forest dark, for the straightforward pathway had been lost."

When *Vultures* debuted almost two years ago it changed my life—I had finally published a book. An anthology titled *Dark Ends* and a novella titled *The World Maker Parable* followed in 2020...and then things unrivaled a bit for me internally. My depression hit really hard around July; I had just started a new job and was also a new father and I felt overwhelmed. I've always had the tendency to place unnecessary pressure on myself as a writer; self-publishing and the desire to be discovered, for people to read and enjoy my work, only seemed to make it worse. I was mired in this notion that I had to keep pushing out new content lest I be forgotten as a writer—and that's not healthy. It absolutely affected my writing. I will be completely honest, the longer I put off starting the follow-up to Vultures, the more I worried I would never get around to writing it, that Vultures was and forever would be one part of an unrealized whole—but I am happy to say that is not the case.

The updated edition of this book pleases me to no end. I have put my heart and soul into making this the best it can possibly be, which is a thank you to the people who have picked up, read, and loved Vultures, who have continually come back to read more of my work. I consider this the ultimate Vultures experience in a way and I hope those of you kind enough to have purchased this copy do as well.

I have a lot of people to thank and to acknowledge, now. Firstly, thank you to Clayton Snyder, Krystle Matar, Justin Wallace, Sarah Chorn, Nick Borrelli, and Tom Clews for often and always providing progressional feedback, moral support, and hilarity when it was most needed. This past year has been one unlike any other and I count myself fortunate enough to have such admirable and willing people as friends.

To Justine Bergman and Timy Takács, fantasic organizers of tours and supporters of self-publshed science fiction and fantasy.

To Angela Boord and Bjorn Larssen for their valuable knowledge on marketing and self-publishing services and to whom I presented many half-formed questions.

To Zack Argyle, Dan Fitzgerald, and Virginia McClain, Twitter cheerleaders supreme and generally lovely people all around.

To my wife, Jenny, and our daughters, Celia and Naomi, for giving me the time and space to put this book together and for your unconditional love.

Lastly, to the readers and book bloggers by whom postive word of my books was, is, and will be spread—you are all immensely appreciate by myself and other self-published authors. Without you, where would we be?

PREVIEW
HOUSE OF MUIR

THE MONTH OF JUL, MID YEAR 1169

Collect the bodies. Light the pyres. Burn the dead—what was left of them at least. That was how it'd always been. It was the Vétur way which, to Fiel, had always meant the quickest and the coldest. Bit of irony, that last bit.

How many dead? How many missing? How many missing and presumed? Best not think about the numbers. No sense in doing so when things were so horrifically...horrific. Redundant, that, but considering the state of things who really cared?

She looked at the body in her arms. Limp, cracked flesh mottled dark, garbed in leathers and a cloak, blues eyes wide —dead. Mostly.

Mostly—was that truly so or was this shock and grief and

games the mind played when the ugliness of war and life crept in and gripped you by the throat? It couldn't be. It wasn't—her Serece yet lived. She *had* to.

Yet. And yet...the absent thrum of blood through veins, the absence of a pulse, and, most importantly, the myriad threads of mirkúr leaking from Serece's wounds and shattered flesh informed Fiel of what her heart had told her hours ago, of what her eyes confirmed not minutes prior to the moment currently at hand: her beloved niece was dead.

"I should have been here, child," Fiel whispered. What would she tell Undrensil? What would she tell Artemae? How could she tell them both their last remaining child was gone, struck down in the city from which, centuries ago, their people had been exiled? What a rusted dagger twisting in a festering wound was life.

Tears crept from Fiel's eyes. Trailed down her cheeks and splashed Serece's face like a sad rain. Her niece was well and truly gone. Dead. Murdered. A memory momentarily exhumed in tarnished flesh.

But you'll not burn here, child. No dead left behind—Fiel's way, and maybe Undrensil's as well. Definitely not her sister-queen's; Artemae was colder than loneliness. No—Fiel would bring the princess home. It was the very least she could do. After all, so much of this was her fault. Hounds and fowl had a nasty way of breaking worlds, as her illum dreams had shown, and Fiel would be damned again if she let another one fall.

This was only the beginning.

. . .

BEHTRÉAL RETCHED BLOOD. Had no idea where he was, only knew something was wrong. He had felt fine upon departing Helveden, felt nothing save guilt and purpose as he had hurtled through the screaming night. Nothing—until he fell from darkness and hit the ground with such impact he thought he might have broken everything of his body, if his current form could be called such a thing.

He retched again—he'd done a lot of that. So much blood. The last moment of Theailys An's life snapped across his mind and Behtréal shrieked; it felt like a knife had been plunged into his chest and twisted repeatedly. Screams in his head. He fell to the grass and hugged himself, convulsing— what was happening?

Night swirled. He crawled, directionless. Felt his way through mystery with pain like he'd not known for years; with relative ease and the assistance of the moonless sky for he was shadow, shade, and silhouette and everything of dark- ness bowed to him and him alone.

Shelter. Sanctuary in the hollow of a tree. Smelled of earth and rain and rot—a pleasing fragrance relative to the flaming ruin he had left. He could still smell burning flesh, could taste the ash and smoke and fear and death and it was strong enough to make him gag. What a monstrous thing he'd done...

"Necessary," hissed Te Mirkvahíl. "It was requisite. You wish to see your wife and son? You wish to see them and the whole of Ouran'an restored? Then remember—sacrifices must be made. What better than the city and the people—the empire—at whose hands Zorahl fell?"

Behtréal closed his eyes, listened to the voice ramble. It

was right, of course. *If only they knew,* he thought, *what their deaths will bring.* Glorious resurrection. Reclamation unlike anything the world had seen—he would rewrite history and quell the mirkúr plague that'd sent his people to their end millennia ago.

"Just...need to rest..."

CAILEAN CARRIED Leyandra all the way to the Hall. Not sure how he did it, where he found the strength. Not sure how he made it through the smoldered corpse of Helveden, through a sea of bodies. Demons all around. Hungry, cackling, whispering fucks, feeding on the ruin like the carrion shits they were. He'd fell every fucking one of them—vowed vengeance.

The Hall. Dead light. A trail of blood and gore and flesh and demon smoke. He clutched Leyandra's corpse tighter as he went, choking back tears at the coldness of her flesh. Swallowing the urge to wail. Could have let the flames take her, let the wind sweep her ashes from this place. *Could have*—but he had not. No fucking way he was going to leave her body to rot in the solitude of smoke and flames and farmland grass where demons gorged.

Through the slaughtered halls. Back outside, beneath an oak tree. Knelt. Laid Leyandra on the grass and wept, screamed as he had never screamed before—he had found Theailys An, still in a patch of blood-smeared grass. Dead. Had been for a while by the looks of it. By the coldness of his cheeks and hands—ice, like a body robbed not only of physicality and soul.

"Fuck..." Cailean punched the grass. *"Fuck. Fuck!"*

"Like a bad dream." Bar stood a couple feet away. *"Is this what you've let your life become, my sweet?"*

Cailean tensed his jaw, looked up at the manifestation. Cursed the memory of his lovely Bar. "Fuck you."

Bar smiled sadly, clasped his hands behind his back. *"You were never going to save them. The coin does as the coin wills—Entropy is king."* He knelt, cupped Cailean's cheeks. *"You've nothing left, my sweet—find sleep. You deserve it so."*

"Not interested in that kind of sleep," Cailean snarled. He pulled away, stood despite the heaviness afflicting mind and body. "Not yet."

Bar rose, smiled. Sunset eyes gleamed brightly in the misery of night. In a twist of light he went, and Cailean was alone.

He looked at the bodies. Chest was tight, throat was dried and ached like shit from smoke and ash and screaming. Looked at the oak tree—something to it, not sure what. He procures an ink-black flask, poured its contents 'round his friends.

"Ig tahn na'tuul." May you rest. How long, how many years since last he'd said those words, the mantra of the Galrun Muir? Seemed appropriate, now. The only fucking thing that made a lick of sense.

Put the flask to his lips and drained what yet remained. Felt the fire in his blood, felt purpose roar to life inside his mind and chest like a furnace waking after centuries of sleep.

The whiskey he had poured—the sip of the Galrun Muir—would keep the flames contained; purify their bodies and ascend Leyandra's soul. Theailys was but flesh and bone.

Cailean snapped his thumb and index finger, summoned flames of blue and set the circled sip alight. Watched a moment as it ate the dead, purified what had been soiled; as a wisp of light ascended from Leyandra's corpse and vanished in the night.

Then, Cailean vanished too.

ABOUT THE AUTHOR

Luke Tarzian was born in Bucharest, Romania. His parents made the extremely poor choice of adopting him less than six months into his life. As such, he's resided primarily in the United States and currently lives in California with his wife and their twin daughters. Somehow, they tolerate him.

Unfortunately, he can also be found online and, to the dismay of his clients, also functions as a cover artist for independent authors.

www.luketarzian.com
www.tarzianbookdesign.com

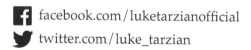 facebook.com/luketarzianofficial
twitter.com/luke_tarzian

Printed in Great Britain
by Amazon